Daniel and Job

To MARY

William A Rich
2-6-95

William A. Rich

ISBN: 978-1-6319255-4-2

Daniel and Job

This book is dedicated to the insatiable readers in my family: my mother Toni, my late father Charles E., my wife Marlene, my late sister Phyllis and my brother Charles A. Rich.

The Chapters

Chapter 1:   Jessie   page 1
Chapter 2:   The Book of Job   page 16
Chapter 3:   Jebediah   page 26
Chapter 4:   Kandar   page 53
Chapter 5:   Shahlaya and the Vargon   page 74
Chapter 6:   Rev-Tech Bionics   page 103
Chapter 7:   The Battle   page 128
Chapter 8:   Reunions   page 166
Chapter 9:   Aftermath   page 199
Chapter 10: Revelations   page 244

I would like to thank my wife Marlene for her contributions
to the proofreading and editing of this book,
and for bearing with me while I prattled on about it at length.

I also thank my friend Kathy Carroll for her research,
for her contributions to the proofreading and editing of this
book and for reminding me that there are rules for punctuation
and grammar.

"That which you seek is coming!" whispered the voice,

And the boy awoke with a start.

Chapter 1

Jessie

Jessie increased her pace as she approached her car. She was doing her absolute best not to look suspicious. The afternoon sun had seared the previous night's rain from the pavement and the door handle was hot. She entered the vehicle, closed the door and quickly started the engine. Backing out of the parking space, she breathed a long sigh of relief. She then drove calmly up to the security gate. As the guard neared her car, she hit the "play" button on her CD player. The song was an oldie: "Had to Cry Today" by Blind Faith.

"Hi, again!" Jessie addressed the man, smiling, as she rolled down her window.

"Okay, Young Lady, I guess everything is in order," Jenkins said, scanning his clipboard and glancing through the open window.

"You haven't stolen anything, have you?" he added, with a hint of a laugh.

"God, no! What's to steal?" she asked, grinning and looking up into her rear-view mirror. She could see Mr. Marx running out of the main entrance, waving and screaming. He had a walkie-talkie in one hand and he was yelling into that, as well.

"Oh, you'd be surprised," Jenkins replied with a smile. "You can go now, Miss. Have a good evening!"

"You, too!" Jessie responded flirtatiously. She reached down to raise the volume on the CD player and to drown out the commotion behind her, just as Steve Winwood sang the first line of the song. The lyrics seemed strangely prophetic and she wondered if today would truly be memorable — or even if what she had just done might have been illegal. She hit the accelerator hard and her tires threw up a dense cloud of dust as she pulled out. Jessie could just barely hear Mr. Marx screaming: "Stop her! Stop her!"

Finally noticing Marx, Jenkins cupped his hand around his ear to ascertain what his boss was yelling. When he finally pieced things together, he instinctively pulled his sidearm and started to take careful aim at the accelerating car.

"No! No! You moron! Are you freaking crazy?" Marx screamed, waving his arms. "I said: 'stop her,' not 'kill her'!" The middle-aged man continued to run towards the sentry gate breathing heavily.

"What am I going to do with you blockheads?" Marx yelled, wheezing.

Just then, two black Hummers came roaring around the side of the building. They pulled up alongside Marx and Jenkins.

"Which way'd she go, Boss?" the first driver asked Marx.

"That way, not two minutes ago!" Jenkins replied as he pointed down the road.

The two vehicles started towards the highway, pausing for a break in traffic.

"And try not to kill her, for God's sake!" Marx barked, coughing.

Finally, both vehicles pulled out from the Rev-Tech driveway and onto the main road, kicking up another annoying dust-cloud. Marx waved his hand in front of his face to shield himself from the flying filth.

"They can't be too far behind her," he muttered, as he continued his hacking.

*****

Jessie was just a few blocks down the road: waiting for a traffic light, enjoying her music and occasionally checking her mirrors.

"Oh, my God! OH — MY — GAWD!!!" she shouted as she spotted the two dark vehicles speeding out from the Rev-Tech entrance. They were still stirring up dust and flashing their lights. The signal

turned to green and she stomped on the gas pedal.

The four-lane highway was narrowing to two lanes and Jessie knew that it would end abruptly just about three miles past the crest of the hill. She could see both of the vehicles gaining on her in her rear-view mirror. From the top of the hill, she saw a gravel road leading into the woods, but she didn't want to hit the brakes and give her pursuers any hint of her intentions. Luckily, the grade ascending the slope had slowed her car sufficiently so she could skid into a right turn. Their vehicles had disappeared from her mirror as she began her descent, so she was confident that they wouldn't notice her maneuver.

She floored the accelerator and headed into the woods. After a quarter mile, the gravel gave way to dirt and it wasn't easy to stay on the path. It was getting dark and the overhanging trees made it that much darker. She realized that she couldn't keep driving without headlights. Jessie switched them on and, almost immediately, saw headlights switched on in her mirror. They had not only followed her, but they had gained ground on the rough terrain as well.

And just when she thought that things couldn't possibly get any worse, Jessie's car began to slow. She looked at her gas gauge: it was still at half a tank. Then her car came to a complete halt. She pressed the gas-pedal harder and she could hear her front tires spinning. She was stuck. The dirt road was soaked from the recent rain and her car was mired in a sea of mud.

"God! They're going to kill me!" she sobbed in desperation.

She grabbed her keys and her purse. She threw the door open and leapt out of her car. The two Hummers pulled up behind her. The first one veered to her left; the other went slightly to the right but blocked any possible retreat. She quickly lost one shoe in the mud, but she still did her best to run. Two uniformed men got out of the lead vehicle.

"Miss Drake, stop right there. You have to come with us," the first one shouted.

The two black-suited occupants of the other Hummer had also joined them in the mud. They were approaching from her right with guns drawn. "Lady, you're going to regret what you're doing to my shoes!" warned one of them.

Jessie didn't care about anyone's shoes. At this point, she didn't even care about the photograph — or her story. She didn't care about anything except getting out of this mess alive. In a sun-lit clearing, not more than thirty feet ahead of her, Jessie glimpsed a young blind man with a rather large dog.

"Miss, I'm sorry to have to do this, but you're giving me no other choice!" the closest uniformed guard warned. He raised his pistol above Jessie's head and came down hard with it. She stumbled forward, briefly making eye contact with the dog as she fell into the mud: unconscious.

*****

"Lie still. That's a nasty bump," a voice whispered.

Jessie opened her eyes, but she couldn't quite focus them yet. "Where are my glasses?" she asked. She had no idea to whom she was speaking, but she didn't sense an immediate threat. Her still-murky mind was formulating an escape. So far, it consisted of: eyeglasses first, then run!

"I guess these are clean enough." It was the same voice — a male voice. He put the eyeglasses over her nose and let her adjust them herself. He turned and sat on a chair just a few feet away against the opposite wall of the small room.

Jessie was lying on a bed, fully-clad, with a cover pulled up over

4

her muddy garments. She raised herself up on her elbows. "You're the blind boy," she said to the young man with the dark glasses.

The dog had been sprawled on the floor. Now he sat up with his ears at alert.

"That's what they say," the boy responded with a hint of a smile. He kept his hand on the dog's head — petting him smoothly. The dog looked up at him.

"Oh, I'm such an idiot! I'm *so* sorry. I really am. I didn't mean it to sound like that," Jessie protested. "I'm *totally* not insensitive about people with problems — not that you necessarily have problems, mind you."

"Really, no apology is necessary," the boy interjected good-naturedly.

"I mean you seem to be a nice-enough person. Of course I don't exactly *know* you, but that doesn't mean that you're *not* a nice person," she continued.

Jessie paused for a second, fumbling for words: "After all, we've only just sort-of met. Although, I guess we really haven't been properly introduced."

For the briefest moment, there was an awkward silence.

"Oh, Jessie, put a sock in it!" she continued in frustration, "I really don't mean to ramble. It's just that I'm *so* truly sorry. I suppose I'm not making a very good first impression, am I?"

"Excuse me, but —," the boy began.

"Young man, please don't interrupt me while I'm trying to apologize!" Jessie admonished him.

"But —," he began.

"Ah!" she interjected while raising her finger. She looked at the boy's dark glasses, then back at her finger. She lowered her hand discretely. "What I actually meant to say was: you're the visually-impaired gentleman with the really big dog. I saw you just as I was falling."

The boy smiled widely, obviously amused at Jessie's embarrassed soliloquy, and replied: "That was yesterday. How are you feeling?"

"A little woozy. Do you have any water?"

"There's a glass right there at your bedside. Let me get it for you," he offered as he started to rise.

"No, please don't get up on my account," she insisted. "I'm sure I can reach it just fine." She stretched for the glass. Her hand was still shaky from her recent experience. She managed to get the glass to her mouth and she took a sip of the cold water. It was actually quite refreshing and she was rather proud of herself that she had only spilled a little. Her first instinct was to apologize for spilling on the bed, but then she thought: "Why should I apologize? This guy didn't see anything!"

"Have you got a washroom?" she asked.

"Right through that door," he replied, gesturing to his right. He rose and offered his hand to assist her. The dog immediately stood up as well.

"That's a lot of dog you have there. Does he bite?" she wondered aloud, before venturing to leave the safety of the bed.

The young man smiled: "Not unless I ask him to. Job is a good dog."

"So, your friend's name is Job? – I'm Jessie," she proclaimed as she cautiously stood up.

"I'm sorry, I really should have introduced myself earlier. My name is Daniel. Welcome to my little home." He helped her to the washroom, reached inside the doorway to switch the light on for her and turned to leave. Job never left his side.

"Will you be okay in there?" he inquired.

"Thank you, Daniel. I think I can handle things pretty well on my own from here. Could you please close the door?" she asked politely.

He pulled the door behind him and walked a step before he heard the lock click. Jessie looked around the bathroom for potential weapons and an escape route. She was pleased that the accommodations looked clean, but she was shocked to see a toilet with a raised flush-tank and a pull chain. "What century is this guy from?" she muttered.

Aside from a toothbrush and a waste basket, there was nothing that could be used as a weapon. The window was high and much too small to be considered a possible exit. It was apparently only meant for light and ventilation.

She used the facilities and, glancing into the mirror, whispered: "Jessie, you are one big mess!" She washed her face and ran her fingers through her dark hair. Her clothes were filthy, wrinkled and still somewhat damp. She couldn't wait to get home, take a shower and put on some clean clothes. Then, she remembered the uniformed men who were chasing her. Her mind was suddenly filled with questions. Were they still lurking outside? Would somebody be waiting for her at her apartment? Who is this Daniel and whose side is he on? She looked into the mirror once again and sighed: "What am I so worried about? This blind kid can't see me anyway!" Then she unlocked and opened the door. When she re-entered the bedroom, there was a clean plaid shirt and a pair of jeans lying across the bed — quite obviously a man's clothes.

7

"I thought you might want to change," Daniel suggested. "These will probably be a little big for you. They're mine. I'm really sorry that I don't have anything better to offer."

"How thoughtful," Jessie responded. She held the pants up against her waist and decided that the "loose" look was definitely better than the "disheveled and muddy" look that she was currently sporting.

Daniel sat in his chair. Sunlight streamed through the bedroom window and reflected off his dark sunglasses. Job settled quietly at his side.

"If you want to change, I can…" the boy began, while rising from his seat.

"No, that's okay," she interrupted. "Does this work?" Jessie pointed at the radio, thinking that a little music might be appropriate.

"It should. Just turn the knob on the right," Daniel answered.

She turned the radio on. *"…and that was two from the Beatles, which brings us to the top of the hour. It is now 5 o'clock at 'Oldies 93.1' and here are today's headlines. On the local beat, authorities are still looking for a woman who allegedly stole classified documents from the Rev-Tech Bionics Corporation…."* — Jessie clicked the switch.

Slightly disappointed that she didn't have music to accompany her impromptu striptease in front of her blind audience — something which she would never have done in full view of any stranger with sight — she slowly and methodically removed her blouse and her pants. She stood in her undergarments for a moment: rolling her clothes into a ball and eyeing the clean clothes on the bed. Finally raising her courage, Jessie asked: "What happened to the four guys who were chasing me?"

Daniel fidgeted for a moment, and cautiously replied: "They went away."

"They just 'went away'?" she asked incredulously.

"Well, believe it or not, Job here and I can be very persuasive," he responded.

Jessie had no idea what these two characters could possibly have done to save her from four armed attackers, but then she suddenly remembered pointing to the radio.

"YOU'RE NOT BLIND!" she screamed and hurled her clothes at the seated boy.

"I never said that I was. That's just what 'people' say. You can't always believe what 'people' say, now can you?" he laughed, slightly embarrassed, while catching her balled-up garments.

"And after all of my apologizing!" she whined.

"Well, I kept trying to—" the boy interjected.

"When were you going to tell me? — When I was stark *naked?* You! — YOU PERVERT!" she yelled as she glared at the boy. "Get out of here! I mean: RIGHT NOW!"

"I'll clean these up for you," he said, hurrying through the doorway with Job following close at his side. As he shut the door behind him, Daniel heard the sudden impact of a shoe against it.

"Job, I think that may have been meant for me!" the young man stammered, knowing full well that it was and that he had probably deserved it.

Daniel grabbed a wire hanger from the hall closet. He draped Jessie's pants over the hanger and buttoned the blouse over them. He concentrated on them briefly, watching the particles of dust waft to the floor before he hooked the hanger over a nail on the wall. Jessie's clothes were now neat, clean and dry.

"I think we should take a walk and come back a little later when she cools off," he whispered to the dog.

Jessie was furious with the boy. She sat on the bed to put the pants on and tears welled-up in her eyes. For a moment, she thought she was safe and now she felt that she couldn't trust this "Daniel" character. He was misleading her the whole time and yet he hadn't actually lied to her. She wouldn't have stripped naked in front of him: blind or not. She just wasn't that kind of girl! But she was having a little fun with him, so was it all that wrong that he was having her on as well? Would he have stopped her before she had gone any further? He didn't *seem* to be that rude, but now she just couldn't trust him and she felt as though there was no one who could help her out of the mess she was in.

"Men!" she intoned. "You just can't trust *any* of them!" She picked up her other shoe and threw it at the door. At least Daniel had managed to find the one that she had lost in the mud! Her head was still hurting from the previous day's incident and she really didn't feel like running or fighting with anyone.

She looked around the room and spotted her purse on the floor next to the dresser. She picked it up to inspect the contents. Everything seemed to be there; so, at the very least, Daniel wasn't a thief. Most importantly, the camera was still there. She was beginning to wish that she had never taken the photo. Her life was obviously never going to be the same again. She checked to see if the door was locked. Surprisingly, it wasn't. She opened it just enough to make sure that Daniel wasn't around and then she pulled it shut. She locked it from the inside.

"I give up! I just can't deal with any of this," she whimpered. She was a strong-willed girl, but the odds seemed so incredibly stacked against her. "Maybe if I go back to Rev-Tech and just give them the stupid camera, they'll let me go?" she muttered.

Saying it aloud didn't make that plan sound any more credible than she had originally thought. Rev-Tech was worse than the government. At least with the government, you'd have your day in court. With Rev-Tech Bionics, you might just disappear — never to be heard from again — or, at least she had heard rumors to that effect.

She lay down on the bed, propping her head on her left hand and eyeing the door. She had no idea when her apparent rescuer planned to return or how she intended to treat him when he did. He owed her an apology. Yes, at the very least an apology; and a better explanation of what had happened to those four men who were chasing her. She also wanted to know exactly what his intentions were. Was he planning to hold her against her will? Did he think he was going to make her his sex slave? "He has no idea whom he's dealing with!" she exclaimed. "Jessie Drake isn't *anybody's* slave!"

"But then, he *is* kind of cute — for a kid," she added. Daniel was a very attractive young man, at her best guess he was probably 15, maybe 16 at the most. She was all of 22 and not prepared to go to jail for messing around with a minor.

"I wonder when his parents will be coming home?" she asked aloud. She was also starting to wonder if her predicament could get any worse. "I might just tell them a thing or two!"

*****

Jessie slept for about an hour. She heard the front door close and the shuffle of feet approaching the bedroom. Someone was whistling a pleasant, but unfamiliar, tune. There were five knocks on the door. "At least whoever this is has some manners," she muttered.

"Who is it?" Jessie demanded.

"It's me. Daniel. I'm truly sorry about our little 'misunderstanding' earlier. Would it be alright if I come in and talk to you for just a minute?" he asked politely.

"Are you going to pretend to be crippled this time or do you just feign blindness?" she asked sarcastically. She walked across the room, unlocked the door and sat back on the bed. She slipped her shoes on and held her purse by the strap: a ready weapon.

Daniel turned the doorknob and stuck his head into the room rather sheepishly. Job pushed the door wide open. "I really am sorry if I misled you. I live here by myself and it makes life a lot easier for me if the people in town think that Job is a service dog. They ask very few questions and allow him to stay with me wherever I go."

"That's really no excuse," Jessie responded coldly. "So, where are your parents?"

"My mother died when I was born and my father left years ago," the boy replied.

He reached outside the door for her clothes. "Here are your things. I'll leave you to get dressed so you can be on your way. I'm very sorry if I've offended you. Can I at least offer you something to eat before you go?"

Jessie was pretty hungry. She missed a good three meals since yesterday's lunch.

"I'll have a couple of cheeseburgers, if you can manage that," she requested.

"Actually, there isn't a fast food place for at least fifteen miles and, although I've been known to hunt, I haven't seen one of them there 'wild cows' in ages!" Daniel said, trying to make her laugh, but Jessie wasn't amused.

"So, what exactly have you got?" she asked, nonplussed.

"Can you deal with fresh catfish? I caught them myself this morning," he answered, hoping she'd accept his offering.

"It isn't exactly on my list of favorite things to eat, but I'm hungry and I don't feel like walking on an empty stomach," Jessie replied. She was starting to warm slightly to the boy. At least he's beginning to show some manners, she thought.

Daniel turned to leave the room with Job at his side: "I'll be grilling the fish outside if you need anything." He pulled the door behind him and Jessie heard the outside door shut as well.

She got up, locked the door again and redressed herself quickly, but with no great confidence that she had total privacy. As soon as she finished, she opened the bedroom door and walked straight through the kitchen and out the front door. Daniel was setting plates of food on a picnic table. When she turned to look back at the house, she was shocked to see what a dilapidated shack it appeared to be from the outside. The inside was small and sparsely furnished, but gave no hint of the outward appearance of the place.

"My, what a lovely home!" she enthused sarcastically.

"It works for me," he replied, ignoring the barb. "Fix a plate for yourself. We have catfish, tomato salad, fried potatoes and fresh grilled corn. All of the veggies are from my garden over there. I don't have any fancy soda pop, but the water in that pitcher's cold and pure."

Jessie took a plate and filled it with half of everything that was edible. She was famished and everything smelled so good. Daniel hadn't planned on her appetite. He put the rest of the tomato salad and the corn on his plate. Then he gave the remaining catfish and potatoes to Job.

"If I had known that you weren't going to eat the catfish, I would have taken more," Jessie said, raising her fork to her mouth.

"I love catfish, but Job needs to eat, too," Daniel answered.

It was becoming clear to Jessie, that the boy and the dog really were inseparable. She admired the loyalty that they demonstrated towards one another. She also felt a little ashamed that she hadn't considered anyone else's needs before she started eating.

"You're quite the chef, Master Daniel," she noted. "I can't remember the last time that I had a home-cooked meal that could top this." For once, she wasn't being sarcastic. The food was surprisingly good and it didn't take her long to finish everything on her plate.

"Thanks for the compliment," the boy replied. "I'm not sure if you're planning to leave right now, but the sun's going down and I'd suggest that you wait until morning. These woods can be a mite scary after dark and we've still got to dig your car out of the mud."

"Well, you probably know best, Daniel. Thank you very much for dinner. Would it be okay if I stayed overnight in that same room?" Jessie asked. She knew that it had a good strong door with an equally good lock that worked from the inside.

"That's fine with me. I can sleep on the couch again," the boy responded.

She hadn't really thought about it before, but, if she was in his bed last night, it was quite reassuring to know that he was somewhere else.

"Good night, Daniel, and thanks again for the food. I really do appreciate your rescuing me and everything." She walked up to Job and brushed his head with her palm. "And a good night to you too, Job. You're a really nice dog."

Job looked up into her eyes without making a sound. She walked up the couple of wooden stairs to the front door, opened it, and went straight to her room. She wasn't actually sleepy, but she was fatigued and her head was still sore.

"Maybe there's something that I can read around here," she muttered, as she glanced around the room. There was a small shelf on one wall, but there weren't many books to choose from: just a Bible, some textbooks and a few skinny, old, leather-bound volumes. As an aspiring investigative-reporter, those immediately attracted her attention.

She carefully picked up the first one from the left, which bore the hand-printed title *The Book of Job*, and she placed it on the pillow. She turned on the lamp atop the dresser and proceeded to get herself ready for bed. She locked the door, kicked off her shoes, stripped down to her undergarments and headed for the washroom.

When she returned, she climbed into bed, propped herself up on the pillow and carefully opened the aged, leather-bound booklet. She noticed that the text was printed in the same hand as the title and she began to read…

Chapter 2

The Book of Job

My Pa never abided having pets. He always told me that attachments don't do you any good. It just gives other people a weapon to hold against you. If something is precious to you, then they'll do their best to take it away. I grew up hearing that and I believed it. But there were times when I wanted to have a friend and there were no friends to be had in the wilderness.

Anyways, one day last spring, I was out fishing the creek by the old cave. I had heard our local bobcat yowling in the distance most of the morning, but we were used to hearing Old Bob. Pa always said that "when you could hear him, you knew where he was at." That made good sense to me.

So, I was fishing for a couple of hours and I caught three good-sized catfish. And I kept feeling like I was being watched. I'd look over into the dark of the cave and, every now and then, I thought I'd see the red glint of something's eyes watching me. I knew it wasn't Old Bob, 'cause I heard his voice off in the distance and I didn't think it was a bear, because a bear wouldn't have been that patient. He would have come right out and eaten the fish and had me for the main course.

After a while, I realized that I hadn't heard Bob for quite some time. I had gathered my things together and I was getting up to leave, when I saw that old bobcat up on the ledge looking down on me. He was growling low and looking really mean. For the briefest moment, I froze. Then, as he went down on his haunches to leap, I threw the creel of fish at him. I turned and started to run, but I stumbled for just a second. I heard Bob screech and I sensed an impact behind me as I got up and ran straight for home. When you're only twelve years old, you don't fool with bobcats: they can make a real mess of you! So,

I ran as fast as I could, yelling: "Pa! Pa! Ol' Bob's on my tail!"

When I got within sight of the cabin, my Pa came running out towards me with his musket. Lucky for me, Ol' Bob wasn't following right behind me. My Pa asked me if I was sure it was that old bobcat. I told him: "It sure looked like Ol' Bob to me, Pa!"

"Well, let's get in the cabin where it's safe," Pa told me. He was a decent human being, but he was a bit skeptical by nature. "Did you catch any fish?" he asked.

"I caught three catfish, but I threw the whole bunch at Ol' Bob," I answered.

"I suppose that was the smart thing to do," Pa muttered, but he looked at me as though he didn't really believe me.

"Get washed up for supper. I guess we're just eating boiled potatoes tonight," Pa said, with more than a hint of disappointment.

*****

After supper, Pa looked out the window and yelled back at me: "Come here, Boy!"

I went to the window and peeked out from under his arm. There was a rather large dog lying in the dirt just in front of the porch. He had my creel in his mouth.

Pa opened the door and walked out. "Does that there look like Old Bob to you, Boy?" Pa dumped the creel out. "Two and a half fish!"

"Did you give this dog our dinner to eat and make up that cockamamie story about Old Bob?" he asked.

"No, Pa!" I yelled. I knew what was coming: my Pa had no patience with liars. He picked up the fish and threw them back in the basket, then he hauled off and slapped me a good one

The dog leapt up — barking and growling. He didn't like that at all.

"Boy, you get in the house!" Pa yelled; and, turning to the dog, he added: "And, You — stay out of it!"

I went inside. My feelings were more hurt than my face was. I knew it was Old Bob. It couldn't have been a dog on that ledge. I went to bed determined that, first thing in the morning, I was going back to the cave near the creek to look for that old bobcat.

*****

I woke up with the first light of dawn. Without even waiting for breakfast, I got dressed and headed out to the creek. As I approached the area where I fell, I saw that old cat lying there. There were flies on him and he wasn't looking good. I ran back home and told Pa how I found Old Bob. He was reluctant to believe me, but he grabbed his musket and followed me down toward the cave. When we got there, he approached the cat cautiously. Pa even poked him with the end of his musket a couple of times to see if he was still alive. He got closer and lifted the cat by his shoulders. Old Bob's head just hung there all loose-like. The cat's neck was broken and there were teeth marks around his throat. We heard a rustling noise coming from the cave and my Pa wheeled around with his gun — ready to shoot whatever was in there. That was when that same big ol' dog walked out.

Pa suspects that dog probably saved my life. Apparently he darted out of the cave, caught that bobcat midair and broke his neck. I took advantage of the situation and begged Pa: "Can I keep him?"

"Under the circumstances, I can't think of one good reason why you can't, but you're going to have to take care of him all by yourself. You understand?" he insisted.

"Yes, Pa," I answered.

Pa looked the dog over real good and said that he probably

wasn't more than a couple of years old, but he had scars that were all healed-over already. "This dog's been through some pretty mean fights. He's a scrapper, but I think he'll be a good hunting dog, if he takes a liking to you," Pa told me.

He thought the dog looked like he'd "been through the war" and seen all sorts of troubles, so I decided to call him "Job," like the man in the Bible.

*****

In the weeks that followed, Pa proved to be right about Job: he was an excellent hunting dog. He could sniff out game and gently retrieve whatever Pa could shoot. One day, Job and I were walking through the woods toward the nearest settlement and we practically bumped into a black bear. I froze in my tracks and Job stayed close to me. The bear took to his hind legs and lumbered toward me making a god-awful noise. Job started snarling and barking like he was possessed by some crazed demon. I had never seen the likes of that before and, apparently, the bear hadn't either. So, the bear got back down on all fours and Job actually chased him up a tree! I didn't want to break into a full run, but I continued down the settlement path as fast as I could walk. When I had gotten a fair distance away, I turned and saw Job in full gallop. He could run mighty fast when he needed to, and, as my friend and protector, he knew that he needed to catch up with me. Job was the best dog that any boy could ever have asked for.

About a month later, we were all out hunting rabbits when we met up with Pierre the Frenchman. He was one of the local trappers. He told us that he had heard a lot of stories about Job and his hunting skills, then he took Pa over to the side to talk to him in private. I didn't like the looks of that at all, but Pa told Pierre that Job had saved my life twice already and he was getting to be "family." I was mighty proud of that.

When we got home, Pa made it clear that I'd better walk the "straight and narrow," if I wanted to keep my dog, because Pierre had made him a really good offer. Then I remembered what he had always told me about "getting attachments" and how people would use the things that you loved against you.

*****

It was getting to be the end of summer and the heat was darn near

u...bearable. I was looking forward to fall and ...atching the leaves c...ange, but, then again ...n't partial to the col..., snowy winters in o...r neck of the w...'t that something...g? — How people n...ever seem to ...y have? ...- I guess that's just w...hat they...

...Job... ...rds the ...k, when there was th...is huge cra... ...tra... ...lightning streaked st...rai... ...could be — not a c...lo... ..., I saw something q...u... ...of it before, but I k...new that... ...uld sense that Job sa... ...too.

"Could that be Elijah coming back?" I asked him. I bent down to hold onto him, because, truth be told, I was a little scared. I remembered the story of how Elijah went up to heaven in a fiery chariot, but I never thought much about it before. Chariots don't fly — simple as that. But this thing was coming down and it was coming down pretty fast, so how in tarnation did it get way up there in the sky in the first place?

The "chariot" came slicing through the treetops and I felt the earth shake when it finally hit the ground. It made a loud groaning noise as it came to rest, not far from the creek. Job bolted straight for the thing. He had to be the bravest creature on God's green earth, because he wouldn't back down to anything!

Now I wasn't about to let Elijah take my dog away with him, so I dropped everything that I was carrying and ran after Job to make my case for him. I told myself that I was prepared to walk through the very gates of Hell for that dog, but I sure didn't want to have to prove it.

The "chariot" looked like a big, flat, copper spittoon. That was never the way that I pictured a chariot when I heard those Bible stories. Weren't they supposed to be open-back wagons pulled by horses? I thought to myself: "This just *might* not be Elijah!"

I was getting closer to Job, but every time I'd get within a few feet of him, he'd run a little bit closer to the *thing*. It was hissing like a teakettle and there was steam coming off it. By the time I got close enough to Job to lay my hand on him, we were within a foot of it. There were pictures etched on the side of that *thing* and I had seen more than enough of it already.

"Come on, Job, let's get out of here," I was practically pleading with that dog. But, Job had a mind of his own. He leapt up with both paws on the side of the "spittoon" and I was amazed that he wasn't burned. I put my hand next to his left paw and, before I could marvel at how cool it felt, the surface snapped down in three circles right around the places where we touched it. There was a "clang" to my immediate left as a door flew open and, with a sudden "whoosh," two large creatures were hurled out of the opening. They were making terrible noises like they couldn't breathe. I didn't take a good look at them, but they were a lot bigger than Pa — and, then, Job was on the move again! He ran up the ramp, so I got up and raced after him. There was a wall at the end of the ramp and Job jumped up against it. I desperately grasped at his tail as the wall flew open.

As soon as I got my fingers on Job, I saw a hand dart out from around the corner. Someone — or some *thing* — had his hand around Job's muzzle. I thought I heard a voice, then I blacked out.

When I woke up, Job was right there beside me, licking my face. We were still inside the "thing," but now I realized that it was a ship of some sort. I wasn't especially good at reading and writing, but the strange markings that I saw all around it were almost beginning to make some kind of sense. Whatever had grabbed Job was nowhere to be seen, but those long, pale-greenish fingers sure didn't look human. At least Job seemed to be none the worse for wear.

I didn't know how long that I had slept there, but I knew that I didn't want to stay in that strange place any longer than necessary. Job and I got up and walked down the ramp. I saw the two creatures still lying on the ground. I had never seen anything like them before, nor had I ever seen outfits like the ones that they wore. Maybe I should have left them there, but I got to feeling like I should bury them. They certainly looked dead and it just seemed to be the righteous thing to do.

It was getting late and I didn't have a shovel, so I piled rocks over them to keep the animals from eating the carcasses. Pa was going to be mad enough when I got home as it was.

*****

Pa was waiting on the porch with his musket when Job and I got back. "Did you catch any fish?" he asked. I had dropped my gear when I saw the thing in the sky and I had forgotten all about it.

"No, Pa. I'm sorry," I told him and I meant it. It was obvious

22

that Pa had been into his corn liquor and he was a mean drunk.

"Where've you been all day, Boy?" he asked me.

"Pa, I was on that thing that come down from the sky," I answered.

"What thing?" he asked with just a hint of menace.

I knew that he wasn't patient with long stories and the drink wasn't going to help matters.

"There was this great big ship that came down from the sky this morning. It looked like a big flat copper spittoon and there were at least three creatures on it. Two of them are dead so I buried them." I blurted the words out as fast as I could.

Pa looked at me long and hard, then he burst out laughing. "Boy, have you got a touch of madness? Now, you go on inside. I think you may have just bought me a decent bottle of whiskey."

Job and I walked past him and through the door of the cabin. I wasn't sure what he meant, but I knew that it couldn't be good.

Pa followed close behind me. As soon as we were inside, he said: "Daniel..."

I turned around to face him just in time to meet his closed fist. I was thrown against the opposite wall and Job stood between us: growling a deep, angry growl.

"Boy, you knowed the rules. I told you that you was going to listen to me and be respectful of your Pa and now you expect me to believe a cock and bull story about some damned spittoon from the sky? Your Ma would still be alive today if it wasn't for you being borned and I'm sure not about to put up with your insolence!" Pa yelled.

Job was still snarling and showing all of his teeth. He backed up towards me, but he kept his eyes solidly on Pa. I felt Job's tail slide

23

between my legs as he sat on my feet, glaring and growling at my old man. I was terrified that Pa was going to hurt him.

"Well, Boy, this is the way it's going to be. You're getting out of my house right now and I'm selling that damned dog of yours to Pierre. Do you understand me, Boy?" he threatened.

Pa took one step closer to us. Job backed firmly against me and I put my hand up in self-defense. It was obvious that Pa was fixing to hit me again, so I closed my eyes. When I opened them again, Pa's clothes were lying on his shoes, but there was no sign of him and I never did see him in the flesh again.

For a few seconds, I stood there terrified and holding Job for dear life — wondering where Pa went and feeling guilty that it was my fault that he was gone. I closed my eyes tightly to distance myself from what had just occurred and I could suddenly see what Pa was seeing. So it didn't take me too long to figure out where he went, because I was witnessing it first hand in my own head. But it took me a real long time to figure out how this all happened and what it all had to do with Job and me.

I hereby testify and bear witness that these events happened in the year of our Lord: eighteen hundred and fifty.

Dan'l Johnstone

*****

Jessie snapped the book shut. Then, she reopened it and re-read the last few lines. "Things are getting curiouser and curiouser," she whispered. She got out of the bed to put the thin volume back on the shelf. She was starting to yawn and the ordeal of the last couple of days was beginning to get the best of her. She was just about to head back to bed when she decided to take a quick glance at the other thin books. She picked up the next one titled: *Jebediah.*

"I wonder if this is another dog fantasy?" she asked aloud. Then she got back into bed. She anxiously flipped open the dusty leather cover and began to read the hand-printed, yellowed pages.

Chapter 3

Jebediah

"Jebediah? Lord, have mercy! What do you think you're doing?" a voice from the past screamed from behind him. Pa staggered around slowly to see his younger sister Martha removing her just-dried clothes from a rope.

"Martha? How did you get here?" he asked.

"A better question would be: what are you doing standing naked as a jaybird in the middle of the street?" she responded. He looked around and noticed that all of the passersby were whispering and giggling.

"Jebediah, you're looking fit!" a vaguely-familiar voice yelled from a coach wheeling past. Pa could hear several people laughing raucously from within the coach.

"For decency's sake, cover yourself!" Aunt Martha threw him a towel.

"I don't know how he did this, but I'm going to kill that little witch — and his big dog, too!" Pa muttered angrily. He had done a lot of drinking in his day, but nothing like this had ever happened before. He wrapped the towel around himself and looked around.

"Boston?" he asked incredulously.

"Of course, it's Boston!" Martha answered. "You go off to God-knows-where for years without so much as a letter and then you show up drunk and stark naked in front of my house! What *will* the neighbors think?"

She was finished with her laundry and she held the full basket in front of herself. "I'd go over there and hug you, dear Brother, but things look bad enough already. Now, you get inside here this instant!" She held the door open for him.

He entered her house. He was quite familiar with the place. With my Ma dying when I was born, Aunt Martha had practically raised me until I was eight. That was when Pa decided to give up his law practice to begin his "great adventure." He was caught up with the fervor to go West.

Pa sat on a chair in the small kitchen. Aunt Martha threw a shirt and an old pair of trousers at him. They belonged to her late husband, my Uncle Bob. "There, now. You put those on!" she barked, although the gesture was self-explanatory. "I'll have none of your gallivanting around here naked in this house!"

"Now, are you going to tell me what this is all about?" she asked.

"Martha, I wouldn't know where to start," he muttered, "And you would never believe me, even if I knew how to tell you."

*****

Telling the truth was something that my Pa prided himself on. But every time he told his story to someone, he was met with disbelief, laughter or, worst of all, concern. He took to drinking heavily, but Aunt Martha would have none of that in her house. For the next several months, he wasted a lot of time drinking and sleeping in gutters, but that wasn't tolerated well in Aunt Martha's neighborhood. She finally imposed upon the local deacon to do whatever he could to sober her "dear Jebediah" up.

Pa spent a few months in the Boston Asylum for the Mentally Unfit, but, eventually, he got back to practicing law again. He no longer yearned for his "great adventure" and he rarely talked about Job or me. At one point, I read that he spoke at a law conference where an ambitious lawyer named Lincoln introduced Pa as "the most eminent drunken prevaricator in all of Boston." I would reckon that's considered "high praise" so far as lawyers go.

*****

When Pa disappeared from the cabin, I found that I could put my mind in his place so that I could see and hear whatever he was experiencing. I never knew how I could do that or what to call it, but it was a gift that apparently came along with the power to send people away. I didn't invoke that ability much beyond occasionally "checking up" on him. A number of years later, I heard that he had died and I found that my notions to visit his thoughts no longer worked. I don't know if that disproves the existence of Heaven or if it just means that his brain was no longer in touch with his soul.

In the days that followed my Pa's departure from our cabin, Job and I set about to moving our home, piece by piece, to the site where the ship had landed. I also planted a whole thicket of junipers around it, so that it would eventually be surrounded by tall trees. It took a couple of years to completely cover the ship from view, but, as luck would have it, it was already nearly obscured by trees, both standing and felled by the impact, in the first place. That saved the two of us a lot of time and trouble.

Much of our day was taken up by mere survival: hunting, fishing, planting and fetching firewood and water. We did our best to avoid the locals. Luckily, the closest settlement was a good piece down the path, but, as time went on, Pierre the Trapper became a problem. He was always poking around, looking for Pa and asking if I'd be willing to sell Job to him. And, I would always tell him the same tales: "Pa up and left" and "No deal."

One day, Pierre showed up with the local padre. They accused me of doing away with Pa and the priest wanted me to confess my sins. I told them: "I never killed nobody — as God is my witness!"

But Pierre was determined to get Job: even if it meant having me hanged as a murderer or burned as a witch.

The discussion was getting rather heated and Job got agitated. He leaned against my legs and, the next thing I knew, both Pierre and the padre were gone. I had suddenly inherited Pierre's clothes, his gun, his skinning knife, some traps and all of the poor padre's things as well.

When I connected with the priest's mind, I could see that they were both standing naked in some kind of a fountain in Rome. I wouldn't have known the place by the looks of it, but the padre was obviously familiar with his surroundings. I still don't know what I'm supposed to do with his prayer beads.

*****

By the following spring, I had the cabin finished so that you could walk straight through the backdoor and into the ship. And, it really wasn't all that long before the cabin and the junipers blocked the view of the ship on all sides. On those few occasions when someone happened upon us, I learned that I could read the greatest fear in their mind and I would make them associate that particular fear with our place. That way, if someone happened to be terrified of snakes, they would think this area was just crawling with rattlesnakes and vipers. That usually was sufficient to prevent repeat visits.

Job and I spent a lot of time trying to repair the ship, but parts and materials simply weren't available. So, we periodically traveled to colleges to make subtle "suggestions" to the professors. We didn't expect to be taken seriously by the smart folk, but we could plant ideas in their minds without them even realizing where those ideas came from. I didn't always rightly understand the things that were in my own head, but I knew that they worked and that it was necessary to deliver the messages to the people who could understand them.

It took quite a long time for me to notice it, but, so long as Job and I stayed together, neither of us seemed to age all that much. Truth be told, I never wanted to be away from Job no ways. He's my best friend and confider. I always seem to know what he's thinking and what he needs. Likewise, with him. If I drop a tool or forget where I put it, I'll turn around and he'll have it in his mouth or he'll be standing over it. In all my days, I've never seen a more faithful companion — man or beast — to anyone.

It was like it was preordained that we should live long enough to repair the ship, although I didn't rightly know why. All of the creatures who came with it were either dead or gone and I had no use for the thing. I had acquired some familiarity with what the etchings meant both inside and outside the craft, but there was always a level of understanding that was just missing. It was a great puzzle to me: all of the pieces were there, but it was still a jumble. Sometimes I felt like Job understood our purpose way better than I did. But, understand it or not, I continued to work on the ship.

Decades would pass between major breakthroughs in science and technology. Job and I knew that we had to be patient — and what more prophetic a name could I have given him than the name of the most patient man in all of the Bible! So, we waited and we just enjoyed being alive. We were forever young and we could romp up and down those hills like a boy and his pup. We avoided contact with other people, because people always ask too many questions. We didn't want to hurt anyone or to send anyone away.

Both my reading and writing skills improved rather quickly after being exposed to the ship. My vocabulary got better as I needed to understand more things and to translate those ideas into something useful. Eventually I came to realize where all of this suddenly new-found knowledge was coming from: it all came from the hand that grabbed Job.

That hand belonged to a creature named Kandar. A being who traveled so far in this ship that we can't even see the planet from whence he came and we can only barely see his sun in our night sky. Some of Kandar's knowledge has been revealed to me and I have never known of a more amazing creature.

*****

Jessie closed the book. She wasn't accustomed to going to bed this early and her head still hurt from her injury, so she dug through her purse to find some aspirin. She took two pills and swallowed them with water from the glass on the nightstand. She put the book back on the shelf and looked around for something to wear.

There was a man's robe hanging in the closet, so she threw that on over her undergarments and slipped her shoes back on. She thought she could hear someone whistling and strumming a guitar outside. She had heard that melody earlier. It was a haunting air: a waltz with a minor-key quality to it. Jessie knew a little bit about music, but she wasn't at all familiar with this particular piece.

She unlocked the bedroom door, walked through the kitchen and straight out the front door. Daniel was sitting at the make-shift picnic table playing a guitar. He saw her, stopped playing and closed the 3-ringed binder in front of him.

"I'm sorry. I didn't mean to wake you," he said apologetically.

"That's okay, I wasn't sleeping anyway," Jessie replied as she approached the table. "Are you any good with that thing?"

"Not particularly. I'm self-taught," he responded, with a slight laugh.

"You were playing something before I came out. I'm sure I've heard you whistling that tune once before. What song is that?" she asked.

"It's called 'She.' It's just something that I made up awhile back," he replied rather sheepishly.

"Could you play some of it for me? It really sounded nice," she prodded him.

Daniel paged through the binder to find the song again and he began to play the guitar. He picked through an intro and continued instrumentally into the verse.

"Don't be shy," Jessie interrupted him, "I can see you have words for it!" She stood behind the boy and leaned over him to read the typed lyrics.

"Come on. You can sing in front of me!" she urged him on, teasingly.

Daniel stopped playing and started from the beginning again. This time he sang the words: "I broke through the shell of the wind. — Felt it shatter across my face. She rode a cloud from where I was going, While..." He suddenly stopped playing and looked away.

"That's so pretty. Why'd you stop?" Jessie asked. "What's wrong?"

Daniel was a little choked-up and tried to conceal his embarrassment.

"Nothing's wrong. I'm not all that used to playing in front of people," he said. "Besides, my voice isn't the best tonight and I guess

I just don't feel like playing right now."

"So, you compose your own songs and you write your own stories. You know, you're actually very talented!" Jessie remarked with a hint of admiration.

"Stories?" Daniel locked his eyes on hers.

"Yes, I was reading some of those short stories that you left on the shelf in my room," she responded. "They're interesting. I mean: you have a lot of imagination."

Job stood up and got a bit closer to Daniel.

"Nobody was supposed to read those. I really wish you hadn't," the young man mumbled, looking down at the ground in front of him.

"Daniel, I didn't mean any harm. The stories are nicely written. I'm not exactly a teacher, but I studied journalism and I think you have a flair for writing," she replied, not wanting to upset the boy.

"Well, what's done is done," Daniel said quietly. He petted Job with long, reassuring, calming strokes.

Jessie sat next to Daniel and put her hand on his. She didn't mean to do anything to upset him and she was genuinely taking an interest in him.

Daniel locked his fingers around hers and looked up at the early night sky.

"Job, there's a faint star just below the moon that isn't supposed to be there," he told the dog. Job looked up and then back at Daniel.

"I guess we should all turn in for the night and get some sleep. I have a feeling that tomorrow is going to be a busy day," Daniel announced.

"Good night, Daniel, I hope you're not angry with me." Jessie stood up, still holding his hand.

"No, we're good. I hope you'll sleep well," the boy replied.

Then he added: "There is just one thing. Why were those guys chasing you?"

Jessie was wondering when that question would come up. "Daniel, I didn't do anything wrong. Honestly, I didn't! It was all one big misunderstanding," she explained.

"Those cars were from Rev-Tech and there was something on the news about classified documents being stolen from there," he persisted.

Jessie sat down again. "I didn't steal anything. I was just trying to get a story and I took some pictures that I guess I shouldn't have taken."

"What kind of story were you trying to do?" he asked.

She looked him squarely in the eyes and asked, "Can I trust you? I mean, after that 'blind' stunt that you pulled earlier: should I even *dare* to trust you?"

"Well, I protected you from those guys who were chasing you and I brought you here to safety, didn't I?" he answered.

Jessie pondered that question for just a moment before responding: "Daniel, I'm a reporter and my first assignment was to apply for a job at Rev-Tech Bionics Corporation. There are a lot of government trucks going in and out of there and it seems like there's some kind of top-secret lab in the main building complex. My boss thinks that it's in the public interest to expose these things. Who knows if they're making weapons in there?"

"So, what's in the photo?" Daniel asked.

"I'm not really sure. As I was leaving the interview, I noticed that the door to a laboratory was half-open, so I stuck my hand inside and snapped a picture," she admitted.

34

"Then maybe we should take a look at your photos," Daniel suggested.

Quite reluctantly, Jessie replied: "The camera is in my purse." She stood to go back to her room. Daniel and Job followed her through the kitchen and waited just outside the bedroom door. For a moment, she debated the possibility of running right past the two of them and straight out the front door with it, but she returned with the camera. It was a rather cheap one, hardly the tool of a professional journalist.

"I'm sorry, but I really don't want you to touch this, because I'm afraid you might accidentally erase my pictures," she insisted.

"Okay, here's the plan," Daniel said with some authority. "The only way we can square you up with Rev-Tech is if we can prove that you don't have any 'top-secret' or 'classified' information in your camera. You don't want them chasing you for the rest of your life, do you?"

"No, but, this story could be important," she whined in protest.

"Important or not, your story isn't worth dying for," Daniel answered.

"Alright, just hold the camera in front of you. I won't even touch it," he assured her. He lifted his right hand and swept it through the air in front of her camera, pointing at the wall with one gesture. The first photo frame lit up the wall. He held his hands parallel and a few inches apart in front of the projected image and spread them wider. The image enlarged.

Jessie's jaw dropped: "How did you—?"

"Hidden features — all of the new cameras have them," he interrupted. The first photo was just the sign in front of the Rev-Tech building, so he scrolled to the next picture with a wave of his hand.

One by one he scrolled through the first five photos.

"Now, that's amazing! Are you some kind of ventriloquist or something?" Jessie asked, spellbound.

"Ventriloquist?" Daniel laughed. "Do you think that I can throw my voice to make Job talk or are you suggesting that he's talking through me?"

"No, no, not ventriloquist," she said, embarrassed by her obviously poor choice of words, "What's the word that I'm looking for?"

"I can't throw my voice, but I know someone who throws shoes — maybe you've got a word for that?" Daniel interjected, good-naturedly.

"So, would you like another demonstration of my throwing skills?" she threatened, as she lifted her foot and bent over slightly to meet it.

"No, thanks. Let's just try some other words instead: magician? Hypnotist?" he suggested trying to divert the subject.

"Yes. Hypnotist!" she decided. "Are you just making me think I'm seeing this?"

"No, nothing like that at all. Really! These are just 'hidden features,'" he insisted. The first five pictures were all innocent enough, but he stopped at the sixth one.

"This could be a problem, but I think I can fix it for you," he offered.

The photo showed the inside of the lab. A rather large orb was visible on the table and a lab worker had his back to the camera. Daniel cupped his hands around the image of the sphere: "First, we'll remove this." He moved the orb outside of the photo frame onto another section of wall.

"Now, we'll make this little adjustment," he added. He cupped his hands around the image of the lab assistant and simultaneously moved and enlarged it to obscure the area where the sphere had been.

"You can't do that. I mean, that just isn't possible!" Jessie gasped.

"Well, you saw it with your own eyes. Cameras are a lot more sophisticated than you would guess from reading their manuals. There are tons of features loaded into their internal memories that most people just don't know how to access. By next year, they'll release the new version of that camera and all of these hidden features will be their 'big new improvements' to get people to buy the very same thing that they already have."

That almost made sense to Jessie. She knew how they would always market new improvements in technology just as soon as you managed to pay off last year's model.

Daniel waved his hand again and the image on the wall scrolled back to the first photo. "So, that was the last photo you took?" he asked.

"Yes, so far as I can recall. I was leaving the building when I snapped it and I wasn't about to stick around there to take any more," she replied.

"You've *really* got to show me how to do all that stuff!" she insisted.

"Maybe when we have more time," Daniel answered. He waved his hand from the illuminated area of the wall back towards the camera. The photo frame disappeared from the wall. Jessie looked at her camera screen and paged through the photos. All six photos were still there, but now the sixth one simply showed the back of the lab assistant in front of the table. The sphere was missing from the photo.

"But now, where's my story?" Jessie pleaded.

"Your well-being and your future are much more important than some story," Daniel tried to comfort her. "Tomorrow we'll take that camera back to Rev-Tech and show them that no harm was done or else you'll be running for the rest of your life."

Jessie was disappointed. She turned and stepped back into the bedroom. "Maybe you're right. I'm not even sure if I saw what I think I just saw. Maybe I'd better just get some sleep."

"Good night, Jessie," Daniel said with a warm smile.

"Good night. And, thanks. I think," she responded with some hesitation. She closed the door and locked it. She removed the robe and put it back in the closet, kicked off her shoes and crawled back into the bed. She was disappointed that her story would never be printed and that she still had no idea what the sphere could possibly be — or even what she had just witnessed.

Daniel looked at the image of the sphere still on the wall. "Job, that isn't good," he whispered. He extended his hand towards the image and the globe floated above his palm as a three-dimensional hologram. Then he added quietly: "Vargon, if you please: retrieve this device and deliver it to the ship." With another wave of his hand, the image disappeared from the room.

*****

The phone rang next to the President's bed. He grabbed it on the second ring. "Yes?" he intoned, slightly annoyed.

"Mr. President, I really am sorry to bother you at this hour, but we've gotten a rather strange report from the SETI Institute," the voice replied.

"And you are?" the President asked.

"I'm sorry, Mr. President, I'm Colonel George Wagner," the officer answered.

"Of course. I believe we've met," the POTUS responded.

"Yes, Sir, we have," Wagner assured him.

"So, what's the problem? SETI needs funding?" the President asked.

"No, Sir. They're getting a regular signal," the Colonel told him.

"What are we talking about — their TV service?" the weary elected official joked with some irritation. "Because I'm tired and I've got a very busy schedule tomorrow."

"No, Sir. Mr. President, a couple of days ago, they detected a regular transmission aimed at us from deep space," the officer informed him.

"And, have they deciphered the transmission?" the President asked.

"Not yet, Sir, but they're working on it and they're convinced that it's the real thing this time," Colonel Wagner answered.

"We're talking about actual alien contact here?" the POTUS wondered aloud.

"It's almost an absolute certainty, Sir!" the officer replied.

"Keep me informed, Colonel," the President said as he hung up the phone and climbed back into bed.

*****

The next morning, Jessie awoke to the smell of breakfast cooking in the kitchen. She used the washroom, dressed herself quickly and emerged from the bedroom.

"That aroma is absolutely irresistible!" she said as she brought her appetite straight to the table.

"Good morning, Jessie! It's only bacon and eggs," Daniel smiled.

"I'm sorry, I'm forgetting my manners! Good morning, Daniel!" she responded. Then, as she bent towards Job and patted his head, she added: "And a good morning to you too, you big, handsome fellow!"

Job raised his head into her hand, so she bent down to wrap both of her hands firmly around his face. She kissed him lightly on the head and stood up briefly. Then she sat at the kitchen table with her legs crossed under her. She wasn't at all accustomed to being waited on, but she was quickly learning to enjoy it.

"How did you learn to cook?" she asked.

"Practice makes perfect. I've been on my own for quite some time now and, you know, you just have to learn to do things for yourself or else they never get done," he replied. "As soon as we're finished eating here, we're heading right over to Rev-Tech to straighten things out for you."

"Who are you going to be? My lawyer?" she suggested sarcastically.

"You could do worse," he responded with a grin.

They took their time enjoying breakfast and, when they were preparing to leave, it suddenly dawned on Jessie to ask: "How are we going to get there? My car's still stuck in the mud!"

"We'll take mine," Daniel replied. "Just wait here. I'll be back in no time!"

He and Job walked off into the woods and within a couple of minutes she heard the roar of an untamed engine. Daniel pulled up in front of the house in an old army-surplus Jeep with Job seated in the back.

"Hop in!" he shouted above the noise of the engine.

"My, you *are* full of surprises!" she replied in amazement.

Daniel took a circuitous route through the woods that seemed to go on for miles. When they finally emerged onto the highway, Jessie realized that they weren't far from the side road that she had taken just a couple of days earlier. She was curious whether her car was still there and she also wondered if the Hummers were still parked behind it.

They drove back down the four-lane highway to Rev-Tech Bionics. Daniel looked at Jessie to reassure her: "Everything is going to be fine, you just let me do all of the talking." He slowed the Jeep as they approached the sentry gate and came to a halt.

"Good morning! We're just here to visit your boss," Daniel told the guard.

"Uh, yes, Sir," the guard replied without challenging the young man's intentions. He lifted the gate and waved them through.

Jessie couldn't believe that it was so easy to get into the complex. She had to sign in at the gate and concoct a whole story about wanting to apply for a job there! Daniel, on the other hand, pulled straight into a parking space marked "reserved" and parked his Jeep. "What a brazen young man!" she thought.

Daniel walked around to the passenger side and offered Jessie his hand to help her out of the vehicle. The three of them entered the facility through the main doors.

Jessie had just been there, so she knew she had to sign in at the desk. The seated guard pointed to a clipboard without paying much attention to the two young visitors. She wrote "Jessica Drake" on the top line and slid the clipboard over to Daniel. He wrote: "Wilbur Post and Ed," and slid it back towards her. She read it and covered her mouth with her hand, stifling a snicker. If she hadn't been so terrified of what they might do to her, she would have thought they were just a couple of high school kids pulling a harmless prank.

The guard at the desk silently reviewed the names and said: "Miss Drake and — uh — Mr. Post, you can go straight to the main office." He buzzed them through the security gate.

"So far, so good," Jessie whispered.

Daniel led Job and Jessie right past the secretary's office and knocked on the already-open door of Jonathan Marx, the executive officer. Mr. Marx glanced up at the boy and smiled: "Mr. Johnstone, please, come right in!"

Jessie gasped at the mention of the name.

"Jonathan, I've got a guest here whom I'd really like you to meet," Daniel said, leading the young woman into the room. "This is my dear friend: Jessie."

Mr. Marx bolted upright. "How did you find her?" he shouted.

"I don't know what's going on; but I'm getting out of here!" Jessie shrieked.

Daniel pushed the door shut behind his back, preventing her escape. He grabbed her arm lightly. "Just a second, Jessie, please don't panic. Just stay calm and everything is going to be alright."

"What do you mean 'everything's going to be alright,' Daniel? We have video of her taking photos in an unauthorized area and we sent four good men after her two days ago. We haven't heard a word from any of them since!" Marx barked.

"Calm down, Jonathan. There was no harm done. I've seen the pictures and I've persuaded Jessie to surrender her camera to you.

You can examine it yourself — or even send it down to the lab to make sure that nothing's been altered on it. There is absolutely nothing on this camera that is worth all of the trouble that we're in," Daniel cautioned.

"So, how is it that *we're* suddenly in trouble?" Marx screamed.

"You sent four men after this young lady and she can file battery charges against them. She can sue all of us for everything we're worth. Your men approached her with guns drawn and, right in front of me, one of them hauled off and hit her on the back of the head with his pistol!" Daniel yelled back. "I own this company and I am not about to lose it over their stupidity!"

"You *what*???" Jessie screeched.

"I own the company and I am really sorry about the way that my employees have treated you. If they ever show up again, I can assure you that they'll all be fired," Daniel responded. "Now if we can all calm down for a second, we can clear Ms. Drake of any wrong-doing."

"Please have a seat, Jessie," Daniel offered as he pulled a chair out in front of the desk. "And, Jonathan, you sit down, too!"

Jessie sat down. "I knew I shouldn't have trusted you — I knew it! I thought you were my friend and all the time you owned the company that caused all of my problems!" she muttered. Jessie was furious.

"Okay, so what's on the camera?" Marx asked.

Daniel handed the camera to him: "Here! Look for yourself. There's nothing on here that is worth the world of hurt that this young lady can put us through."

Marx paged through the photos, then he clicked the intercom button: "Maxine, have somebody from the lab come in here. I have a camera that they need to examine."

"Yes, Sir," a female voice responded.

Jessie stared at Daniel, fuming. She could only *barely* contain her anger.

"Miss Drake, Daniel, can I offer either of you something to drink while we're waiting?" Marx offered politely. The realization that their positions had suddenly reversed was finally beginning to sink in. He enjoyed his job and he was actually relieved that the photos didn't reveal anything that he was trying to keep from Daniel.

There was a knock on the door.

"Come on in," Marx responded loudly.

A lab technician entered the room: "Mr. Marx, did you need something?"

"Yes. Take this camera back to the lab and make sure that nothing's been deleted from the memory. And don't take all day, I need you to get it right back to me as soon as possible," Jonathan told him.

There was no small talk in Marx's office. Finally, Daniel broke the ice: "So what exactly was Miss Drake *not* supposed to have on her camera?"

Marx fidgeted: "Well, there's no particular project that I can think of off the top of my head, but we can't be too careful. We both know we do a lot of government contracting and there's no room for industrial spies in our facilities. Those men were just supposed to retrieve that camera and nobody was supposed to get hurt."

"Would you like to look at the bump on the back of this young lady's head?" the boy asked him.

"No, I don't have to see it, Daniel. Ms. Drake, I really *do* apologize for the way that you were mistreated by our employees. I hope that we can come to some kind of mutually-beneficial agreement to prevent any sort of legal action," Marx added by rote.

Within fifteen minutes, the lab tech returned with the camera. He entered the room and handed it to Jonathan: "Mr. Marx, I can assure you that there are only six photos on that camera's internal memory and that none of them have been altered."

"Thanks, Walters, that will be all," Marx replied, and the lab tech left the room.

"Well, there you have it. — Much ado about nothing!" Daniel said, patting Job on the head. "Please notify the local authorities that there is absolutely no reason for them to continue looking for, or bothering, Miss Drake any further. She has been through quite enough already."

"Sure, Daniel. I'll get on that immediately," Marx replied, and to Jessie he added: "My apologies to you once again, Miss Drake, I am truly sorry about all of this. If you need anything, please let me know and I will attend to it personally. Have your lawyer contact me at any time and I will do my best to set things right for you."

"Thank you, Mr. Marx, I can assure you that you'll be hearing from him shortly," Jessie replied coldly, knowing full well that she didn't have, or even know, a lawyer.

Daniel, Jessie and Job rose to leave the office. Daniel looked back at Marx: "Take care, Jonathan, and let me know if you ever get your hands on anything that's worth all of this intrigue!" The boy retrieved the camera from the desk and handed it back to Jessie as they approached the open door.

They had just gotten a few feet down the corridor from the office when Walters ran right past them. He continued through the doorway, panting: "Mr. Marx, the artifact from lab B is missing."

"What? It can't be!" Marx replied. He clicked the intercom button and added a curt: "Stop them!"

As Daniel, Jessie and Job got to the lobby, two guards blocked the door.

"What's the problem?" Daniel asked.

The first guard answered: "I'm sorry, Mr. Johnstone, but we were asked to detain all of you for just a moment."

Marx ran up from behind them. He looked at Daniel, Jessie and the dog and then he made eye contact with the second guard.

"Search Mr. Johnstone's Jeep!" he wheezed.

The guard walked outside and looked the Jeep over thoroughly. Within a couple of minutes, he returned, appearing somewhat bewildered.

"I'm not sure what I'm looking for, but I can't find anything that would be considered 'unusual' in Mr. Johnstone's vehicle," the guard addressed his boss.

Daniel removed his sunglasses and stared at Marx: "So, Jonathan, is it okay if we go now? Or, would you like to frisk us first? Bear in mind, that, if you touch this young lady, I'll see that you're put up on sexual assault charges!"

Marx waved them toward the exit and started to walk back towards his office.

"Oh, and Jonathan: I want a written report detailing exactly what it was you were looking for in my Jeep. You'll have it on my desk by Monday. Got it?" Daniel shouted.

Not at all amused, Marx turned back and yelled, "Young Man, just because your grandfather founded this company doesn't mean that you can order me around!"

46

"Jonathan, you're absolutely right about that. It's not because he founded it; it's because I *own* it! And, that's why you'll have that report on my desk on Monday. Do you understand me?" Daniel replied firmly.

"Yes, SIR, Mister Johnstone!" Marx retorted with no lack of sarcasm as he marched back into his office and slammed the door.

"Give me a second," Daniel told Jessie as he walked back towards the secretary's office and stuck his head through the open door. Job followed close behind.

"Maxine, please call up 'Legal' and have them send a copy of Marx's contract to his office. I think he needs to be reminded that he's just an employee here," the boy ordered the young woman.

"Yes, Sir, Mr. Johnstone, I'll get right on it," she replied, reaching for her phone.

"Thanks, and have a great afternoon!" Daniel smiled.

The young lady smiled back at the boy: "You too, Sir."

Daniel and Job rejoined Jessie in the lobby and the three of them exited Rev-Tech. They headed straight for the Jeep. Daniel put his sunglasses back on.

"Up you go, Boy," he told Job. He offered his hand to Jessie, who was obviously still fuming. "Jessie, I'm really sorry about all of this. I promise I'll make it up to you somehow, but first I think we should get out of here."

She ignored his hand and got into the Jeep on her own. He started the engine. As he pulled up to the sentry box, he waved to Jenkins. The guard raised the gate and Daniel accelerated out onto the highway driving much too fast. The grinning boy turned to Jessie and asked: "Did you ever think you'd be doing 65 miles an hour down this highway with a 'blind boy' at the wheel?"

He was trying to get her to smile, but it quite noticeably wasn't working.

"Just take me to my car," she replied coldly.

"Look, Jessie, I'll admit that I should have told you that I own Rev-Tech, but, if I had: would you have believed me?" Daniel asked.

He drove just past the gravel road where she had left her car and pulled over on the shoulder. He stopped the Jeep and turned towards her: "Look at me, Jessie. You saw how I live. Do I look like I could possibly own a big company like Rev-Tech?"

She peered at him. "What are you? — Like fifteen or sixteen years old? — No, I guess I wouldn't have believed you." She paused. "But you still should have told me anyway!"

He looked her squarely in the eyes: "Jessie, I really am sorry about all of this. I can give you so much money that you'll never need for anything; you'll never have to work again, but please don't be angry with me."

Her chin started to quiver and her eyes glazed over. She buried her face in her hands and started to weep quietly. The accumulation of stress was taking its toll on the young woman.

"Jessie, I could never do anything to intentionally hurt you. You've come to mean so much to me over these past couple of days. When I saw you running from those guys, I didn't know who you were or why they were chasing you. All I saw was a beautiful damsel in distress and I just had to save you," he said, extending his arm around her shoulders. She initially pulled away, but then she leaned in towards the boy and rested her forehead against his chin.

Job yawned loudly.

"Let me take you back to my place and I'll make you some lunch.

Hit me if you want to hit me, but please stop crying. I did everything that I promised I would do: I cleared your name; the authorities won't be looking for you anymore and I'll make sure that you'll never have to work again. Just *please* don't be angry with me," the young man pleaded in earnest. He had never felt like this before.

Jessie wiped her tears with her hands.

"I'll never have to work again?" she mumbled through a forced smile.

"Never, *ever*," he whispered. "I can even hire somebody to throw your shoes at me for you."

"Now, this is starting to sound serious!" Jessie laughed. She was just beginning to realize how much she liked Daniel. He was an absolute puzzle to her: so young, so wealthy, so powerful, so talented. He was almost magical! She had witnessed things that she still could not believe and she was starting to wonder if any of the stories that he had written could have even a nub of truth to them. She had to go back to the cabin with him. She needed to finish reading those skinny leather volumes to find out if there was any explanation that could solve this intriguing mystery of a young man.

"Take me to your leader," Jessie joked.

Daniel pulled back onto the highway, but, before they got to their turn, Job pushed between them and nudged the boy.

"We seem to have a request from the peanut gallery. Do you mind if we take a slight detour first?" the young man asked Jessie.

"Sure, why not?" she replied amiably.

Daniel continued past his private road and made a left at the next intersection. He drove a short distance and stopped in front of a church.

"Okay, Boy, but we're not staying here all day," he told Job.

The dog jumped out of the Jeep and sat in front of a statue. The church was called Our Lady of Grace Church and in front of it, there was a large statue of a woman standing on a globe, which apparently represented the earth. The sun was glinting off the white marble figure. It might not have been great art, but it was a fair likeness of an attractive young woman with her arms spread slightly from her sides.

Daniel and Jessie got out of the vehicle and walked over to Job. Daniel stooped over the dog, petting him playfully. "Now come on, Job. You know that isn't her."

Job looked up at him, let out a short whine and looked back at the statue. He lay down with his head nestled between his front paws and his eyes fixed on the figure. It was obvious that he didn't want to leave.

"What gives?" Jessie asked.

"Job happened to see this place by accident one day and he's taken a fancy to that lady up there. We'll just give him another minute," Daniel replied.

They started back towards the Jeep. Daniel held his hand out and Jessie put her hand in his.

"So you own Rev-Tech and your dog is an art lover?" she joked.

"Yeah, something like that," he replied. Daniel helped her into the vehicle and walked around to the driver's side. "Come on, Job, let's go get something to eat!"

Job got up rather slowly, then he ran to the Jeep and jumped up on the back seat. He looked back at the statue and continued to stare at it as Daniel started the vehicle and headed back toward the main road. He made a right turn. The boy was smiling widely as he made a quick left about a quarter mile further down the road and followed the winding dirt path back up to his shack. In all of his years, Daniel had never met anyone quite like Jessie and he was feeling a closeness to her that he had never before experienced.

He wanted to know everything about her: where she lived, where she had gone to school and, most importantly, if there was another man in her life. By the time they got back to Daniel's home, it was well past noon and he had promised her lunch.

"I've got some chicken breasts in the freezer, if you can deal with grilled chicken?" he asked Jessie.

"Chicken is fine with me," she responded.

He unlocked the door and held the screen door for her as she ascended the couple of wooden steps to the kitchen.

"This is going to take a little while," he added.

"Well, I've probably been fired from my newspaper, but it looks like someone is going to fix things so I'll 'never *ever*' have to work again. So, I guess I've got time," she laughed. She still wasn't sure if she could believe everything that Daniel was telling her, but she certainly admired the way that he dealt with Mr. Marx at Rev-Tech.

"I'm going to freshen up a little bit while you're fixing lunch," she added.

Jessie walked back through the house to her room. She locked the door behind her and kicked off her shoes. She wasn't prepared to read a whole novel, but, apparently, Daniel had quite some imagination and she was becoming engrossed in his quaint style of storytelling. If the books were truly written by him, then he clearly had the makings of an author. She returned to the shelf and noticed that the next two thin books were titled: *Kandar* and *Shahlaya and the Vargon*.

"In for a penny, in for a pound," she whispered as she selected the book called *Kandar*. She lay on the bed, propped herself up with her pillow and opened the book.

Chapter 4

Kandar

Kandar was pressed into military service while still in school on his home planet of Ionus. The Forever War with the planet Bardok was beginning its second millennium and he fully understood that conscription was necessary. He was an exceptionally athletic young man, but what made him truly extraordinary was his mind. He scored high, not only in intelligence, but in the areas of telepathy and telekinesis. Many people on Ionus could read the thoughts of someone in close proximity, but Kandar could both project and read thoughts from kilometers away. Similarly, there were other cadets in his class who could move small objects with their minds, but, on more than one occasion, Kandar had actually lifted full-grown adults.

It was not surprising then, that he would end up in the fighter-pilot training program: a place where his attributes would certainly be useful. Unfortunately, he was a pacifist by nature. The thought of attacking an enemy with the intention of killing him did not sit well with Kandar, but he was loyal to his planet, to his Ionian culture and, of course, to his family and his young wife Shahlaya. Just recently married, they had met at school where they had both majored in Alien Cultures.

Kandar and Shahlaya shared an interest in all alien life-forms and they had done undergraduate research on several planets, but one life-form that particularly fascinated Kandar was the Vargon. He had never met anyone who had actually seen one, but it was something that had long existed in the mythology of his planet. In fact, it was Kandar's intention that, if he survived the war, he would search for the creature to pursue an advanced degree. In the meantime, while other pilots had named their ships after their wives or their

53

sweethearts, Kandar christened his ship *Vargon 1*.

*****

Kandar's first mission was a scouting patrol. He and his small squadron were to do reconnaissance near Mundago, the third moon of Bardok. It would be a test not only of Kandar's flying skills, but also of his mettle as a warrior.

Doing battle with the "brutes of Bardok," as he called them, was frightening enough, but recent reports indicated that they had created a death ray, which appeared as a cool, bluish-white beam until it hit a target. If that target was metallic, it would begin to glow red at the contact point and the red would continue to expand until the entire object was quickly engulfed. Within just a few seconds, the glow would intensify and the object would disintegrate. If the target was organic, it would slowly glow white and then, in a burst of blinding light, it would simply disappear. Kandar and his fellow cadets jokingly referred to this new weapon as the "moon-beam," because of its color and its cold, non-threatening appearance.

As Kandar and his squadron entered the orbit of Mundago, enemy vessels began to pop up on their sensors. There were at least six ships directly ahead: five fighters and what appeared to be a battle-cruiser. Immediately, Lokar, Kandar's group leader, communicated to the Ionian command center both their position and the number of vessels that they were about to engage. There was no response. Never having seen battle before, Kandar was the newest pilot in the squadron of four. The left and right wing-men broke formation and attacked the enemy fighters nearest them. Kandar followed Lokar's lead and went straight down the middle. Lokar immediately targeted an enemy fighter, hitting the pilot with his pulse

54

cannon. The ship careened wildly towards Kandar's ship, but Kandar used it as "cover" to launch his own attack on a second fighter. He successfully targeted that ship's propulsion system and left it drifting in space.

Things happen very quickly in battle and Kandar noticed that he had lost his left wing -man and that the third enemy fighter was missing, as well. A battle-cruiser and two other ships remained to be reckoned with and Lokar was going for the kill on the cruiser. Kandar and Mordan attacked the two fighters.

The enemy ship closest to Mordan's fighter accelerated into a suicide run. The Bardokians were not known as elegant tacticians. Their ships collided in an enormous explosion while Kandar scored his second "kill" of the day. All that was left was the battle cruiser, which Lokar was hitting with every weapon at his disposal. Kandar did his best to attack the cruiser from a different angle to divert attention from Lokar's ship.

Unfortunately, both Kandar and his group leader recognized the cold, bluish-white beam that hit Lokar's fuselage. The ship quickly took on a red glow and, just a second later, Kandar saw a burst of white light in the cockpit. He would now have to fight this battle alone.

He swept toward the enemy ship in a helical arc, firing all of his forward weapons at the Bardokians. The space between Kandar and the enemy ship was filled with the glow from his pulse cannons; and, the flashes and explosions from their return fire were all around him. Then, he reversed his spin to avoid the same fate as Lokar. Suddenly, he noticed that a "moonbeam" had hit the tip of his right wing. With only seconds to react, Kandar killed all of the lights on his fighter, jettisoned his canopy and ejected from his ship. As he watched the wing glow brighter, he focused all of his mental capacity on his ship's throttle. He pushed it full-forward and fired all of his thrusters to launch the embattled *Vargon I* into the prow of the enemy battle cruiser.

Kandar floated helplessly in space and watched the explosive impact. His tiny vessel did minor damage to the enormous enemy ship, but the metal-on-metal contact spread the devastating effect of the "moonbeam" to its source. He watched quietly as the entire ship became engulfed in the horrific red glow. He could see bursts of white light from within the portholes. No one on board could have expected that a squadron of four fighters would dare to take on a cruiser equipped with their dreaded "death beam" and it was apparent that no one was attempting to escape in the life pods.

Minutes passed as the battle-cruiser morphed from glowing wreckage into a faint cloud of dust suspended in the orbit of Mundago. Kandar looked for any signs of life. There was none in the direction where the battle-cruiser had been. Then he thought the first Bardokian that he had attacked might still be alive, so he did his best to rotate and look back in the direction from which he came, but that pilot was slumped over in his cockpit — still smoldering from the fire that erupted in his propulsion system.

It was difficult for Kandar to believe that he, a pacifist, could have done so much damage or taken so many lives. As he floated helplessly in orbit around that moon, he started to realize the utter hopelessness of his situation. His air supply was dwindling and, although they had reported their position prior to engagement, he had no confidence that help was on its way. He feared what the Bardokians might do to him, if he were captured alive. His only hope was that he would die before an enemy ship could arrive and find him.

Kandar's thoughts went to Shahlaya. She was the love of his life: the only female for whom he had ever found a fascination or an infatuation. He desperately made an attempt to contact her telepathically, but he was much too far from Ionus to project his thoughts to her. He hoped that she would someday learn of his fate.

Kandar recalled one of his earliest memories: a scientific expedition led by his parents. He was only a toddler, but he wandered away from the camp into a village of "savages." By the time his parents found him, he was telekinetically suspending a burning torch in front of the tribal chief. And, it was with great difficulty that they got him back, because the savages had claimed him as their "god." Now he was drifting alone in space and the so-called "God of the Savages" was clearly unable to even help himself.

Although religion was frowned upon on Ionus, Kandar did believe in a Creator. As he looked out at the vastness of space, he chose to drink in the marvels beyond his reach. He could see Mundago at his feet, Bardok just beyond it in the distance and there were stars in every direction. It was so quiet — so beautiful — so cold. The air in his flight suit was almost gone.

That was when he glimpsed something shiny. Something moving in the distance. It wasn't moving at all like a ship. It was actually quite erratic. It would change both speed and direction much too quickly to be any sort of vehicle.

"Come to Kandar," he intoned softly. Then, it suddenly appeared in front of him: a small spherical creature perhaps a meter in diameter, with different colors washing over its glistening surface.

"Are you what I think you are?" Kandar whispered. "Are you a Vargon?"

There was no response. Little was known about Vargons. According to legend, they were intelligent creatures that consumed base matter and converted it into pure energy. It was also believed that they were capable of expanding to many times their normal size or of shrinking to mathematical unity — and that was where the legend got even stranger: the Vargon could become not just a point, but a vector. It could launch itself in virtually any direction like a cognizant, mobile black hole — and it could take, whatever it chose to encompass, along with it.

Kandar marveled at his new companion. He gazed, absolutely beaming with delight, at this: his final and most wonderful discovery. His air supply was nearly exhausted and he was sad that he couldn't share this new knowledge with Shahlaya. He extended his hand toward the Vargon and with his last gasp whispered, "Please, help me, if you..."

Kandar blacked out.

*****

When he awoke, he was in his own bed and Shahlaya was tending to him. He looked around the room and tried to raise himself up on his elbows.

"Lie back, Kandar," Shahlaya whispered.

"How long have I been here?" he asked.

"Not long. Just a very short time," she replied. "I was in the lab with the Professor when the creature materialized. It opened up and — there you were! Dr. Markus had to help me to get you out of your pressure suit or else you would have suffocated."

"Is it still there?" Kandar wondered aloud.

"No, it disappeared as quickly as it came," she said.

"It was a Vargon, wasn't it?" he asked.

"Professor Markus certainly thinks so," she responded. "He couldn't have been any more excited to witness such a thing! So far as he's concerned, you've already done all of the research you needed to get your degree. Aren't you thrilled?"

"That is good news. Have you notified anyone that I'm here?" Kandar inquired.

"Not yet, but we probably should. How do you feel?" Shahlaya asked.

"A little light-headed; and very disappointed with myself. I didn't think I could kill anyone, but I've killed hundreds of Bardokians. Not innocents, mind you! I didn't attack a village or anything like that. I destroyed two fighters and a battle-cruiser — in self-defense," he added.

"A battle-cruiser?" Shahlaya almost laughed, then she realized that Kandar wasn't joking. "What about your squadron?"

"They're all dead," he answered, "I need to report to my Commander."

He sat up on the bedside and rose slowly.

"I should clean up and change my uniform," Kandar said.

He dressed quickly and kissed Shahlaya goodbye.

"I'll be back as soon as I can," he told her as he left.

*****

He made his way to a shuttle. This was the quickest public transportation available that could get him back to his base. Most people referred to the shuttles as "Clouds." They were unpiloted space-transports capable of carrying a dozen passengers. The majority of them traveled predetermined routes, but some could be hired and programmed for private use, as well. Kandar was sharing this Cloud with what appeared to be some young recruits. He stood toward the front of the vehicle staring through the windshield and wondering how he was going to explain his situation to his Commander.

When he finally arrived at the base, he checked in with the sentinel on duty and was ordered to wait. The sentry scanned his data screen and looked up at him.

"Kandar is on a mission; so you, Sir, must be an imposter," the sentinel told him, while drawing his weapon. "Sit right there with your hands on your head." Then the guard spoke into his communicator: "We have a situation at the main gate — a possible security breach. I need an identity match."

Within a minute, another soldier arrived with a small box-like instrument.

"If you're who you say you are, this won't be a problem," the second guard said.

Kandar picked up the instrument by the sides and held it up to his eyes.

"Flight-Lieutenant Kandar, AW1624, fighter-pilot, match confirmed," the instrument intoned.

"Take me to Commander Korbay immediately," Kandar ordered them.

*****

When they arrived at the Commander's office, he was already alerted to their presence. He stood at the door and invited Kandar inside. Then he gestured toward the guard to leave and added a curt: "That will be all."

"Young Man, I remember you. You're the new recruit who

60

scored at the top of his graduating class and right now you're supposed to be on a mission around Mundago," Korbay started calmly, and then he screamed: "So why did they wake me up in the middle of the night and why am I staring at your sorry face here in my office?"

"I'm sorry, Sir, I..." Kandar tried to interject.

"Sorry? Sorry??? No, you're pathetic!" Korbay screamed. "Where is Lokar and the rest of your squadron?"

Kandar looked down solemnly: "They're all dead, Sir."

"Dead?" the Commander asked.

"Yes, Sir. We engaged the enemy at Mundago and only I survived," Kandar replied, and then he added weakly, "I suppose you could call it a small victory for Ionus."

Korbay looked at the duty roster: "Lokar, Mordan and Jordak — the rest of your squadron are all dead and you're here declaring victory?" He grabbed Kandar by the collar.

"Sir, we engaged five fighters and a battle-cruiser. And we destroyed them all. I'm lucky to be alive," Kandar whispered.

"If you can't substantiate your claim, you might want to reconsider your good fortune!" the Commander muttered, releasing his grip. He sat at his desk and scrolled down the screen of his computer. He checked the communications from Air Wing 1624. The last message received from Lokar indicated the truth of what Kandar had said: they had engaged five fighters and a battle-cruiser in the orbit of Mundago mere hours before.

"How is that possible?" Korbay asked loudly. "How *could* that be possible? Not even considering the fact that there were only four of you against five enemy fighters *and* a battle-cruiser, but how are you standing in front of me when it takes nearly a day just to get to Mundago? There is *no way* that you could get back this quickly! —

and, where is your ship?"

"My ship was destroyed, Sir," Kandar replied meekly, "I was drifting in space, nearly out of air, when..." Kandar paused.

"Yes, you were drifting and then what?" Korbay interrupted him.

"I was rescued by a Vargon, Sir," Kandar answered reluctantly.

"Oh, a Vargon! A mythical creature just comes along and brings you safely back home?" the Commander looked at him with disgust. "Do you really expect me to believe this rubbish? Is that the best you could come up with?"

"Sir, I know it sounds unbelievable, but both Professor Markus and my wife saw the creature," Kandar responded.

"I know Markus. And I fully intend to talk to him about this matter," Commander Korbay countered, then after a moment of reflection, he asked: "And how precisely did you destroy a Bardokian battle-cruiser?"

"Sir, we lost both Mordan and Jordak while destroying the enemy fighters, then Squadron Leader Lokar attacked the cruiser. I was attacking from a different angle when I saw the Bardokian death-ray hit Lokar's ship. The impact was so close to him that he had no chance to eject. He died within a second or two." Kandar hesitated.

"Go on," Korbay demanded.

"Sir, I was hitting the battle-cruiser with all of my forward weapons when a 'moonbeam' hit the tip of my right wing. I immediately jettisoned my canopy, switched off all illumination and ejected from my ship. Then I telekinetically fired the thrusters of my fighter: impacting the cruiser at full speed," Kandar got the words out, but he was becoming less certain of the reality as he remembered it.

"And the impact of a small fighter took down a battle-cruiser?"

Korbay asked in disbelief.

"No, Sir, my ship was engulfed by the red glow of the moonbeam when it made metal-on-metal contact with the battle-cruiser. The battle-cruiser effectively destroyed itself," the junior officer explained.

Commander Korbay had never heard a more brilliantly simple strategy in all of his years of service. He looked out of his window mumbling: "The moonbeam is like a virus. Once a ship is infected, it can spread the infection by direct contact. Brilliant!"

"Lieutenant, did you have any idea that this strategy would work?" Korbay asked.

"No, Sir, it was the desperate act of a dying man," Kandar replied sheepishly.

"Well, thank you for not dying, Young Man! You have done a great service for Ionus. Now, go home and get some rest," the Commander reassured him as he opened the door. "If Professor Markus can verify your story, I'm putting you in for a medal."

"Yes, Sir. Thank you, Sir," Kandar saluted the Commander, wheeled around and left the office. He was exhausted and couldn't wait to get back home to Shahlaya. All in all, he felt that things went much better than he had envisioned and, on the trip home, he felt much more relaxed than he had been on the way to the base.

*****

When Shahlaya came to wake Kandar, it was already past midday: "Kandar, there are people here to see you! You have to get your uniform on — and hurry."

Kandar got up and dressed quickly. Commander Korbay was waiting in the next room with two armed guards and Shahlaya was doing her best to keep them occupied. Kandar entered the room cautiously and saluted the Commander: "Flight-Lieutenant Kandar reporting for duty, Sir."

Korbay returned his salute: "At ease, *Captain* Kandar, we came here to deliver the news of your promotion. No mere Flight-Lieutenant has ever received the Order of Ionus, so I thought I'd give you time to upgrade your uniform before the formal ceremony. I'd also like to personally thank you for your service to our planet and to congratulate you in advance of receiving the actual medal."

"Thank you, Sir, I am honored — and a little confused," Kandar answered.

"Young Man, Bardok was on the verge of winning this war with its new weapon, but your brilliant maneuver — your *discovery* — will save our planet!" Korbay enthused.

"Thank you again, Sir," Kandar responded.

The two guards saluted Kandar and turned to leave. He returned their salute and held his until Korbay returned it. As the Commander stood in the doorway, he turned back and added: "By the way, I spoke with Professor Markus about your Vargon. If you can persuade those things to join our side, I'll even make you a Commander!" Korbay laughed and waved at Shahlaya as he departed.

"Kandar, I'm so proud of you!" Shahlaya gushed as the door closed.

"Thank you, but I wish I had never been put in this position," he replied. "I'm no hero. I watched my entire squadron die and I just got lucky."

"No, Kandar, it wasn't luck. Your quick thinking saved your life," she insisted.

"At the cost of how many Bardokians?" He paused. "I did some research and our intelligence sources estimate the full complement of a Bardokian battle-cruiser at 480 of those reptiles. Mind you, I don't like the beasts, but no good can come of this."

*****

In the days that followed, Commander Korbay dispatched two remote-controlled drones with every fighter squadron. All Ionian pilots were trained to defend themselves against the Bardokian "moonbeam" using Kandar's successful strategy. If their vehicles were hit by the moonbeam, they would eject immediately and try to direct their damaged vehicles at their attackers. If a battle-cruiser was present, they were instructed to aim their drones for it in the hopes that they would be hit by the moonbeam en route.

Day after day, this strategy met with great success until the war machine of Bardok was virtually destroyed. On the celebration of the New Year, a mere two months after the Battle of Mundago, Kandar was presented with the Order of Ionus. The very next day the Supreme Commander of Bardok sued for peace.

Captain Kandar became the hero of the people of Ionus. With the end of the Forever War, he was discharged from active service and freed to do whatever research he chose to pursue. And, the government was more than willing to subsidize his efforts. Unfortunately, the government was also run by a military which, having concentrated on a war for well over a thousand years, was not accustomed to maintaining an economy during peacetime. To those in power, Kandar destroyed their reason for being and came to represent all of their failings, as well.

*****

"Dinner is served!" Daniel intoned loudly, with a mock English

65

accent.

Jessie quickly closed the book and placed it back on the shelf. She glanced in the bathroom mirror to make sure that she was presentable and went to open the bedroom door. She really didn't know what to make of the stories or of the young man whom she assumed had written them.

"That chicken smells great!" she noted, as she walked out the front door.

Job eyed her suspiciously.

"Well, there's plenty here, so I hope you're hungry," Daniel replied.

"Hey, what do you do around here for fun?" Jessie asked.

"Job and I go fishing; we do our gardening," Daniel answered. "I like music so we listen to the radio or I mess around with the guitar. I don't suppose that sounds all that exciting to a 'city girl' like yourself."

"What makes you think I'm a 'city girl'?" Jessie inquired.

"Well, you're educated; you're a reporter. You just sound a lot more sophisticated than I am. I didn't mean to imply anything bad," he said apologetically.

"More sophisticated than 'Mr. President of His Own Company'?" she laughed.

"Owning something doesn't necessarily mean I'm smart or sophisticated," Daniel replied. "What do you like to do for fun?"

"Let's see: going out to dinner, going to movies—concerts," she answered. "Going shopping. Spending money. I *really* enjoy spending money! That's something I wish I could enjoy a lot more often, but I don't have all that much money to spend."

She laughed, just a bit embarrassed by her comment. She didn't want to sound like a gold-digger, but the absolute truth was: she really *did* like money. Everyone she *knew* liked money. So, why is it that this guy who apparently has *tons* of money is living in this rustic little hovel?

She filled her plate, carefully avoiding her earlier mistake. Daniel hadn't eaten much at breakfast and Job looked hungry, too.

"I wish this could go on forever, but I guess you've got a life to get back to," he said, hoping that she'd reveal something about her personal life.

"Actually, I've really enjoyed this time with you, but I guess I should go back to my apartment," she responded. "I haven't checked my mail, or my *e-mail*, in days. I've got clothes to wash, my cell-phone needs charging: there are probably a million things that I'm not even thinking of, that I really need to attend to."

"Can all of that wait until tomorrow?" Daniel asked, reaching over the table to touch her hand.

"Hmmm. You drive a hard bargain. Okay, I'll stay one more night — no 'hanky-panky,' mind you! You still look like a kid to me and I don't want you to think that just because you own your own company that I'm going to be 'easy'!" she warned him, only half-jokingly.

"You've got a deal! No 'hanky-panky,'" Daniel agreed, perhaps too quickly. "Now eat up and don't be afraid to go back for seconds."

"You're going to make me fat," Jessie warned him.

"I'd love you no matter how fat you got!" Daniel blurted, and, in an embarrassed effort to save face, added: "I'm sorry, I didn't mean that the way it sounded."

"No apology necessary. It must be those raging teenage

hormones!" she replied coyly. "Exactly how old are you, Young Man?"

"I can't tell you that, but I'm a lot older than I look," he mumbled with his mouth full of food.

Job put his front paws up on the picnic table and laid his head down between them, glaring directly at Jessie.

"Was it something I said?" she asked the dog, and then to Daniel: "He doesn't bark much, does he?"

"I haven't heard Job bark since right after I got him. He's not much of a talker, but he's an excellent listener. Aren't you, Job?" He wrapped his arm around the dog and kissed him on the head. He rubbed the dogs face playfully with both hands.

"Job and I have had lots of long conversations over the years without a word being spoken," Daniel said. "We each just seem to know what the other one's thinking."

Jessie looked back toward the house.

"So, what's behind the house? The trees around it are so dense, I don't even think I could squeeze through there," she asked.

"Not much. Just more trees," Daniel answered cautiously. "I don't even have windows toward the back of the house, because there's nothing back there to see."

"I'd be afraid that critters might nest around the back or on the roof," she said.

"So far, I haven't had any problems like that. I guess Job's scent scares most of them away," Daniel joked.

They had finished eating and Jessie was careful not to be too inquisitive.

"Can I help you with the dishes?" she asked.

It was the first time that she had offered to be of any assistance since she arrived and Daniel wasn't sure if it would be proper to accept her offer. After all, she was his guest.

"I think I can handle things just fine," he replied. "But thanks for asking. That's really mighty kind of you to offer."

"Here, I insist." Jessie began to stack the dirty plates. Daniel rose and ran to hold the door for her as she carried the dinnerware into the kitchen. She scraped the dishes into a garbage receptacle next to the sink.

"Do you prefer to wash or dry?" she asked.

"Really, you don't have to do either," Daniel answered. "You've got such pretty hands. You shouldn't be putting them in soapy water."

Jessie giggled, "You really *are* a character, Daniel! I put my whole body in soapy water: that's how I get it clean!"

Daniel's face was quite obviously taking on a red glow. He hadn't intended to think about her bathing, but now he just couldn't get the image out of his head.

"Why, Daniel, I do believe you're blushing!" Jessie teased.

"I'm sorry, I'm just not used to having a young lady around here," he confessed.

She turned toward the sink and began to rinse the dishes. Daniel stood close behind her and put his hands on her hips. He leaned over her right shoulder and kissed her lightly on the neck.

"Uh-uh, Mr. Johnstone, remember rule number one: 'no hanky-panky'!" she said sternly; and then she turned around and looked up at him with the most beautiful smile he had ever seen. She put her arms around him and kissed him fully on the lips.

Now Daniel was completely at a loss. He had never kissed a woman like that before. It wasn't like kissing his Aunt Martha or a cousin. He drew her close to his chest, resting his chin on her head and whispered: "I'll take care of the dishes. You had better go to your room or else your 'rule number one' will be in serious jeopardy."

Jessie leaned back slightly and smiled. "If you insist."

She dried her hands on the dish towel and added: "Sweet dreams, Daniel." She walked the few steps over to the bedroom door and, smiling back at him, closed it slowly behind her.

"Good night, Jessie," Daniel replied as the door clicked shut.

He quickly cleaned the dishes and left them on the rack to dry, then he turned to Job, patiently waiting on the floor, and said: "Old Fella, we've got some work to do."

*****

"Mr. President, Colonel Wagner is on line one," the secretary informed him.

"Yes, George, what can I do for you?" the President spoke into the phone.

"I'm sorry to bother you again, Mr. President, but the SETI Institute believes that they've deciphered that repeated message," the officer replied.

"And, what exactly does it say?" the President asked impatiently.

"It's difficult to be certain of how to translate proper names, but the best they can come up with is: 'Surrender Kandar, the war criminal; and, return his ship and the Vargon!'" the Colonel answered.

"Do we have any idea who, or what, they're asking for?" the Commander in Chief inquired.

"We are researching those names, but, so far, we haven't got a clue," the officer replied. "Should we attempt to respond?"

"Give me a second," the President said, as he scribbled on a notepad. "Tell them to send this: 'Take Kandar, his ship and the Vargon and go. We will defend our planet and the rest of its inhabitants against any invading force.' Have you got that?"

"Yes, Sir, Mr. President, you're putting the burden of finding this Kandar person back on them," the Colonel stated.

"Exactly! Now we'd better hope that they know precisely where he is, so they don't have to destroy this whole planet looking for him," the President responded. "Let me know if there's a reply to our message and, in the meantime, I think we had better plan on filtering all the media to prevent a panic. If word gets out that an alien invasion is imminent, who knows what people will do?"

"Mr. President, I'll get on that message to SETI right away. I'm sure you have other channels for dealing with the media," Colonel Wagner replied.

"Is there anything else, George?" the President asked with some annoyance.

"Actually, Mr. President, there is something important that I should have mentioned earlier," the officer added reluctantly.

"And that is?" the POTUS prodded.

"The source of the transmissions is closing in on us at an amazing speed."

"Thank you, George. Keep me informed," the President said as he terminated the call. He held down the intercom button: "I need all of my top media advisers here within the hour."

*****

Job rose and followed Daniel through the living room to the back door. The boy unlocked the door. They passed through it and he quickly locked it behind them. They ascended the ramp and Daniel turned his attention to the sphere that the Vargon had delivered from

Rev-Tech. It was obviously not of this world. The boy waved his hand at the wall and a work surface jutted out from it. With another motion of his hand, the sphere rose up and rested on the table.

There was a shallow trough along the front edge of the work surface within which rested an assortment of alien tools. Daniel picked one up and inserted it into a crevice in the sphere. With the flick of a button, a panel flipped open and Daniel reached into the compartment to remove the glowing power source. "Well, Job, that should disable it. And now we can use this bit in the weapons array."

The sphere was a Bardokian tracking device. It probably had been attached to the outside of the *Dorius*, when they boarded the ship, and it apparently broke off while entering earth's atmosphere. It was very likely to have already transmitted this position and there was little doubt that the faint "star," which they had seen in the sky the night before, was a scout ship.

"It's too late to run, so we'd better prepare for the worst possible scenario," Daniel remarked as he began to check the ship's onboard systems and, with his fairly limited knowledge of the way it worked, tried his best to get it flight-ready.

*****

The sun was just beginning to go down in the west and Jessie didn't feel all that tired when she first snuggled under the covers, but she quickly fell sound asleep. A few hours later, she suddenly woke up: hugging her pillow tightly and breathing heavily.

"Wow!" she gasped as she tried desperately to remember all of the details of the dream that roused her from her sleep. She had never before dreamt anything quite so vivid or erotic in her life. There was no way that she could go back to sleep in her present state, so Jessie unlocked the bedroom door. She tiptoed out in her undergarments, holding the boy's robe modestly in front of her.

"Daniel?" she whispered.

She looked from the kitchen into the darkened living room.

"Daniel?" she called again. The couch was empty, but she could see light under the back door. "Why would there be light *behind* the house?" she wondered aloud, then she added: "Oh well, it's your loss, Mr. Rev-Tech!"

She walked back through the kitchen to the bedroom and locked the door behind her. She tossed the robe on the bed and glanced at the thin volumes on the shelf.

"If I'm going home tomorrow," she said quietly, as she picked up the last book entitled: *Shahlaya and the Vargon*. "This may be my last opportunity to research my handsome young subject."

She fluffed up her pillows and slipped her legs under the covers. Jessie wasn't sure how much mischief she would have gotten into with Daniel, but she just couldn't help but smile when she thought of him — especially after having dreamt so sensuously about him.

"Maybe this will take my mind off my handsome, young Mr. Johnstone!" she ventured as she opened the final volume.

Chapter 5

Shahlaya and the Vargon

Nearly a year had passed since the end of the Forever War and Kandar was fully enjoying civilian life. His desire to research the Vargon was on temporary hold. Now Professor Markus had something more important to pursue: the exploration of a moon in a neighboring solar system. It was well known among Ionian scientists that there were two planets traveling in tandem around that star. These were not habitable planets, but gas giants. What made them interesting was that, although they revolved around their sun always equidistant from each other and in parallel orbits, their daily rotations were in opposite directions and they shared a moon that traversed a near-perfect lemniscate while orbiting around them. This moon appeared to have an atmosphere and, quite possibly, could sustain life. The scientists called the moon Dorius.

Under the direction of Professor Markus, the Ionian government had sponsored the construction of a deep-space exploration vehicle that was now nearly complete. This ship needed an extended range, because it would have to travel farther into space than the nearest vortex. And, unfortunately, using a vortex would have transported them far beyond the moon that they sought to explore.

This ship, christened *Dorius,* was large enough for a crew of three and equipped with everything that they would need for their research and exploration, plus a weapons array previously unseen on even their best fighters. Markus was the designated leader of the mission while Kandar and Shahlaya were chosen for their respective military and scientific expertise.

The mission was nearly set to launch when a pre-flight examination revealed that Shahlaya was pregnant. That rendered her ineligible for any extended deep-space flight. Professor Markus was disappointed, but he had every hope that Kandar would remain in the program. In fact, Shahlaya encouraged Kandar to continue with the mission, but he chose to stay close to home so he could be there for the birth of their first child. The mission to Dorius was now on temporary "hold" while alternate crew members were being tested and interviewed.

*****

Just a few days after Kandar learned of Shahlaya's pregnancy, he stopped at his former Air Wing base to spread the good news to his old military friends and to look over his last ship: the *Vargon II*. On a whim, he asked Commander Korbay for permission to fly the fighter and was somewhat amazed that he relented. He never told the Commander where he intended to go with it. He knew that Korbay held him in high regard, but the truce with the Bardokians was tenuous at best and Ionians were not welcome within the bounds of Bardokian space.

Still, it was a great opportunity to do some research in the area where he had seen the Vargon. Kandar contacted Shahlaya telepathically and explained that he would be away for just a couple of days, doing research, but he gave no indication of any potential danger being involved.

He borrowed a flight suit and entered the *Vargon II*. The cockpit sealed around him as he started the thrusters and the ship hovered momentarily before he took off on a steep angle. There was a loud "crack" as the ship accelerated through the atmosphere. This ship was much faster than the *Vargon I* had ever been. The trip that had previously taken nearly a day could now be made in half that time.

Kandar needed to think about things. His wife was pregnant with their first child and he had just taken himself off the Dorius Mission. He had prepared for that mission for months and now he needed to do something equally stimulating to make up for it. He needed to see the Vargon again. He needed to learn something more about that species for his own peace of mind. His contact with it had been so brief and he really knew nothing more now than what he had read in the books of mythology.

He was absolutely certain that he could find it again, if he just went back to where the now-famous Battle of Mundago had taken place. He hadn't been there since he lost his first ship and he wasn't sure if he wanted to confront the ghosts of his past, but just seeing the Vargon again was more important than any excuse for *not* going that he could conjure. And so, he steered his ship toward Mundago in the hopes of rediscovering the exact location where the battle had occurred. "Perhaps," he thought, "that was an area the Vargon frequented."

In a matter of hours, Kandar could see that moon growing larger in the distance. He set his course for the equatorial region and the globe of Mundago continued to grow until it filled the forward view of his canopy. As he entered the moon's orbit, he located debris from the battle on his sensors. Kandar cut his propulsion system and his outboard illumination; and, he let the *Vargon II* drift with the dust and the pieces of the destroyed fighters. In the year since the Forever War had ended, the orbits of the charred remains had decayed somewhat and he realized that eventually all of this would fall toward the lunar surface and no evidence of the battle would remain.

He was pondering this when his sensors picked up two fighters coming towards him at high speed. They were obviously not Ionian.

He stayed calm as the Bardokians flew past, but, as soon as they started to bank for a return run, he fired his thrusters. He felt assured that he could outrun them as he pulled up and out of the moon's orbit.

Kandar was right about being faster, but he also knew that he could not outrun their pulse cannons - or their dreaded "moonbeam." The two Bardokians followed him, flying practically wing to wing and, when they realized that they couldn't catch him, they began to fire their cannons at his ship. Kandar had already opened his mind to their thoughts, so he was prepared for evasive action. He rolled down and backwards to avoid being hit by cannon fire and then he aimed his ship directly at his attackers. He fired at the propulsion systems of both ships and ripped through the space between them. He left the Bardokian ships drifting in space, but the *Vargon II* had taken considerable damage. Returning to Ionus was no longer a possibility.

Kandar guided his ship toward the cratered moonscape of Mundago. It was a moon without an atmosphere and presumably devoid of life. It was ironic that Kandar would have died here a year ago and now he had stupidly thrown away his miraculous "second chance" to return once more and face that same fate. He struggled to control the *Vargon II* as he skimmed the rocky surface. The ship hit hard and he studied the canopy as it began to crack. He sealed his visor. Now, his pressure suit would have to suffice. Finally, all forward motion stopped and there was little point in staying with the ship, so he jettisoned the useless, shattered canopy.

He stood upright in the cockpit and surveyed the area. He realized that he could communicate his location to Ionus, but there was nothing they could do to save him. He also recognized that there was a very real chance of his message being intercepted by the Bardokians and used as a premise for war. That was not an option.

Many Ionians felt that he had almost single-handedly put an end to the Forever War and he refused to undo his legacy. In the meantime, it was highly likely that the two Bardokian pilots, whom he had just encountered, were communicating with their base.

Kandar couldn't leave his battered ship intact for the Bardokians, but neither could he bring himself to commit suicide while destroying it. He threw one leg over the side of the vehicle and, half standing on the wing, he reached down inside the cockpit for the medical emergency kit, the spare oxygen tank and extra ammunition for his sidearm. He dropped those to the lunar surface and re-examined the cockpit for anything useful that he could salvage. He needed to destroy the ship without leaving any identifiable evidence that could be traced back to him or Ionus.

Finally, assured that he had everything that he dare take with him, he started the self-destruct timer. Kandar jumped down from the *Vargon II's* wing, gathered up his resources and clipped the containers to the belt of his pressure suit. He leapt towards a nearby crater. The gravity of Mundago was less than half that of Ionus, so he could cover a great distance with a single leap. A second leap put him over the rim of the crater. He had no idea what he would encounter on the other side of the mound of rock and moon-dust, but he needed shelter from the impending explosion. The lights on his helmet illuminated the shadow-enshrouded area where he was about to land. Luckily, there was no immediate danger and he landed upright and without injury.

He could see the self-destruct countdown flashing in the display within his visor. The numbers had changed from black to red as the last few seconds elapsed. He leaned against the wall of the crater as he felt the ground vibrate slightly and saw debris hurled over the rim. It was apparent that the detonator had accomplished its mission.

Kandar surveyed the inside of the crater. His helmet was functioning properly, so he could read the diameter of the basin at slightly over 85 meters. For his own peace of mind, he had to determine that no recognizable evidence of his ship remained, so he turned around and leapt back out of the crater. There was not much left to examine except a large concavity where the *Vargon II* had stood just moments before. He took a few steps towards that newly-formed depression and stopped. He slowly turned and viewed the lunar surface in all directions. There was very little to see except rocks, dust, craters and what appeared to be a mountain ridge.

Without hesitation, Kandar started leaping towards the mountain. According to the read-out on his visor, the distance was slightly under a kilometer. If there was any form of shelter on Mundago, he would have a better chance of spotting it from a higher elevation. It only took a few minutes to arrive at the base of the mountain, but Kandar could see that all of his activity had nearly exhausted the air-supply in his suit.

He connected the spare oxygen tank to the secondary intake of his pressure suit. Without much exertion, he had perhaps another hour to live. He climbed the ridge slowly taking very deliberate steps — testing the density and rigidity of the surface as he walked. There was a wide ledge just a couple of meters below the peak, so Kandar stopped there to look around. He was at least half a kilometer above the lunar surface. In all directions, as far as he could see, there was nothing to shelter or save him. He sat on a small boulder and looked upwards.

Somewhere among those stars and planets were two Bardokian

pilots — possibly dead, perhaps awaiting rescue. Kandar could no longer sense their minds, so he wasn't sure of their status. They were simply too far away. He concentrated harder. If there was any friendly creature within a hundred kilometers, he had to make every effort to contact it. For just a moment, he thought he felt something.

He looked down, sweeping the lunar landscape again from left to right, but he saw no evidence of a life-form. So, Kandar stood tall and grasped the side of the mountain to steady himself. He looked upwards and scanned slowly in all directions. Suddenly, he saw something shining. Off in the distance, there was something approaching, but it was moving quite erratically. He focused all of his mental capacity on it, but his mind was blocked.

"What have we here?" Kandar asked aloud. The shining "light," that he saw from afar, finally came down to his level and floated alongside the mountain just a few meters beyond his reach. Kandar could see the beautiful colors washing over the orb just as he'd witnessed roughly a year ago.

"My Friend, I've returned for you — and you for me," Kandar whispered. "If I might impose upon you once again. Would you mind taking me home?"

The Vargon came closer, as if to examine him, but stayed well over the edge of the mountain. It seemed wary of him. Kandar could feel its mind, but he couldn't enter it. The Vargon seemed to understand him, but he lacked the ability to respond in kind.

"You helped me once, what is different now?" Kandar asked quietly. Then, he looked down and realized that there was a significant difference. He slowly released the belt that held his medical kit, his weapon and the extra ammunition and he dropped it over the edge of the cliff. He asked the Vargon: "Is that what you're waiting for?"

The Vargon hovered nearer. Kandar could finally reach out his hand and touch it. He could feel the contentment of this being as it opened itself ever so slightly to his mind.

"We are really two of a kind, My Friend. I've been a most unwilling participant in war, but I mean you no harm. I truly mean no harm to anyone," Kandar said quietly. With that, the Vargon levitated Kandar for a moment and then it encapsulated him.

Once inside the Vargon, Kandar floated in amazement. He could see through the creature as the colors washed over it, tinting his view of the many stars above him and Mundago below. He still had a few minutes of oxygen left, when, for the briefest moment, everything suddenly went black.

*****

When Kandar checked his oxygen level again, there was no significant change. It was as though no substantial time had passed. But looking through the Vargon, he could easily recognize that he was somewhere else. He felt the weight of added gravity within his body even though he was still floating inside the creature. And, through the translucency of the Vargon, he noticed what appeared to be interior lighting and he thought that he could see two figures approaching.

The creature opened up and deposited him upright on the floor. He was in the laboratory of Professor Markus and both he and Shahlaya were standing nearby: watching in utter astonishment. Kandar opened his visor and took a deep breath.

Turning around, he said, "Professor Markus and Shahlaya, may

I introduce you to my dear friend, the Vargon."

The creature floated there before them as if to acknowledge them. Kandar rested his hand lightly on it and added, "And my dear Vargon, please let me introduce you to my loving wife Shahlaya and a great man of science, my mentor, Professor Markus."

The three of them gathered around the Vargon, stroking it lovingly like a new pet. They were all thrilled to be in the company of such a legendary being and their minds were filled with both questions and amazement. But, perhaps, most importantly, their hearts were filled with contentment.

Kandar had finally made a significant emotional connection with the Vargon. He could communicate basic thoughts to it, but he could not see within nor experience the memories or the cognitive processes of the creature. It wasn't perfect communication, but he knew that the Vargon could read both his mind and his heart.

It was unfortunately necessary to report the loss of the *Vargon II* to Commander Korbay and Kandar dreaded that task, but he did so. The Commander was far from pleased at the loss of one of his best fighters, but he considered the contact with the Vargon and his high esteem for Kandar in his final judgment on the matter. Korbay assured him that no further inquiry would be made.

*****

The Vargon seemed comfortable with the trio. It came and went periodically over the next few days. It allowed the Professor to make unobtrusive measurements and it demonstrated a few of its abilities for them. One thing that they found amazing was that the creature could magnify Kandar's mental abilities in extraordinary ways. Without any assistance, Kandar could levitate things, but the Vargon could amplify that mental power to such an extent that the experimental subjects would instantaneously disappear from their presence and reappear in another place of their choosing. At Kandar's disposal, the Vargon seemed to act as a funnel between dimensions. This ability went far beyond telekinesis. This was teleportation and, while that had been successfully accomplished under strict laboratory conditions using very elaborate equipment, no ordinary creature had ever been able to achieve it naturally. But, the Vargon was in fact no such ordinary creature: it was truly inter-dimensional.

One day, Kandar asked the Professor to explain exactly how the Vargon "worked" and if the Vargon could actually shrink to a mathematical point.

Markus began: "We view the Vargon as a sphere in our four dimensions of space and time. If the Vargon gradually moves from this point here, all the way across the room, it would appear to diminish slightly in size. Without time there is no motion, so in a sense, the Vargon will have moved in space *and* time. But its dimensionality is the same, because, even though you see it as being smaller, a short walk across the room will assure you that its actual size is unchanged."

Kandar and Shahlaya nodded in agreement.

"Now, imagine, if you will, how the Vargon would appear in a linear world of two dimensions," the Professor continued.

"You mean the linear dimension plus time?" Kandar asked.

"Precisely!" the Professor answered.

"Well, the intersection of a hollow sphere with a line would be two points," Kandar replied.

"Yes, and what would happen if the Vargon gradually lifted itself out of that linear world?" Markus asked.

"The two points of intersection would appear to approach each other until they met as a single point," Kandar speculated.

"A tangent point! And that tangent point is all that would connect the Vargon to the time sequence of that environment," the Professor continued. "If the Vargon leaves the line, it could rejoin that linear world in a different place or at another point in time."

"Now consider how the Vargon would appear if it intersected a world of three dimensions, that is: a two-dimensional plane plus time," Markus went on.

"Obviously, the Vargon would appear to be a circle: the intersection of a sphere and a plane," Kandar answered.

"And, if the Vargon decided to lift itself out of that world, what would be the apparent effect on the circle?" the Professor asked.

"It would seem to get smaller?" Shahlaya interrupted.

"Yes! But, has its size changed? Has the Vargon actually gotten smaller in any sense of the word?" the Professor inquired.

"I don't think so!" she replied

"No, it hasn't," Kandar interjected. "The Vargon stays the same regardless of the space it's viewed in. It is only the way that we perceive it that changes."

"You are absolutely correct! So, can the Vargon actually shrink to a mathematical point?" Markus asked them.

"Yes and no. It seems to disappear from our view — to become infinitesimally small, but only because it is rising into a higher dimension. So, no matter what angle we view it from during that process, it appears to be diminishing in size!" Kandar answered.

"Very well phrased. And, if the Vargon leaves our apparent four-dimensional world entirely, it can reappear anywhere in time within our space. A black hole appears to be infinitesimally small, but it has an enormous mass because the majority of that mass has been lifted into a higher dimension. It is essentially a dead star of tremendous gravity held tangent to our space at a single point. A vortex has an aperture that is tangent to our space and an outlet that we've found to be fairly permanently affixed to another place in our universe. If one of those tangent points is disrupted, then there is no telling where a vessel would re-emerge in time or space!" Markus continued to lecture.

"So, the Vargon can travel through space *and* time?" Shahlaya asked.

"In theory, the Vargon can travel in *many* spaces and *many* times!" the Professor speculated. "This creature exists beyond my own comprehension. I can't even begin to imagine all of the possible worlds — no — *universes* — that this being has seen!"

"So, what do these higher dimensions look like?" Shahlaya wondered aloud.

"All dimensions exist around us always," the Professor replied. "The 'higher' ones are simply beyond our perception and our comprehension. Just as a being in that planar world would have no concept of height, we can only see and understand that segment of reality that intersects with our particular universe at this particular moment."

*****

As the days passed, Professor Markus began to publish his findings. News of the Vargon and the ongoing experiments extended well beyond scientific publications into the mainstream media. Once again, Kandar was the hero of Ionus. First lauded by the military and the general population for his extraordinary role in ending the Forever

War, now he was being praised for bringing the Vargon to his planet. He had suddenly become the hero of the scientific world as well.

So, it came as no surprise when he was summoned before the Grand Regent of Ionus. It was the Day of the Long Eclipse and Kandar would have to travel from Ionus to its larger moon Inovar, the location of the Ionian Ruler's palace. It was a great honor to be invited there, but it was also a wonderful opportunity to view the eclipse from Inovar as it passed between Ionus and their sun. Kandar had always hoped to see the eclipse from that perspective, but neither he nor Shahlaya had ever before done so.

Shahlaya wasn't specifically mentioned in the invitation so she kissed Kandar "goodbye" and promised that she would join him later that day on Inovar. He left her early in the morning — anticipating great things and hoping to experience the eclipse with her after his meeting with the Grand Regent. For transportation, he boarded a Cloud that was programmed for direct flight to the palace.

Once there, Kandar was somewhat surprised to find that there was no great fanfare to celebrate his arrival. He announced himself to the guards and they escorted him to a room where he was to await his audience with the Grand Regent. He was not really comfortable waiting and wondering what was to come, but he had learned to be patient in the military. Still, the longer he waited, the more he felt that something just wasn't right.

Finally, he was escorted into a larger room. Commander Korbay was seated at the table alongside several other military commanders. Kandar was led to a seat at the end of the table where he stood awaiting the entrance of the Ionian Elder.

As the Grand Regent entered, all of the commanders rose and

bowed. Kandar did the same. And, when they were asked to be seated, they did so in unison.

"Kandar, you've become quite the celebrity on Ionus," the Ionian Ruler began.

"Your Eminence, I've done nothing to deserve it," Kandar stood and replied in all true modesty.

"Oh, indeed, you have," the Grand Regent continued. "You almost single-handedly ended the Forever War with Bardok and now you've brought the Vargon to Ionus. Isn't that worthy of your celebrity?"

Kandar was becoming suspicious of this line of questioning and he chose his words carefully: "I cannot take credit for ending the war. As for the Vargon, Your Eminence, I was blessed to have it save my life and bring me back home to Ionus on two occasions. I have no control over the creature — it comes and goes as it pleases."

The Ionian Elder turned to the sentries at the doors and said, "Bring them in."

The soldiers opened the doors and held them wide. Kandar was shocked to see four uniformed Bardokians leading in a Bardokian official and his translator. The Grand Regent gestured the official towards a chair. He glared at Kandar as he sat. The four guards stood in two rows behind the official and the translator who stood beside him.

The sight of the reptilian creatures, breathing their methane through nose-tubes, surprised Kandar. Although he was accustomed to studying alien creatures, this was not at all what he was expecting when he arrived at the palace.

The official spoke to the translator in loud, rough tones. The translator listened carefully and then he screamed, pointing at Kandar:

"That man has committed an act of war against Bardok! He attacked and destroyed two of our fighters, killing both pilots — and, he has stolen our Vargon!"

"What have you to say in your defense, Kandar?" the Grand Regent asked. "They have brought identifiable parts of your fighter with them. Is there any way that you can deny any of these charges?"

"With all due respect, Your Eminence, I did not attack those fighters. I merely defended myself. I did not intend to injure the Bardokian pilots and I did not 'steal' the Vargon. As I said earlier, it comes and goes as it wishes," Kandar responded.

"But, you were there. You entered Bardokian space without permission. In effect, you invaded Bardokian territory and, when their fighters defended that territory, you attacked them instead of surrendering," the Regent continued.

Commander Korbay stood to answer: "Kandar is no longer a military pilot. He is a scientist. And, although, he probably should have done things much differently, I am absolutely certain that he meant no harm in going to Mundago."

"He destroyed two ships!" the Ionian Elder interjected.

"In a fire-fight, a man's military training takes over! Of course, he fired back. Those pilots were trying to kill him!" Korbay rejoined.

The Bardokian diplomat stood and, looking at all of the Ionians seated around the table, began to scream in his native tongue. Kandar didn't need a translator to get the gist of what was going on. He didn't speak Bardokian, but he could read mental images and none of those were favorable. The translator stood, repeating: "This man has committed an act of war against Bardok! This 'Demon of Mundago' has attacked and destroyed two of our fighters, killing both pilots —

and, then there is the matter of the Vargon!"

"Kandar, you have put me in a very unenviable position," the Grand Regent said quietly.

"I'm very sorry, Your Eminence, I fully understand the situation and I take full responsibility for my actions. I humbly apologize to the Bardokian people and I will surrender myself to them to pay restitution as they see fit," Kandar responded solemnly.

"That is all well and good, but that is not enough," the Ionian Ruler replied.

"Your Eminence?" Kandar inquired for further clarification.

"You don't seem to understand. In order to avert a war, they are demanding the return of the Vargon and they want you — and all of your family — to pay for your crimes," the Regent explained.

"All of my family?" a trembling Kandar asked.

"I'm sorry, Kandar. If we want to avoid another war with Bardok, we have to surrender you and all of your family to these — *reptiles*," the Grand Regent responded.

The translator glared at the Ionian Ruler and whispered to the Bardokian official. The official's expression immediately changed to one of anger as he stood, bellowing at the Grand Regent and all of the other Ionians at the table. The translator screamed: "We will not be insulted here. If war is what you want, then that you shall have!"

The Bardokian official pushed the table slightly, and turned to leave. The rest of the Bardokians followed closely behind him with their hands on their weapons.

"Wait, just one moment!" the Ionian Elder yelled. Then, looking at Kandar, he added, "I'm sorry, Young Man, but, as much as I admire you for all that you've done for Ionus, both as a military officer and as a scientist, I cannot allow our planets to go to war again. There are simply too many lives at stake."

The Grand Regent turned to the Bardokian official and shouted: "We will agree to your terms to avoid war."

The Bardokians stopped at the door as the official conferred with the translator.

The translator turned to the Grand Regent and said: "Then it is agreed. Your Kandar, this 'Demon', — and his family — are ours to do with as we see fit. And, the Vargon will be returned."

"Yes," the Regent answered reluctantly.

The translator added: "Now you will provide us with the coordinates for Kandar's home and the homes of his family members."

Kandar hadn't realized that this information had already been gathered in advance of the meeting. Commander Korbay had the data on a hand-held transmitter, which he reluctantly handed to the Grand Regent. Korbay looked at Kandar and whispered, "I'm sorry, Captain."

The Ionian Ruler passed the transmitter to the Bardokian official who handed it to one of his guards. The guard conferred with the translator briefly and then attached it to his own communication device. The translator told the assembly, "It is done. The coordinates have been sent to our warship and these sites will be destroyed momentarily."

"The people who live in those areas are innocent of any wrongdoing!" Kandar shouted. "You can't let the Bardokians kill everyone who just happens to *be* there!"

"Kandar, the debt is on you. I have no choice in the matter," replied the Regent.

Kandar stood silent and heartbroken. His entire family would be destroyed in just a matter of moments and there was nothing that he could do about it. The four Bardokian guards surrounded him: two on each side. They motioned him towards the door.

The Bardokian official and the translator led the way and Kandar followed them out. As soon as they left the building, Kandar did his best to connect with the mind of his father on Ionus. It was such a great distance that he could not be certain that his father got the message, but he warned him of the imminent destruction of their entire family. Then he focused on Shahlaya. He was fairly confident that he connected with her mind, because he could clearly see that she was aboard the Cloud for Inovar. At least he knew that she would not be at home when the Bardokians destroyed it.

Clearly, there was nothing that the Ionians could do to help him, so he would have to save himself. He was being led toward a Bardokian diplomatic shuttle, which was just two docking bays farther than the *Dorius*. He was angry and desperate. He had no time to devise an elaborate plan of escape, so he tried to enter the minds of the Bardokian guards. What he saw in two of them, made him even angrier. He could clearly see the image of the *Vargon II* as they pursued it near Mundago. Two of these guards were the very pilots that he was accused of killing!

It was obvious to Kandar that there was no way he could prove this to the Grand Regent nor to the high-ranking assemblage of military officers, but, more importantly, it wouldn't do him any good if he could. Unless he could save himself, he was apparently facing torture and death at the hands of the Bardokians.

Instinct and rage got the best of Kandar. Using his mind, he pushed the Bardokian official forward, landing him flat on his face. The two guards in front ran to assist the old reptile, while Kandar grabbed the guard to his right and hurled him across their backs.

The guard on Kandar's left reached for his weapon, but Kandar telekinetically fired the weapon while still holstered — burning the guard's leg severely. The translator stood helplessly in all of the confusion, so Kandar grabbed his weapon and ran for the *Dorius.* He looked over his shoulder at the Bardokian delegation and fired at them to keep them from following. By the time he got to the *Dorius,* the Bardokian guards from the diplomatic shuttle were firing at him, as were the other four.

He boarded the vessel and quickly sealed the hatch behind him. He was fairly certain that Bardokian side-arms would not damage the ship, but he was not going to wait around for them to find something bigger. The *Dorius* was already prepared for take-off and provisions were well-stocked. He ran to the pilot's seat and immediately launched the ship. His pressure suit was still hanging in the airlock, but the ship was pressurized so he was fairly safe — for the moment at least.

"I am Kandar. All commands are 'my voice only,'" he ordered the computer.

As the ship exploded through the atmosphere, Kandar could feel the stress on his body, but he was a strong, young man and he knew he could withstand the gravitational forces. He set his course for Ionus and left the controls on autopilot for a few moments while he returned to the airlock to don his flight suit.

Once he was back in control of the ship, he immediately started scanning for the Bardokians. He had a faster ship and a good lead. He wasn't even sure if they would be following him or if they would go back to file a complaint with the Grand Regent. So, it was most important that he open his mind to Shahlaya, to see if he could locate her and, hopefully, rendezvous with her.

The Bardokians still were not on the scanner, but, through the forward canopy, Kandar could clearly see the shadow of Inovar as it began its sweep across Ionus. If Shahlaya were not in danger, he would have enjoyed watching this eclipse. He tried desperately to make mental contact and he suddenly realized that she was getting very close. There was just a speck of light between him and Ionus, which still wasn't covered by the shadow. He could feel with absolute certainty that she was on that Cloud. It was approaching him on a fixed course and he was accelerating toward it.

He would have to maneuver his ship around the space transport and dock with it to transfer her through the airlock, because Cloud passengers do not wear pressure suits or helmets. It might be difficult, under the hurried circumstances, but it wasn't impossible. He had no choice; he simply *had* to make it work.

As the Cloud got closer, he could see Shahlaya standing at its bow, looking for him through the front portal. That was when he noticed the Bardokian ship had appeared on his sensors. It was quite some distance behind him. More importantly, he noticed that something larger, but much farther away, was coming up from behind the Cloud.

The *Dorius* was closing the distance rapidly, but Kandar was beginning to worry whether he would be able to extract Shahlaya from the transport before the ship behind it arrived. Kandar was crestfallen as he witnessed the "moonbeams" hitting all around the Cloud. Then, suddenly, its propulsion system went offline and Shahlaya was jolted forward against the handrail. Kandar immediately realized that her transport had been hit.

"Vargon, if you can hear me: please save my Shahlaya!" he screamed.

It was almost a prayer — and, it was almost answered. Kandar watched the Cloud taking on the familiar red glow just as he saw the Vargon appear inside of it. The creature vanished as quickly as it came. Kandar cut his engines and turned back toward the cargo bay. The Vargon reappeared only a few steps below him and, as it opened, he could see Shahlaya. The creature levitated her and shrank itself down. It became half its normal size and hovered below her, still levitating her above itself. It was isolating her from the surface of the ship.

Kandar stopped on the steps. Shahlaya stood tall above the globe and raised her hands before her face. She could see that her fingers and palms were glowing white.

"Kandar, I can't save our child," Shahlaya sobbed, as she realized what was happening. She instinctively held her arms out towards Kandar and then, not wanting to share her fate with him, lowered them to her sides.

"Shahlaya!" Kandar cried, but there was nothing either of them could do. The white light spread across her entire body within seconds and the glowing white figure, standing above the Vargon, vanished in a blinding flash.

"Shahlaya—" Kandar whispered. She was gone forever and he was temporarily incapacitated by the brilliant light. He felt a slight collision as the Bardokians docked with the ship. The Vargon had disappeared. Kandar was alone.

When the door to the airlock opened, Kandar was still sitting on the steps below the pilot's compartment. His face was in his hands and tears ran down between his fingers. He had just watched his wife die and there was apparently no fight left in him.

He could hear the Bardokians barking commands at him, but he didn't understand the language. As his vision began to improve, he could see that they were gesturing for him to stand up, so he did so. This time they put a neural suppressor on his head. This was supposed to scramble his thoughts, to confuse him so that he couldn't focus his mind on anything for more than a moment. It was obvious that they wanted to take him and the *Dorius* back to Bardok with them. They pushed him into the small sickbay and locked him inside.

The neural suppressor might have been enough to incapacitate even Kandar under most circumstances, but this was suddenly a very different Kandar. This was not the pacifist or the scientist, but the Kandar who had just witnessed his wife's murder and who was himself awaiting torture and death.

Kandar's mind was flooded with disparate images. He revisited his childhood in one instant and he was seeing his wedding day the next. He was among the savages, then at Mundago and back at Inovar. He was desperately trying to focus on one thought — any thought. Any thought that would allow him to regain control of his mind — and the ship.

The Bardokians had just released the *Dorius* from their docking clamps. One of them had ascended the steps to the pilot's seat and he was trying to familiarize himself with the Ionian control panel. The other stood outside the sickbay, staring through the glass at their prisoner. As he stood there, he readjusted the atmospheric composition for all of the ship except the sickbay. When the methane level rose sufficiently, he removed his helmet and called to the pilot that it was safe for him to do the same.

The Bardokian pilot removed his helmet and spoke to the ship's computer, but the computer failed to respond. Then he tried speaking to it in his best imitation of Ionian, but there was still no acknowledgment. In Kandar's confused state, he wasn't entirely sure of how long this went on.

Finally, Kandar forced his mind to focus on a single, simple thought and mumbled the directive, "unify." And, somehow, the Vargon heard this and expanded itself around the freely-drifting *Dorius*. There was a startled scream from the pilot. Then, everything went black for a moment as the Vargon launched itself, and the ship within it, through a higher dimension and across the universe.

*****

When the Vargon re-emerged, it was exhausted and in need of nourishment. It left the ship in the upper atmosphere of a planet similar to Ionus, while it went to the nearby moon to feed. But, the ship was not in a stable orbit and the occupants were being tossed about inside it, as it quickly lost altitude.

Kandar was thrown to the floor and the neural suppressor was dislodged, but he was still locked inside the sickbay. The ship was plummeting through the atmosphere and the two Bardokians were in a complete panic. The pilot was desperately trying to get the propulsion systems online and the other guard was trying to find an escape pod.

Kandar stared through the window at the nearest guard and telekinetically tossed his weapon from its holster. As the blaster hit the floor, he hurled the guard at the airlock. The frightened Bardokian stood there paralyzed as Kandar mentally opened the door behind him and pushed him into the chamber. Kandar sealed it after him.

Then Kandar projected the thought of an escape pod into the mind of the pilot. The Bardokian left the command seat and came down the few steps with his weapon in his hand. Kandar threw him across the cargo bay and against the airlock door. The Bardokian was knocked unconscious and the pistol fell from his grip.

Still locked in the sickbay, Kandar telekinetically opened the airlock once again and forced the second guard inside of it. He then resealed the hatch. Kandar pressed the intercom button: "*Dorius,* this is Kandar. Emergency landing procedure." The ship seemed to slow slightly. "Emergency landing procedure — NOW!"

He reset the atmospheric composition for the rest of the ship from the control console, then Kandar used his mind to unlock the sickbay door just as the ship began to hit the tops of the trees. Before he could even open it, he was thrown hard against the deck. He cracked his skull; his ribs were crushed and he was bleeding profusely. Death seemed imminent, but, so long as he could remain conscious, it was not completely unavoidable. Kandar telepathically projected a distress call to any creature able to sense it. He was hoping to find an intelligent being — both willing and capable of preserving his mind, his life-force, his essence.

When the ship came to a halt, Kandar guided the creature in unlocking the outer hatch — and just as he heard it open, he assisted the difference in atmospheric pressure by telekinetically hurling the two Bardokians out of the airlock. It was unfortunate for the "reptiles" that they did not come from an oxygen-rich planet. They were methane breathers and their helmets were still inside the ship. Kandar could feel their panic as they gasped desperately for what they considered "breathable air." He knew that these were the same Bardokian pilots whom he had encountered on his ill-fated trip to

Mundago and he had neither pity nor time for them.

Kandar focused on the two native creatures who were just outside the ship. As the apparent leader of the two reached the inner airlock, Kandar opened both it and the door to the sickbay. He desperately reached out and grabbed the closest alien. He sensed that this was a brave creature with a noble spirit and he spoke the words: "Kogitarus argossum Kandar!" But, as fate would have it, just before the words left his mouth, the second creature made physical contact with the first and, with those words, Kandar transferred his spirit into the two of them.

And, although it has taken several decades to reconstruct these memories from the mind of Kandar, this was how Job and I received the essence of this incredible being. Our longevity, our ability to teleport things, all that we know and understand of the ship comes from Kandar and from the even more amazing Vargon.

I, hereby, attest and bear witness that all of the foregoing is true to the best of my knowledge and understanding on this 21st day of July, in the year of our Lord: 1884.

Daniel Johnstone

*****

Jessie's immediate reaction was to burst out laughing. She had read a lot of tall tales in her day, and written quite a few as well, but this took the proverbial "cake." Was Daniel writing fiction or was he actually insane? Could he possibly believe any of this to be true? She closed the book and rose from the bed.

"Good grief!" she mumbled as she put the thin volume back on the shelf. Then she remembered something. She sat down on the bed for just a moment and whispered, "I wonder—?"

She bolted upright and grabbed the robe from the closet. She went to the bedroom door and quietly unlocked it. As she cracked the door open, she peeked through the narrow aperture and saw that the kitchen was dark, so she crept out.

With the light emanating from her bedroom doorway, she could see Daniel's guitar leaning against the wall and his three-ringed binder of songs rested on a table. She tiptoed across the room and grabbed the binder. And, with that tucked under her arm, she quietly returned to her room.

She left the door ajar and sat on the bed. She paged through the book searching for that one song that Daniel had started to sing. She turned page after page, skimming through songs that were totally unfamiliar to her. Finally, she found the one simply called "She." There was no sheet music, just lyrics and chords, and she read these words:

She[1]

I broke through the shell of the wind —

Felt it shatter across my face.

She rode a Cloud from where I was going,

While moonbeams gave her chase.

She grew bright while the sun became shadow,

Since it could not out-shine her, and then:

My eyes grew salty and vision escaped them.

I was never to see her again.

I was never to see her again.

---

[1] Copyright, ©, 2015 by William A. Rich. All rights reserved.

Jessie dropped the binder to the floor. Were these simply pretty words? Merely flowery poetic images? Tears were welling up in her eyes and, at first, she didn't want to believe what she was thinking. Suddenly, she stood up and screamed aloud, as the realization touched her. She began to sob uncontrollably. It suddenly all made sense to her: Job and his statue; and, this hypnotic little waltz that was apparently Kandar's song for his beloved Shahlaya — a beautiful account of what had to be his most horrific nightmare.

*****

"Jessie, are you okay?" Daniel yelled as he burst into the room. He took a step in her direction and extended his arms out towards her.

"What are you?" Jessie sobbed, keeping her distance.

Daniel looked down at the binder and bent to pick it up. He tucked it under his left arm and said, "I'm just Daniel."

"No, you're not *just* Daniel!" she sobbed. "You're some kind of alien!"

Daniel was hurt. He stood there looking at her. She was crying and he could feel tears running down his own cheeks.

"No, please, listen to me," he pleaded, "I'm the same person that I was an hour ago. I'm just Daniel. You shouldn't have read all of this stuff. It's not my fault if you stick your nose into other people's business!"

"So, what *is* this 'stuff'? Fiction? Are you just making up stories or are you some kind of mental case? What's the deal?" she blurted without giving him a chance to reply.

"You know — I don't even care. I'm getting out of here!" she screamed, gathering her belongings. She intended to push past Daniel and head towards the door. Job sat in the doorway and growled menacingly.

"Wait a minute, you can't leave like that!" Daniel said, grabbing her arm.

"What? You're going to hurt me now? Are you going to eat me or feed me to your Vargon?" she snarled.

"I'm sorry, I don't mean to hurt you. I'll let you go and you can leave if you want to, but I really think you should get dressed first," he said, reminding her of her current attire. "And, I would very much prefer it if you'd just let me explain everything before you go running off into the night. You know it can be dangerous out there!"

"Your dog is growling at me! It's starting to look pretty dangerous in here, too!" she exclaimed. "Both of you get out of here and let me get dressed."

"Job, let's go," Daniel said to the dog and, turning to Jessie, added: "Think about what you want to do while you're getting dressed. If you want a story, then you'll let me explain everything to you — or else you'll be walking out of here with nothing."

Daniel led Job out of the bedroom and pulled the door behind him. He slowly took two steps and heard a shoe hit the door. As he wiped his tears from his face, a slight grin broke his troubled countenance. He took another step as the second shoe met the door. Daniel's grin widened to a full smile. He looked at Job and whispered: "I think that girl loves me."

*****

Daniel sat in the kitchen for what seemed like an eternity. Job was obviously concerned about the present state of affairs. He was sitting on the floor next to Daniel's chair, but the boy held the dog's front paws and upper torso on his lap. He kept petting Job's head and hugging him, reassuring him that "everything will be okay."

Job insisted that there were more important things that needed to be done and that time was of the essence. War was imminent and there was no time for this emotional nonsense. Kandar's essence was getting stronger in Job.

"Well, what are you waiting for? Isn't this about the time that you're supposed to knock on the door and stick your head in to apologize?" Jessie yelled somewhat angrily from the bedroom.

"Coming, Dear!" Daniel replied loudly. He did his best to suppress his smile as he eased Job to the floor and stepped toward the bedroom. He knocked on the door with the five-knock "shave and a haircut" rhythm and said: "I'm sorry, Jessie. Is it okay if I come in and apologize?"

"I guess so," Jessie responded with a hint of reluctance, "but this had better be good!"

Chapter 6

Rev-Tech Bionics

"Jessie, I'm really sorry if you think that I've lied to you about anything. I don't have a lot of time, but I'll do my best to explain whatever is bothering you. Where would you like me to start?" Daniel asked.

"The beginning might be a good place; don't you think?" she snapped back.

"Well, are you going to reserve judgment until I'm finished, or are you going to walk out of here as soon as things start sounding weird?" he inquired.

"We'll see," she responded coldly. "Start talking, Mister. The meter's running!"

Daniel walked over to the bookshelf and glanced at his booklets.

"Have you read all four of these?" he asked. She just sat there and glared at him in response, so he continued, "Of course you have: or else we wouldn't be having this conversation."

"You asked me how old I am," he began. "Well, actually I was born in 1838, so that puts me at over one hundred and seventy-five years old."

"That's it, Buddy. You are delusional!" Jessie barked as she stood to leave.

"Wait a minute, Jessie!" Daniel said as he blocked her path. "You're supposed to be a reporter — either you want to know the truth or you don't. Why would I make this stuff up? Do you think I'm trying to make myself sound crazy? Do you really think I want to look stupid? I haven't trusted anybody enough to tell them my story in nearly seventy years!"

Jessie stood with her arms folded in front of her. She was looking angrier by the second. Daniel was beginning to wonder if it was even worth the effort to try to explain anything to her in her current state of mind.

"Look, it's obvious that you don't want to believe anything I'm telling you. You read my story as best I could tell it at the time. You saw what I did with your camera and you know that I own Rev-Tech Bionics. Have you ever stopped to wonder where that name comes from?" Daniel asked.

"No, not really, but what does that have to do with anything?" she replied.

"Rev-Tech is short for 'reverse-technology.' I started the company with a friend of mine in the late 1940s," he continued. "After the crash at Roswell, I knew that I had better accelerate the repairs on the ship, so I befriended and confided in a young physicist named Albert Bascombe. He fronted the company for me until his death two years ago."

"I needed to reverse-engineer replacement parts for the ship and Bascombe had the brains and the wherewithal to do just that. I couldn't take a prominent position in the company, because, as you may have noticed, I don't show my age much," Daniel joked, hoping to relax the situation.

"Okay, let's see now: so you're pushing two hundred years old; aliens really *did* crash at Roswell; you've owned your own company for some seventy years and you've got an alien stuck inside you," Jessie interrupted, counting off each point on her fingers as she spoke. "Is that about right?"

"No, it's not like in the movie *Alien* or anything like that," he countered.

"Well, that's good, because we don't want anything eating its way out of your stomach and making a big bloody mess now, do we?" she scoffed.

"Kandar makes his thoughts known to me only when necessary. He's in Job, too. Sometimes, I feel like he's even smarter than I am, because poor Job took the brunt of the transference," Daniel continued, ignoring her sarcasm.

Jessie bent down towards Job, and teased: "So, who's a good doggy-woggy? Is Kandar a good doggy-woggy?"

"I wouldn't do that," Daniel warned her and then he spoke to the dog: "Job, please don't get upset with Jessie, she doesn't know whom she's dealing with."

"Oh, she doesn't does she?" Jessie remarked.

The dog glared at the young woman.

"There! Now you've done it! You might just want to look down," Daniel said in exasperation.

"I might want to look down where?" Jessie asked as she gazed downwards. That was when she realized that she was hovering several inches above the ground. She closed her eyes tightly and demanded: "Whoever is doing that — would you please stop it and put me down!?!"

Alighting gently on the carpet and with her eyes still shut, she added, "Am I back down yet?"

"Yes, for the moment, but be very careful of the way you talk to Job. Kandar does *not* have a sense of humor," the boy warned her.

"Okay, Daniel, I'm trying to stay calm. I really want to like you guys, but I'm getting scared here. I mean *really* scared!" Jessie whimpered, taking a deep breath.

"What can I do to make you feel better?" he asked.

"You mean like 'be normal'? — I think we're well past that

stage!" she replied.

"Jessie, I know things are looking bad right now, but I'm really a decent human being. I'm not a vampire; I'm not going to do anything to hurt you. But, there is one other thing that I should tell you about," Daniel said, "and it isn't good."

"Actually, there are probably a million things that you should tell me about, but you go right on ahead and humor me," she said half-jokingly.

"Here, maybe you'd better take a look for yourself," he told her, as he opened the front door. He held the screen door for her as they stepped outside.

"Okay, what am I supposed to see? It's still dark out, what's the big deal?" she asked.

"Look up," he told her with a touch of foreboding.

Jessie looked up at a sky utterly filled with stars. She had never seen so many shining points of light in all of the years that she had lived in that area. For a moment, she forgot about the subject of conversation.

"Alright, so it's beautiful. I've never seen such a starry sky," she whispered.

"That's the bad news: they're not stars," he warned her as he walked back through the front door. "Job and I are pretty sure that they're Bardokians and they've come for Kandar. I never realized it before, but the Vargon didn't just bring the *Dorius* here — he took it back in time. That's why it's taken them over one hundred and sixty earth years to traverse the distance that the Vargon covered in mere seconds."

"If Job and I can't turn them back somehow, they might just destroy this whole planet in their search for Kandar, his ship and the

106

Vargon," Daniel intoned with no hint of humor.

"You're really serious about this, aren't you?" Jessie asked.

"Dead serious," he replied. "It's almost dawn and you're going to have to leave. I'm sorry that I didn't have time to dig your car out, but you can take my Jeep. The keys are right on the kitchen table. Job and I are going to finish preparing the *Dorius*. I've never piloted an Ionian ship before, so I'm hoping and praying that Kandar will guide me, because Job sure isn't built to be a pilot."

"Wait a minute!" Jessie interjected. "The world's about to be destroyed and you want me to just hop in a Jeep and drive off?"

"If I can't avert this war, there is no place on earth that will be safe; but, if they detect the *Dorius* here, this will be ground-zero for the first wave of attack. You can't afford to be here and I don't want you to get hurt," Daniel said.

The sun was rising over the trees and Daniel realized that there was no time for any further explanation. He held the door for Job to come back in. Daniel grabbed the keys from the kitchen table and leapt down from the doorway. He placed the keys in Jessie's hand and closed her fingers around them.

"Take the Jeep and get out of here as fast as you can," Daniel whispered and, almost as an after-thought, he added: "I love you, Jessie!" He placed his hands on her shoulders and pulled her slightly forward. He kissed her on the lips and turned to run back into the shack. Job was sitting just inside the front door.

"Come on, Job, we've got things to do," Daniel said as he passed the dog.

He turned back for one last look at Jessie, but she was already gone.

"That was fast!" Daniel muttered. Then, looking down outside the doorway, he saw her clothes lying in a pile over her shoes.

"Job! Jessie was nice! Why'd you have to go and do that?" Daniel yelled, "Bad dog!" He had never punished the dog before, but he took one quick, angry swipe at him — contacting only his tail. Job spun around more out of shock than anger.

*****

Jessie let out one long, blood-curdling, unintelligible scream. The young scouts immediately spun their heads to look at her and, seeing them, she screamed again at the top of her lungs. A couple of the younger boys screamed back in terror. She was sitting inside of her car, scrambling to cover her naked body with her hands and arms.

"Daniel!" she screamed, "Job! You! — *You!* — How *could* you?"

"Where the—" the Scoutmaster paused, turning to look at the young boys, and, then back at Jessie, continued, "*Heck* did *you* come from?"

"Never mind that!" she yelled, huddling behind the steering wheel. "I want all of you to turn around: *right now!*"

"Okay, boys, the show's over. Everybody turn away from the vehicle!" he shouted.

"You, too!" she screamed at the Scoutmaster.

Reluctantly, he turned his back to Jessie. She looked around at the boys and, still hunched down behind the wheel, she reached for a blanket that was on the back seat. She had never been so humiliated in her entire life. She struggled to wrap it around herself.

Finally, Jessie rolled down the window and asked: "What were you guys doing to my car anyway?"

"Well, Lady, I don't know where you came from, but the car looked empty when we found it stuck here, so we were going to push

108

it out of the mud. That's what scouts do. That's how we earn our merit badges — we try to do 'good deeds,'" the Scoutmaster explained, gesturing animatedly. "But now, because of you, they're all going to want an extra badge for 'Nature Study'!"

"By the way, do you really intend to drive away like that?" he added, out of curiosity.

Jessie thought for a moment. Besides not having clothes, she didn't have her keys or her license either. She pounded on the steering wheel in frustration and the horn blared loudly, startling her and some of the younger scouts as well. She took a second to compose herself.

"I'm sorry, I'm going to have to ask everybody to face away from my car one more time," she requested rather adamantly.

"Okay, Scouts, I want all of you to stand at attention on this side of the road, facing away from this lady's vehicle," the Scoutmaster bellowed. "Line up! *Atten-tion!*"

As they all did their best to comply, Jessie rolled the window back up, opened the door and stepped out of her car. She had managed to wrap herself in the blanket, so she could walk in it with one hand free. She popped the trunk open and walked towards the back of her vehicle. There was a jacket and an old pair of sandals in there.

"Lady, are you done yet?" the Scoutmaster asked. "These boys are getting a little rambunctious."

"I'm almost there — just one more minute, please!" she insisted, while she slipped on the old sandals and the jacket. She reached under the jacket to discretely lower the blanket to form a make-shift skirt.

"Okay, 'at ease' or whatever," she told them as she snapped the trunk shut.

"I'm sorry I startled your boys. If you still would like to push my car out of the mud, I'd really appreciate that, but right now I have to go get my keys — and my things," she told the Scoutmaster, and barely audibly she added: "And I'm going to kill a certain young man and his alien-infested dog!"

She closed the door of her car with a slam and waddled up the path where she had first seen Daniel and the dog. She had no idea how long it would take her to find that old house, but she felt angry enough to raze it with her bare hands and she simply couldn't wait to get those hands on Daniel. With each step, she muttered aloud: "How dare you? How dare you humiliate me like that? You're all apologetic one minute and then I'm buck naked and sitting in my car the next. I listened to you and I put up with all of your exasperating nonsense. I even let you kiss me after I was absolutely convinced that you were stark-raving mad!"

She hadn't gotten very far when she noticed a sizeable snake sprawled across the path in front of her. Jessie was absolutely terrified of snakes and she immediately froze in her tracks. Then she recalled what Daniel had written in one of his books about how he used people's fears to keep them away from his home.

"Nice try, Mister Alien! So now you're trying to scare me off with an imaginary snake, huh?" she exclaimed. She grimaced as she picked up the snake and hurled it into the bushes. Her shoulders shook uncontrollably with revulsion. The snake hissed as it hit the ground and slithered off.

"Wait a minute—" she wondered aloud. "Can you pick up a snake, if it's only in your head?" She wasn't sure, so she continued down the path, wiping her hands briskly on her jacket.

She soon found an old creek that she assumed was the same one that Daniel had mentioned in his first story. She also saw a cave and a rocky ledge where he might have encountered Ol' Bob and met Job. It was a beautiful wooded area and she would have thoroughly enjoyed the walk, if she wasn't so completely livid.

It didn't take her long before she could see the tops of the dense fir trees with the peak of that ramshackle house tucked between them. Another five minutes and she would have her revenge.

*****

Daniel was still upset with Job, but there was no time for that. The fate of the world depended on the two of them working together now, just as they had always done before. He glanced around his home for one last time, knowing full well that he would never see it again. He would do his absolute best to save his world from the Bardokians, but he had little hope of surviving this day. He had never even flown the *Dorius* before, how could he possibly take it into battle?

The two of them stood in the small cargo bay. Daniel was trying to summon the courage to close both the outer and inner hatches of the airlock. Finally, Job stood up on his hind legs and put his paws on Daniel's shoulders. He held his enormous head against Daniel's for a few seconds — in an obvious show of affection — and, then he pulled it back again slightly: to look him in the eyes.

"I'm sorry, Job. I love you, too, but you shouldn't have sent Jessie away," Daniel told the dog, while he rubbed the dog's head.

"Stay, Daniel!" Job left the words resonating in the boy's head. The dog dropped down to the floor and entered the small sickbay. He turned back towards Daniel for just a second and, with more than a hint of sarcasm, he telepathically added the words: "Good Boy!"

The dog leapt up with his front paws on the command console and pressed his nose against it. The door to the sickbay closed and locked. Daniel walked up to the window and, putting his hands on the glass, watched in amazement as Job continued to press a complicated series of contact points.

Then the lights dimmed slightly in the sickbay and a large drawer began to open slowly from the wall. The drawer extended over seven feet across the room and the lights in sickbay focused on it. It was actually more like a slab that you might see in a morgue. There was a metallic-looking sheet covering whatever — or whoever — was on it.

Job turned away from the console and leapt up with his front paws on the slab. He gripped the top of the sheet with his teeth and pulled it back and down off the creature's face. Immediately, Daniel began to remember what had happened when he blacked out on the ship over one hundred and sixty years ago.

*****

After Kandar had transferred his essence into the two of them, Job looked into Daniel's eyes and peered deep into his mind. He compelled the boy to open the restoration chamber and to drag Kandar's body up onto it. The twelve-year-old Daniel struggled to get the huge alien up there and then, with the dog fully controlling his movements, he cleansed the alien's wounds and applied ointments from the medical supplies. He put a sheet over the full length of the body and keyed in a sequence of instructions on the sickbay console. The drawer of the restoration chamber slid back into the wall without leaving even a hint of its existence. That was when Job looked at Daniel and motioned him out to the cargo bay. Then Kandar, acting through Job, emptied the boy's mind of everything that had happened after he saw that mysterious hand. Daniel leaned back against the wall of the cargo bay and slid down its surface into a seated position. It was best if no one knew the whereabouts of Kandar's body or of the purpose, or even the existence, of the restoration chamber. And, for over one hundred and sixty years, that had been precisely the case.

*****

"Job, please don't!" Daniel begged the dog with his face pressed against the glass.

The dog looked back at Daniel and projected the thought: "Only *I* am Kandar." Then, Job laid his head across the alien's throat. Within a few seconds, the sheet began to move and, just as Job's body began to slide limply off the slab, the alien grabbed him roughly by the scruff of his neck. Kandar sat up on the table and swung his legs over the side. He stood and casually dropped Job's lifeless body onto his former "resting place." The alien glanced at Daniel through the window and then looked down at the control panel. He pressed a series of instructions into the computer and, once again, the slab retracted into the wall and the restoration chamber sealed shut.

Kandar looked up at Daniel. The boy glared back at him and, pounding on the glass, screamed: "You killed my dog! Job was my best friend and you killed him!"

The alien stared back at him and Daniel could hear the words: "*I* am your friend. Without my intervention, both you and the dog would have died a great many years ago. I could have returned to this form long ago, but I stayed with you because we *are* friends. But now, the *Dorius* is complete and I must leave you. The dog is no longer necessary."

"For all these years, you just used me!" Daniel screamed. "You used both of us. We were nothing but your slaves!" Daniel couldn't control himself. He stood there sobbing with his hands pressed against the glass.

Kandar had mastered Daniel's language, but he hadn't

vocalized with this body in nearly two centuries. He continued to connect telepathically with Daniel rather than to attempt to speak with a tongue untrained to vocalize in English. Thus, Kandar answered: "You were my hands and my voice. We worked together. I raised you and I protected you as though you were my own son. And, I shared your world with you, so now I must protect it as though it were my own, as well."

Kandar stretched his arms out to release the stiffness from his huge muscular frame. He opened the sickbay door and stood there for a moment, feeling Daniel's grief.

*****

Jessie had finally succeeded in shuffling her way back to the cabin. She found her clothing on the ground just outside the door and she managed to pull her panties and her slacks up under the blanket. Then she dropped her makeshift "skirt" and sat on the steps for a few seconds to put on her shoes. She picked up the keys to Daniel's Jeep and stuffed them into her pocket.

"Prepare to die, Mister Rev-Tech!" she bellowed, as she swung the front door open. She could see lights toward the back of the house, so she marched straight through the cabin, right out the backdoor and up the slight incline, muttering: "I am going to hurt you in places that you don't even know you have!"

Tears were still running down Daniel's cheeks, as he backed away from the glass. Jessie saw him and was in the process of removing her shoe when Kandar stepped out of the sickbay. She froze mid-bend, staring at the six-foot seven-inch alien. The shoe fell from her loose grip. As it resounded on the metal floor, Kandar turned towards the intruder. Daniel instinctively edged over towards Jessie and stood between the two of them to protect her. Kandar smiled.

114

"Oh…, my…," Jessie muttered, suddenly at a loss for words.

And then, taking a deep breath, the alien intoned: "Rawn!"

For just a second, Jessie and Daniel stood there trembling together in terror. Neither of them was quite sure of the alien's intention or of what he was trying to say.

"Raaawwnnn!" Kandar bellowed again, waving his arms at them in an almost threatening manner.

Jessie grabbed Daniel's shoulder and whispered: "Run!" Then, finding a more appropriate volume, she screamed — right in Daniel's ear: *"Run! — It said 'run'!"*

Kandar smiled as Daniel spun around and lifted Jessie up into his arms. The eyes of the lifelong friends met for one last time before Daniel ran down the ramp and out of the cabin. He carried Jessie all the way to the Jeep without a word being spoken.

Finally, Daniel mumbled: "Oh, God! I hope you brought my keys!"

Jessie looked at him with just a hint of a smile. She reached into her pocket and produced his keys, holding them by the ring and dangling them in front of his eyes.

"Thank you, Lord!" Daniel exclaimed, "I really didn't want to have to go back in there again!"

Daniel lowered Jessie into the Jeep and ran around to the driver's side. He leapt into the seat and started the engine. He threw it into reverse and spun the vehicle around. With little regard for conventional safe-driving technique, he then barreled down toward the main road.

"I know what you're thinking, but I didn't do it!" Daniel said. "Job sent you away all by himself."

"Oh, isn't that a lovely way to put it: 'Job, sent you away'?

Like you guys sent me off to camp, or something?" she began quietly, and then she continued to scream: "Well, you *did!* You sent me off *stark naked to a freaking Cub Scout camp!"*

Daniel covered his face with his hand and muttered: "God, this is not going to be pleasant! Just put me out of my misery!"

"So, when are we going back for my purse and the rest of my things?" Jessie asked coldly, but at a nearly civil volume.

"Now may not be the best time," Daniel answered. "You know, what with the world about to be destroyed and my whole cabin being reduced to ashes by the *Dorius* taking off."

"Okay, then, are you at least going to drive me home?" she snipped.

"The safest place that we can go to right now is Rev-Tech," Daniel answered.

*****

The phone rang inside the Oval Office.

"Yes?" the President answered.

"I'm sorry to bother you, Mr. President," his secretary began, "but there's a Colonel George Wagner on the line."

"Okay, put him through," he replied, then after the connection was made: "Hello, Colonel, what have you got for me?"

"Mr. President, the alien vessels have transmitted the coordinates where they expect to find this Kandar character and his ship," the Colonel informed him.

"Do we have any idea what's there?" the POTUS asked.

"Yes, Mr. President, they're giving us the general location of the main campus of the Rev-Tech Bionics Corporation in Apple Creek, Colorado," Wagner answered.

There was a brief pause. The President tapped his pen on the

116

desk and closed his eyes for a moment: deep in thought.

"Colonel Wagner: why does that name sound familiar?" he began.

"Rev-Tech has been covertly supplying us with computer support and technology for decades, Sir," the officer replied.

"You said 'covertly,' why 'covertly,' Colonel?" the President inquired.

"Evidently, the U.S. government has had a top-secret relationship with this company since the middle of the last century. In fact, we apparently just shipped some kind of sphere to them about a week ago," the Colonel continued. "Somebody found it buried in the middle of the desert and they're supposed to have the best labs for examining and researching these artifacts. Unfortunately, we have almost no information about the guys who run the place."

"I'm not even sure how that's possible, but find out everything that you can about them! If there's an alien running that place, find out who he is. Check his tax records! Do something and do it fast! Let the other aliens have him! If they can travel clear across the galaxy, I don't think we should be making any attempt to resist, so long as they do not attack the American people or any of our interests. Do you have all that, Colonel?" the POTUS asked.

"Yes, Sir, Mr. President," the Colonel answered.

"Perfect, George," the President said. "And, in the meantime, I want all of our resources converging on that area and I want all branches of the military on their highest level of alert."

*****

Kandar sealed the inner and outer doors of the airlock and proceeded up the few rungs to the pilot's cockpit. He was still wearing the flight suit from nearly two earth centuries before, but now

117

all of the damage was repaired just as the restoration chamber had healed his wounds. He began to touch panels and flip switches, preparing for flight.

"*Dorius*, this is Kandar," he began in his native Ionian, "Display the Bardokian attack fleet."

The ship's computer displayed a holographic image of the fleet right in front of him. He studied it momentarily, assessing weaknesses and planning a strategy. Then, he said: "Now put up a display of this planet," and the *Dorius* complied.

"Vargon, my old Friend," Kandar continued, assuming its cognitive presence. "If it pleases you, could you put my ship here?" He extended his finger to designate a point almost directly antipodal to his current position.

The Vargon immediately encompassed the *Dorius* and released it on the opposite side of the planet, but several hundred miles above the earth. Meanwhile, a Bardokian troop carrier and four fighters broke orbit above North America and began their descent, just as Kandar stabilized his orbit and accelerated to maximum speed: circling the planet three times within mere seconds.

As he completed the third orbit, he cut his power and, gesturing with his finger once again, asked: "And now that we have their attention, my dear Friend, can I implore you to put us here?"

*****

Daniel happened to look up and slammed on his brakes. It was still very early in the morning and, luckily, no one was behind him.

"Are you freaking crazy?" Jessie yelled. "You could have killed us!"

"Look at that!" he said as the third band of gold streaked across the sky, "I'm not sure what he's doing, but I'm sure that's Kandar."

"Is that supposed to be some kind of sign or something?" she asked.

"I think he's trying to show them that the *Dorius* is ready for battle. He's trying to get their attention to take the fight out to space. — Away from earth," Daniel speculated.

"But, we're still heading for cover," he added.

Daniel switched the radio on in the middle of a news bulletin: "*...immediate shelter. I repeat: anyone within range of this broadcast should take immediate shelter. Go to your basement or the innermost room on your lowest level. Radar indicates that aircraft of unknown origin are descending over the state of Colorado. We do not know their intentions so we must assume that we are under attack. This is an emergency.*"

He switched the radio back off and headed straight to the Rev-Tech complex. There was a sonic boom as a squadron of fighter-jets screeched overhead. Arriving at the sentry post, he came to a quick stop.

"Jenkins, open the gate and take the rest of the day off!" he yelled at the guard. "Something really bad might happen, so I think you're going to want to be with your family today!"

"Are you *for real*, Mr. Johnstone?" he asked, laughing.

"Absolutely 'for real'! Haven't you heard the news broadcast?" Daniel answered. "If you don't trust me, you can just come along with us. We're heading for the safest place that I know."

"Well, you go on ahead and I'll catch up later," Jenkins responded. As the Jeep sped towards the reserved spaces, he muttered: "That stupid rich kid thinks he's funny!"

Daniel parked the vehicle in his reserved spot, then he ran around and helped Jessie from the Jeep. They quickly pushed their way through the main entrance.

"Where's Job?" asked the guard at the desk.

Jessie looked at Daniel. "Yes, where *is* Job?" she asked menacingly.

"He's gone," Daniel replied with a slight quiver of his chin. He stepped over the security gate, then lifted Jessie over it and held her close.

"You forgot to sign in!" the guard yelled as they hurried past.

"Marx can vouch for us!" Daniel shouted back.

When they arrived at the secretary's open office door, the boy stuck his head in to address the young woman: "Good morning, Maxine!"

"Oh, good morning, Mr. Johnstone!" she replied, smiling at the two of them. "Is that the 'catch of the day'?"

"Actually, Maxine, today's my birthday, so please get on the intercom and tell everybody that they can go home right now: with pay. And, you do the same!" he added.

"Oh, happy birthday, Sir — and thank you very much! I'll get right on that," the young woman replied gleefully.

As Daniel continued down the hallway, with Jessie still nestled in his arms, he heard Maxine's voice on the intercom announcing: "In honor of our Mr. Johnstone's birthday, we have all been granted permission to leave early, with full pay. Please lock up for the day and leave in an orderly fashion."

A happy roar echoed through the complex as the Rev-Tech employees began to shut down their computers and vacate the premises.

"Why didn't you just tell them the truth?" Jessie asked.

"What? That our world's about to be invaded by aliens? Mr.

Jenkins apparently didn't believe me. For security reasons, Rev-Tech is electronically isolated from the rest of the world," the boy replied. "So, who's going to believe me unless they happened to hear that news broadcast for themselves?"

Suddenly, Jonathan appeared at his doorway.

"Back so soon?" he asked sarcastically. "You've never come here twice in one week before. Have you finally discovered 'work ethics'?"

"We're going to the sub-basement for shelter," Daniel responded as he pressed the elevator's "call" button. "You can either come with us or die up here."

"Kid, I've worked here for *years* and there *is* no sub-basement," Marx laughed.

Daniel set Jessie down as they boarded the elevator. Just while the doors were closing, he held up his ID pass and added: "Only Albert and I had the proper keys!"

The boy slid his pass into the key-slot and Marx stood outside the elevator doors, grinning. He watched the "B" light up. Then, a minus sign appeared in front of the "B" and Marx's jaw dropped. He hurried back into his office and depressed the intercom button yelling: "Maxine, cancel Johnstone's last order and dig out the schematics for this building! Nobody is to leave the premises!"

*****

As the elevator opened to the sub-basement level, Daniel switched on the lights and led Jessie into the somewhat-dusty, but elegant, office. There were huge, dimly-lit display cases on both sides of the elevator and two more on either side of a couch.

"My gosh! Why didn't you just live here?" Jessie asked in astonishment.

121

"I guess it looks a lot nicer to you, but Job insisted that we stay near the ship," he answered matter-of-factly. "Now that Job —and Kandar — and the ship are gone, it doesn't rightly matter where I live."

"How long will we have to stay down here?"

"I wish I could tell you, but I don't know for sure," Daniel answered. "Make yourself at home, I have an important call to make."

Jessie sat on the couch and started to unzip her jacket. She looked down and quickly thought better of it. She finally had time to realize that she was sitting there with no bra, no blouse and one shoe. She leaned forward, with her elbows on her knees, and dropped her face into her open palms.

"What's wrong? Why are you shaking your head?" Daniel asked her, as he sat at his desk.

"You've got to be kidding me!" she moaned. "I always thought that I'd be better dressed than this when I died! I am going to be the worst-dressed corpse on the planet!"

Tears began to well up in her eyes and she started to weep quietly.

"Jessie, please, I have to make this call. There's a door next to the washroom over there. That's the emergency living quarters. Reach inside the door and turn the lights on. There's a closet full of clothing to the left. I'm sure you can find something to wear," Daniel said quietly. "Just give me a few minutes and I'll be right with you!"

Daniel lifted the receiver to his ear and, hearing a dial-tone, slid his ID badge into a slot on the side of the phone. It rang one time.

"General Bascombe speaking," a voice answered.

"Jerome, this is Daniel Johnstone, I don't know if you'd remember me, but I was a friend of your father's," he said.

For a moment there was dead silence on the line. The General was dumbfounded.

"Daniel Johnstone? Uncle Danny? Of course, I remember you!" the General finally responded. "My Dad brought me to your house to visit you way back in the sixties. You were still a teenager. You did those incredible magic tricks and you had that wonderful dog! I'm sure you even babysat me a couple of times. How could I forget you? Those were great times for both my Dad and myself!"

"I'm so glad that you remembered me — and Job," Daniel responded.

"That's it! Of course! Job! He was an absolutely amazing animal. I'm sure he's long gone by now. That's a real shame to lose a friend like that," the General replied.

"Yes, Job was truly special," Daniel said sadly.

Then General Bascombe remembered that this was a secured telephone line.

"Mr. Johnstone, I know that my father always spoke highly of you and you were a friend to my family, but why are you calling on this line?" the General asked. "We're sort of in the middle of an international emergency."

"Jerome, codename *Dorius*," Daniel replied.

"Got it!" Jerome responded, as he tapped on a keyboard, "I'm pulling up the file right now. Just give me a second to review it."

"It won't show you much onscreen," Daniel pointed out. "You have to go to the file cabinet and pull up a hard copy."

"Amazing!" the General exclaimed.

"What's amazing?" asked Daniel.

"I opened the computer file and, just like you said, it references a file cabinet!" the officer replied.

A few short minutes later, Bascombe exclaimed: "This is

unbelievable. This is absolutely incredible! Harry Truman's personal seal is on this thing. My Dad never told me about any of this stuff!"

"It was all on a need-to-know basis," Daniel explained. "Your Dad encouraged you to join the military so I would have a trustworthy contact inside the government. We both knew that this day might come and he knew that a liaison in the military would be important."

"That sounds critical," the General responded.

"Are you aware of the alien presence in earth orbit?" Daniel asked.

"Absolutely. That's our 'international emergency.' We've been watching for the past couple of nights. I've never seen these files before, but, just scanning over them quickly: am I to believe that this '*Dorius*' ship is operational?" the General asked.

"I'm pretty sure that Kandar launched about 10 minutes ago. Did you see the three golden streaks in the sky?" Daniel responded.

"No, I didn't actually see them, but the reports are all over the news. The phones at the Pentagon — NORAD — the White House — *everywhere* are ringing off the hooks!" the General answered. "You mentioned 'Kandar.' The President got a coded message asking that we surrender this Kandar and his ship or else these aliens were coming to get him. We had no idea what to make of that. Are we officially under attack?"

"Not yet, but you had better put everyone on their highest alert. I don't know how many alien ships are up there, but I can't even begin to imagine how Kandar can protect us from all of them," Daniel said, with a sense of hopelessness.

"If numbers will help you, based on sightings around the world, we're estimating close to one hundred alien ships," the General replied, "but nearly all of them are maintaining orbit over the western

United States.".

"That doesn't make me feel any better," Daniel sighed.

"What about this other creature?" asked Jerome, as he continued to scan the file.

"You mean the Vargon?"

"Yes, whatever exactly that is!" the General answered.

"The Vargon is a non-aggressive entity," Daniel replied. "If we're lucky, it will assist Kandar in repelling the attack, but it will not purposely do anything to harm anyone."

"Is there any chance that this Kandar will surrender to them in order to prevent a war that we obviously can't win?" Bascombe asked.

"He surrendered to them once and they wiped out his whole family. I think he has a score to settle," Daniel replied.

"Then you have to make him understand that we're not prepared to battle an alien invasion force just to settle his personal vendetta!" the officer implored him.

"General Bascombe: Kandar and the *Dorius* are the only things keeping those aliens from destroying this whole planet. From what little I know of them, they are absolutely ruthless and they have no sense of honor," the boy explained.

"Understood. Keep me posted if you learn anything new — and may God help us!" the General declared, intending to end the call, but before he could hang up...

"Oh, Jerome, wait! On that very subject, I have to advise you to retrieve a small box in the back of that same drawer where you found the *Dorius* file. Pull all of the files forward and reach down behind them," Daniel requested.

"Yes, Sir, just give me a moment and I'll be right back," Bascombe responded.

After a minute or so, the General came back to the phone.

"I've got the package," he said.

"Great! Carefully open the carton and remove the contents. It's a communication device," Daniel informed him. "With the dial pointing at the square icon, you'll be in direct contact with me. This will be our only means of communicating, if either the power grid or the satellites go offline."

"What do the other icons represent?" inquired Bascombe.

"I'm not positive about all of them, but the triangle should be the *Dorius*," the boy replied. "This device is also supposed to incorporate an English to Ionian translator, but I've never had an opportunity to test it."

"Before this is over, I think we'll have a very thorough working knowledge of this thing's capabilities!" the General responded, looking at the communicator in amazement.

"The device activates on contact whenever you pick it up. I'll keep in touch, in case anything new comes up. Take care!" Daniel said as he put the phone down.

He unlocked his lower desk drawer and pulled it open. There was a soft tone as he reached into the drawer to retrieve an exact copy of the General's communication device and held it near his face.

"Jerome?" Daniel spoke into the device.

"Yes, Daniel, I just wanted to make sure this thing would actually work. I have no idea what it runs on, so I'm going to set it down before I accidentally run down the power source," the General replied.

"Good idea! If you have to go out into the field, be sure to take it with you," the boy advised him.

"Oh, and one last thing—" Jerome added.

"Yes, General?" Daniel asked.

"I just can't get over your voice. Uncle Danny, you sound *exactly* the way you did fifty years ago!" Jerome exclaimed in amazement.

"Yeah, I get that a lot. I guess I've taken good care of myself for all these years! You do the same, Jerome!" Daniel replied as he set his own device on the desktop.

When he looked up, he saw Jessie leaning over the opposite side of his desk. She was staring at him with her mouth agape in utter disbelief.

"What?" Daniel inquired.

Chapter 7

The Battle

The Vargon deposited the *Dorius* in the exact position that Kandar had requested. He was toward the back of the Bardokian fleet, situated midway between two fighters, but facing in the opposite direction. Kandar aimed and launched grappling cables from both sides of the *Dorius* — simultaneously harpooning the tail sections of the two Bardokian Warbirds.

As the Bardokians spun their heads in the direction of the impact, Kandar pushed his ship to full speed. The two Bardokian fighters collided behind the *Dorius,* banging uncontrollably into each other. The two pilots were firing wildly in all directions, unable to steer their own ships, while Kandar guided his ship in a wide arc back toward the rest of the fleet.

Through a stroke of luck, one of the tethered fighters hit a Bardokian battle-cruiser with a moonbeam. As the huge ship began to glow red in the distance, Kandar released one of the cables, allowing the attached ship to collide into two other fighters. All three of them exploded in a ball of flames.

Kandar sped onwards with the second ship — weaving in and out between three more Bardokian fighters. He easily pulverized all of them with the "wrecking ball" at the end of his cable. He finally jettisoned the panicked Bardokian as he whipped past another cruiser. The battered fighter plunged right through its hull: causing significant damage.

With few tricks left up his sleeve and no longer having the benefit of surprise, Kandar targeted every fighter between him and the nearest battle-cruiser, with all forward weapons blazing. The *Dorius* was now commanding the attention of the entire Bardokian fleet.

Kandar was revitalized and longing for battle. He was as ready for his own death as he was certain of it.

"For Shahlaya!" he screamed as he attacked the Bardokians with all of the ferocity of a wild dog taking on a bobcat. Kandar could feel the blood burning in his veins. And then there was nothing.

*****

Kandar stared out of his canopy at darkness. So far as his eyes could see, there was nothing. Not a star nor a planet — not a hint of illumination outside of the *Dorius*. For a moment, Kandar just sat there, gawking in utter disbelief.

"Rotate slowly on the horizontal: three hundred sixty degrees," Kandar demanded.

The ship responded, but all was black.

When the motion stopped, Kandar asked again: "Rotate vertically — and slowly — three hundred sixty degrees."

The *Dorius* obeyed, rotating three hundred sixty degrees vertically and then it came to an abrupt halt. In every direction that he looked, Kandar could see only darkness.

"Where am I?" Kandar wondered aloud.

"How will I ever avenge Shahlaya?" he asked in despair.

He stared into the depths of the void beyond his canopy.

"Is this what it's like to be dead?" he muttered, thinking that perhaps he simply hadn't survived the battle. He rose from the cockpit and walked down the few steps to the cargo bay. He sat on the steps and stared at the empty space in front of him. That was where the Vargon had levitated Shahlaya while she and his unborn child were being consumed by the Bardokian death-ray.

"I've lost everything!" he whispered.

Kandar sat there; and, his eyes glazed over.

"Vargon, can you hear me? I've lost everything!" he bellowed.

"I've lived all of these years, patiently waiting to avenge my wife and child," he muttered. "And now I'm somewhere that doesn't exist and the battle is lost!"

"Vargon, are you even there?" Kandar yelled. The Vargon had stayed with them for most of their years on earth. It had always availed itself to their needs. He stood and stretched his tired frame; and, then, he ascended the steps to the cockpit.

He sat in the pilot's seat and leaned forward. With his head in his hands and his eyes closed, he reached out with his mind. There seemed to be nothing but the emptiness of space. The Ionian had no sense of time. So deep was his despair: that the passing moments could have been seconds — or hours. He lifted his head and stared out into the blackness that encompassed the *Dorius*.

"If there is a god out there, then show yourself!" Kandar screamed.

As he sat there, he thought he glimpsed something from the corner of his eye.

"Rotate: vertical axis, plus forty-five degrees," Kandar commanded. "— Stop!"

"And now, rotate: horizontal, plus forty-five degrees." He paused, "— and stop!"

Just as the ship ended its rotation, Kandar spotted the Vargon in the distance.

"Vargon, my Friend, — are you God?" he inquired.

In all the years that he had known the Vargon, he had never before heard its voice. But, suddenly, Kandar realized that there was an answer to his question.

"There are many levels of existence greater than our own."

Kandar pondered the answer for a moment and then he asked: "If you are not a god, then what are you?"

"We are the choir of souls," the Vargon replied.

Kandar was not sure what any of this meant, but he felt compelled to ask the Vargon: "Why am I here? Why didn't you let me have my revenge?"

"You are not the Kandar who was our friend," answered the Vargon.

"Of course I am your friend. We have been great friends for so very long — since the Battle at Mundago. How can I not be your friend?" Kandar inquired, bewildered.

"You are as much the beast as you are Kandar. You have lost your humanity," the Vargon responded. *"Kandar was not a warrior. Your thirst for vengeance is the animal in you. The boy has your humanity."*

The Ionian listened intently, but he would not accept the truth.

"Then why have you allowed me to live? What purpose is left to me, if not to avenge my wife and child?" he asked.

"Kandar, I require no vengeance," a voice answered.

The Ionian held his breath in astonishment. It was the voice of Shahlaya.

"Isn't it greater to live for the living, than to die for the dead?" she asked.

"Shahlaya?" Kandar gasped, "Is that really you? I only wanted to avenge you, so that I could finally be with you."

"I have always been with you, Kandar," she replied. "The whole time that you were with Daniel: I was with you. Your whole family has been with you."

"The boy loves you as though you are of the same blood," the

131

voice continued.

"No, that isn't true," Kandar replied. "Daniel hates me. I know that he hates me. And rightfully so, because I took his beloved Job away."

"You've put a whole world in jeopardy and it is now your obligation to do what you can to save it," Shahlaya replied.

"Then you must help me to return to earth," Kandar implored her.

He sat there quietly, staring at the Vargon and mulling all that was told to him.

"I need to save Daniel. He was like a son to me. I raised him and protected him. I have to go back to save the boy and his planet," Kandar pleaded with the Vargon. "You must help me or, surely, they will all die."

*****

Jessie found a shirt and some gym shoes in the closet, while Daniel stood in the main office area examining the contents of the display cases. Jessie dressed herself quickly and returned to find Daniel unlocking one of them.

"Wax cylinders, 78s, eight-track cartridges, vinyl. You've got quite a collection of music antiques!" she noted, peering into one case.

"Well, they weren't exactly antiques when I bought them," he responded. His interest was focused on another case entirely.

"What are these?" Jessie asked, pointing at some Sony "Elcasets" and DATs.

"Those were supposed to be the 'next big thing'!" he answered, then, smiling, he added: "You have no idea how many times I've had to re-purchase all of the music that I liked — just so they could replace that format with another one!"

132

"Yeah, tell me about it!" she replied, gawking at the collection of players that matched up with the media.

Suddenly, the ground shook and they could hear explosions nearby.

"Oh, my God! What was that?" Jessie screamed.

"I think we're getting visitors," Daniel told her as he hurriedly removed various antiquities from his display case. "And we had better be prepared."

*****

As soon as the Bardokians invaded U.S. airspace, a squadron of Air Force stealth fighters were scrambled from the nearest base. They were not supposed to engage the alien forces, but, when one of the Bardokians strayed from their intended flight-path, the American pilots took aggressive action and destroyed it in a brief skirmish. It was as though both sides were anxious to test their destructive potential.

The three remaining Bardokian fighters easily downed all six American jets and then proceeded to strafe the Rev-Tech campus with their pulse cannons. While precisely-selected buildings blazed, the troop carrier landed and its deadly cargo disembarked. Twenty-four of Bardok's fiercest marines slowly began to fan out across the burning complex.

Jenkins was huddled down in his sentry box when the Bardokian craft landed. He only had a 9mm sidearm with three extra clips, but he was a war veteran and he knew how to use them. He had seen the air battle and now he watched the creatures closely as they exited their vehicle. They were all heavily armed and he had just witnessed the devastation of alien weaponry.

The Bardokians were all walking away from Jenkins' post

when he stood and took careful aim at the nearest one. He hesitated for a moment.

"Screw it!" he muttered. "Rev-Tech doesn't pay me enough for this!"

The middle-aged man was just about to turn and run, when one of the creatures made eye-contact. The war veteran instinctively raised his weapon and squeezed off three rounds. The alien was thrown to the ground. As two other aliens spun around, Jenkins emptied the rest of his clip. He hit both primary targets and also managed to hit two others in the back. While the security guard ejected the spent clip and snapped a second one into his gun, two of the alien marines incinerated the sentry post and its lone sentinel.

Within seconds, shots rang out from the entrance of the Rev-Tech office building. Two more Bardokians fell to the ground and the rest of the alien marines focused their firepower on the doorway. The guard at the door died instantly.

The second guard was crouched behind his desk, dialing the local police, when six of the aliens smashed their way through the doors. Jonathan Marx started to walk down the corridor to investigate all of the commotion. He heard a noise to his left and walked into Maxine's office.

"Psst! Hide, Jonathan!" Maxine whispered from beneath her desk.

Marx spun around as five shots rang out, followed by a muffled scream. He ran out of Maxine's office and headed towards the elevator. He looked over his shoulder for just a second and glimpsed a large figure at the opposite end of the hall. He desperately pressed the elevator's "call" button.

"Daniel! Daniel!" Jonathan screamed, pounding on the doors.

The doors opened, but it was too late. An alien marine picked him up by the neck and threw him headlong through his office window. Marx lay there broken and bleeding. The last thing he saw was four of the creatures congregating inside the elevator.

*****

The Vargon felt Kandar's despair and it knew that the earth was in peril. It moved to one side and revealed a spot of light off in the distance. Kandar rose from his seat, squinting through the canopy at the tiny point.

"That is your universe as viewed from a higher dimension," the Vargon said.

"If that's the whole universe, I couldn't pilot the *Dorius* over such a distance in a billion lifetimes!" Kandar exclaimed in despair.

"Then, prepare to fight — so that others may live," the Vargon ordered him.

And so, it encompassed the *Dorius* and, in what seemed like the blink of an eye, placed it behind the earth's moon. The Vargon had depleted most of its energy. It needed to feed again. Kandar was now on his own.

"*Dorius,* scan for Bardokian ships," the Ionian ordered.

The computer displayed the nearest ships and their positions relative to his. He immediately realized that three fighters were descending from a low earth orbit in attack configuration. Kandar fired all of his thrusters and emerged from the moon's shadow in hasty pursuit.

The Ionian would have to do his best to prevent those ships from attacking earth, but, in revealing his position, he was drawing the attention of nearly every Bardokian on his side of the planet. The odds of survival were incalculably low. Kandar knew that he would be with Shahlaya soon.

*****

A soft tone rang from Bascombe's desk. Reluctantly, the General picked up the alien device and held it near his mouth.

"Daniel?" the General asked.

There was no answer. Bascombe looked at the device and realized that there was an unfamiliar icon illuminated. Out of curiosity, he turned the dial to the circle and pressed the symbol.

"This is Korbay. Is anyone on this frequency?" the Commander asked.

"Uh, Cowboy, this is General Bascombe. Who are you?" the General replied.

"This is Commander Korbay of Ionus. Is Kandar there?" Korbay responded.

"No, Sir. To the best of my knowledge, Kandar is defending this planet against an alien invasion force," Bascombe answered reluctantly. "Where exactly are you and whose side are you on?"

There was no reply.

"Hello?" Bascombe called out, but the circle was no longer illuminated.

*****

Daniel had finally managed to get Jessie inside the living quarters.

"Stay in there, barricade the door and don't make a sound," he insisted.

"But,—" she protested.

"No 'buts,' this is serious! Lock yourself in, barricade the door and keep quiet," he whispered.

Daniel had already upended his desk and moved it to the middle of the floor some fifteen feet away from, and slightly off-axis to, the front of the elevator doors. He had the couches and chairs piled up on either side of it. All of the lights were focused directly on the elevator. Daniel crouched in the shadows behind the desk with what few weapons he had at hand.

There was banging inside the elevator and occasionally the screech of some kind of wild animal. He heard the ominous sound of metal being torn apart and then there was a "thud" — as if something had fallen down the elevator shaft.

The boy could hear a rapid beeping sound and a creature groaning. Then he saw claws pushing between the elevator doors. With another groan, the alien managed to push the doors about six inches apart. It peered through the gap, squinting into the bright light. Daniel recognized that face. He had placed rocks over two such faces, a great many years ago.

Daniel aimed his Pa's musket and pulled the trigger. The hammer snapped down, but nothing happened. The boy cocked the gun again and quickly aimed it at the alien a second time. The lock snapped down once more, but the musket still didn't fire. The boy ducked down. He did his best to adjust the flint. By the time he rose up, the creature was holding the doors wide open and it stood between them, almost grinning at him. For the third time, the boy aimed the ancient musket at the alien.

He pulled the trigger. The flint ignited the powder with a flash and the ensuing explosion launched a lead ball through the middle of the Bardokian's skull. The inside of the creature's helmet was spattered with yellow fluid and orange matter. The alien wobbled for just a moment and then it fell backwards. The doors closed partway, the alien's protruding legs keeping them from sealing.

Daniel and Job

The recoil nearly knocked the boy off his feet. Daniel didn't even have time to reload when a second alien leapt down the shaft from the basement level. The boy fumbled in the dark for Pierre's musket. As soon as the hideous creature showed its face, Daniel fired a lead ball into it.

The boy had made a point of buying fresh kegs of powder every couple of years and the nearly two centuries that he had kept these particular antiques in pristine condition had finally paid off. Now he was doing his best to reload the second musket in the dark. It was something that he had done many times before, but never in the grips of such terror or desperation.

There were two more thumps in the elevator. The boy hunched down behind his cover and froze. He dared not make a sound.

"Daniel? Are you okay out there?" Jessie whispered from behind the door.

The alien nearest the elevator doors looked out and toward its left, apparently looking for the source of that sound. It stepped out into the room. There was a loud "snap" and the creature dropped its weapon, screeching in pain. It had found one of Pierre's old bear traps. Daniel hurled his Pa's hunting knife into the Bardokian's chest, severing the hose to its breathing apparatus. The beast staggered there for a moment while methane escaped into the room. It fell to one side.

The creature behind it fired wildly at the lights. The room went completely black. Daniel still had one surprise left, if it would only work! He had found two of them inside the *Dorius* years ago. He had always kept one at his home and the other one had been on display in this office. Now it was in the back of his belt.

The Bardokian was screaming commands as it made an adjustment to its weapon. Daniel didn't know if it was calling for

138

reinforcements or just yelling at him. This time when the alien fired its weapon, the pile of furniture burst into flames.

Daniel rolled across the floor and fired the old Bardokian pistol. The alien stood there for just a moment with the most bewildered expression on its face. It dropped its weapon and looked down at the hole burned through its chest. Then it slowly stumbled to its knees before it fell face-first into the small inferno that it had just ignited.

The boy stood up slowly, keeping a close eye on the bodies of the creatures, as he reached for a fire extinguisher. He covered his mouth and nose with a handkerchief and quickly doused the flames. He approached the elevator doors and cautiously peered up the shaft. They had apparently moved the elevator to the basement level and ripped a hole in the floor for their descent.

He stood there for a moment, listening carefully. There was a small device on the floor. A light flashed on it rapidly, in time with the beeps. He picked it up and smashed it against the opposite wall.

Then he refocused his attention up the elevator shaft. He could hear gunshots and vehicles. Suddenly, Daniel realized that what could have been a slaughter on the surface was becoming more of a battle. The people of earth were fighting back – and apparently in force.

He picked up his communication device.

"Bascombe here," the General responded, "Is that you, Daniel?"

"Yes, Sir," Daniel replied. "Have you sent reinforcements to Rev-Tech?"

"The Regional Command sent troops in as soon as the aliens began their descent. Are you okay?"

"All things considered, I guess I'm doing fine, but the air is getting pretty bad down here. I think Jessie and I are going to have to evacuate."

"Jessie?" the General asked.

"She's a friend. I'll have to tell you about her sometime," Daniel answered.

"Just be careful! It's still not safe, but, luckily for us, the aliens aren't particularly good fighters once they leave their ships," Bascombe advised him.

"You're right. They're a bit slow and they have to carry their own air supply, which encumbers them quite a lot," Daniel said.

"By the way, do you know of a Commando Cowboy or Corby?" the General wondered.

"Do you mean Korbay? Commander Korbay?" a puzzled Daniel responded.

"Yeah, that sounds right. Is he on our side?" Bascombe inquired.

"I can't say for certain, General," the boy replied. "Korbay was Kandar's commanding officer and perhaps his friend, but he also gave the Bardokians all of the information that they needed to track down and murder his family."

"Well, whatever the case and whatever his intentions may be, I have good reason to believe that he's nearby. I think I intercepted a call from him on the communicator," the General said.

"And you understood him?" Daniel asked.

"Yes, so apparently the translator works, as well," Bascombe added.

"That's good to know. Should I contact Kandar?" the boy inquired.

"If he's up there battling that whole fleet by himself, I think he's probably way too busy to worry about any new developments," the General responded. "You just take good care of yourself and let

140

the military deal with those creatures. — Oh, and by the way, Uncle Danny: you have to promise me that we're going to get together when this is all over with. Okay?"

"Absolutely! I look forward to seeing you again," Daniel replied as he put the device back into his pocket. He then hurried over to the door to the living quarters to check on Jessie.

*****

Kandar was hurtling towards earth in pursuit of three Bardokian fighters. He locked his forward missiles on the two nearest ones and fired. Within a fraction of a second, the Warbirds exploded and Kandar nosed the *Dorius* up to avoid taking collateral damage. He felt the shock of the explosions.

"Damage report!" he yelled at the computer.

"Minimal damage to the exoskeleton; all systems functioning," the *Dorius* replied.

Kandar had lost some ground in his pursuit of the lead vessel. He concentrated on closing the gap between them. He also realized that there were at least five Bardokian fighters closing in on him.

"Those reptiles must either want this ship — or they want me alive," Kandar said quietly, "because they're not using their moonbeam."

He was gaining on the lead fighter, firing all forward pulse cannons. He could see the Bardokian ship in front of him breaking apart.

"Lock missiles on rear targets!" Kandar commanded the *Dorius*.

"Missiles locked," the computer replied.

"Fire!" Kandar shouted. Then he spun the main housing of the ship one hundred eighty degrees within its thruster rings. For just a moment, Kandar was flying backwards towards the cloud of debris left by his previous target, while observing the rear missiles as they approached their destinations.

Unlike the fighter-class vessels that resembled earth's fighter-jets, the *Dorius* was an experimental saucer-shaped craft. It had two thruster rings encircling the central cabin. Kandar then maneuvered those two parallel rings one hundred and eighty degrees in opposite directions, so that they met on the opposite side. This effectively flipped the ship upside down and totally reversed its direction.

The *Dorius* was now coming up from below and heading straight at its pursuers. This maneuver was new to the Bardokians who were totally taken by surprise. Kandar continued his assault.

Two of the five Bardokian ships took direct hits from the missiles. Kandar was firing all forward pulse cannons at the underbellies of the three remaining fighters. It would have been a completely successful maneuver, but Kandar could see that there were several dozen more enemy fighters not far behind them. Completely outnumbered, he was ready to break off the attack.

"Thanks for softening them up for us, Captain!" said a voice through his ship's communicator.

Now Kandar could see there were Bardokian ships exploding quite some distance behind his closest pursuers, so he continued to fire on the three nearest ships. One of them veered off, but Kandar got both of the others with disabling hits from his cannons.

"Scan for non-Bardokian ships within lunar orbit of earth," Kandar commanded.

"Three Ionian fighters and one Ionian battle-cruiser within given parameters," the *Dorius* responded.

"Is that you, Commander Korbay?" Kandar asked.

"Yes, Captain, I'd like to officially request permission to assist you in ridding this planet of these vermin," the Commander responded.

"Permission granted, Sir. Welcome to Earth!" Kandar replied.

The Ionian battle-cruiser launched ten more fighters and, with that, it suddenly became clear that the "brutes of Bardok" had changed their tactics. Kandar could now see the soft white moonbeams flashing out across the darkness of space.

The Forever War had begun anew and Kandar had lost his significance. The Bardokians were regrouping and concentrating on the Ionian battle-cruiser. Korbay and his Air Wing were doing their best to keep the enemy fighters away from their flagship.

"Commander Korbay? Why are you here?" Kandar asked, opening the channel of communication.

"The Grand Regent finally realized that you and your family were being unfairly punished. Also, one of his cousins happened to be a casualty of the collateral damage that you cited at your hearing. So, when he noticed that the Bardokians sent half of their fleet in pursuit of you and left what remained for the defense of Bardok, he decided it was a grand opportunity to rid the universe of the Bardokian menace!" Korbay responded.

The Commander paused to fire his weapons before he added: "We destroyed their home fleet and we got here as soon as we could, but the Bardokians entered the vortex well before we did. We were following their trail and we have no idea how they found you."

"Apparently, they had attached a tracking device to the *Dorius*," Kandar replied. "We found one just recently and it was still functioning."

"Concentrate on the battle, Captain! There are Bardokians

143

descending into the planet's atmosphere. You take care of them and we'll deal with the ones up here," the Commander ordered.

*****

Daniel knocked on the door to the living quarters.

"Jessie, are you okay in there?" he whispered.

"Daniel—" Jessie responded weakly.

"I'm coming in!" the boy exclaimed.

He used his key to unlock the door and then he pushed on it as hard as he could. Cracking the door open, he could see that there was a large dresser up against it. He went back to get Pierre's musket and used it to pry the door open. As soon as he squeezed inside, he spotted Jessie sitting on the floor with her back against the bed.

The room was filled with smoke and methane. The main power had gone out and only the battery-powered emergency lights were operating. The ventilation fans had apparently stopped functioning.

"Hang on, Jessie, I'm going to get you out of here!" Daniel told her.

The boy pulled the dresser far enough from the door so he could open it fully. He then bent down and picked the young woman up.

"Daniel…I…don't…feel…so…," Jessie mumbled as she lost consciousness.

"I'm here, Jessie, you're going to be fine. You just need a little air," he replied.

Daniel carried his young friend out to the main office and he sat her on the floor near the only exit. With the power out, he would need to get her up through the hole in the floor of the elevator. He dragged the bodies of the aliens toward the opposite corner of the room. Then he pulled the dresser out from the bedroom and between the doors to the elevator. He lined it up under the hole.

144

The Battle

Things were relatively quiet inside the elevator shaft. Daniel could no longer hear evidence of a battle. He wasn't sure if that was a good sign or not, but he knew that he'd have to check to see if it was safe before he could bring Jessie out of the sub-basement.

He climbed atop the dresser and carefully rose up through the hole, looking in all directions. The doors were open at the basement level and there was no sign of anyone in the vestibule of the parking garage — so far as he could see. Daniel got down from the dresser and went back into the sub-basement office. Having breathed some fresh air, he was all the more aware of the lack of oxygen and the stench of smoke down there.

He grabbed a wooden chair and set it next to the dresser. He retrieved a pistol belt from one of the dead marines and secured it around his waist. He put his weapon into the holster and slipped his Pa's knife through the back of his belt.

Then he cradled Jessie securely in his arms and he put his right foot up on the chair. With little difficulty, he managed to get his left one there as well. He rested Jessie momentarily on the top of the dresser while he got his knees up on it. He stood carefully, all the while holding onto the girl, and took another quick look through the hole.

All seemed clear, so he picked Jessie up, lifted her through the ragged opening in the elevator floor and placed her on the torn carpeting. He then pulled himself up through the hole and, straddling it, he lifted Jessie once more to get her out to the fresher air of the vestibule. He sat her down against the wall. There was a vending machine nearby, so he used his Pa's knife to break the glass out of the display and he helped himself to a bottle of water. He wrenched the cap off and, pouring some into his hand, he applied it to Jessie's face.

Slowly, the young lady opened her eyes to a narrow slit.

"That's it, Jessie, take a deep breath," Daniel told her.

The girl breathed in the fresh air and began to cough.

"You've got to take the good air in and let the bad stuff out," he advised her.

She opened her eyes a bit wider and continued to take deep breaths.

"You...really...know...how to... show...a girl... a good... time!" Jessie muttered between gasps. "This...has *got* to be...the *longest*...and the *WORST*...first date...of my whole freaking life!"

That was when Daniel heard the "beeping" getting louder behind him. He spun around and saw a Bardokian marine, holding an electronic device in his left hand and a blaster pistol in his right.

"Kahn-DARsssssssss!" the creature hissed, raising the pistol.

"No!" Daniel screamed, instinctively raising his hand in self-defense.

There was no time to reach for a weapon. The boy stood between Jessie and the alien, with his hand held up in defiance. The alien's right hand began to tremble. Daniel could see the strain in the creature's face. It was trying to fire the weapon, but it couldn't. It dropped the tracking device to the ground and gripped the pistol with both hands.

The pistol slowly jerked upward in the Bardokian's hands and aimed back at his face. Daniel pushed his hand solidly through the air towards the creature and the pistol rammed into the alien's helmet — cracking it slightly. Suddenly realizing what was happening, the boy clenched his fist in the air before him and, with a sudden throwing gesture, the Bardokian was launched through the glass of the vestibule.

"Part of Kandar is still in me!" the boy whispered in

astonishment. "Somehow these tracking devices are leading them straight to me!"

He turned to check on Jessie. She was looking past him as she let out a loud scream. Daniel gripped the handle of his Pa's knife and spun around to hurl it in one flowing motion. The battered Bardokian marine was rushing at him as the large blade cut through the air. The throw should have narrowly missed the alien, but Daniel maneuvered it telekinetically to the center of its intended target. The creature fell to its knees and then forward on the knife. Jessie screamed uncontrollably when the tip of the blade erupted from the Bardokian's back.

The girl was getting hysterical. She screamed again. Then, she covered her face with her hands and broke down in tears. She had been terrified just listening to the battle that had taken place in the sub-basement, but now she was witnessing it with her own eyes. The boy sat next to her and tried to put his arm around her, but she immediately leaned away.

"I'm sorry you had to see that, Jessie," Daniel whispered.

"I...am...so...scared," the girl mumbled through her tears.

"I know, Jessie. I am, too," the boy said quietly, "but we're still not safe here. We have to start moving again."

*****

The Vargon had nourished itself and it was fully aware of the battle being waged above its recent home. It could not allow another Forever War — enough blood had been shed already. Although it had avoided direct involvement in the affairs of lesser creatures in the past, it felt an attachment to some of these. It was time to put an end to this.

Kandar was busy hunting the Bardokians who were descending upon the planet. He had the most technologically-superior vessel and an amalgam of amazing skills to pilot it. The Vargon left him to his own devices and did the only thing that it could do.

It transported itself to the middle of the battle-zone and sent a simple telepathic message to all combatants: "The war is over." It then enlarged itself to get the attention of the warriors on both sides. Normally about a meter in diameter, the Vargon expanded itself to twenty meters — large enough to engulf the *Dorius* or any of the fighters. And then, as all of the Ionians and the Bardokians gazed at the shimmering sphere between their battle-lines, it expanded to fifty meters. The noble Vargon's colors washed over it.

A Bardokian pilot took aim at the strange creature and fired his pulse cannon. The Vargon absorbed the beam and grew to one hundred meters in diameter. The cognizant sphere glowed with all of the colors of the rainbow; and then it exploded in a brilliant flash of energy and dazzling light.

Hundreds of small glowing spheres hurtled out in every direction. Combatants on both sides were engrossed by the spectacle, but, before they could reconvene the battle, each of them suddenly realized that one or more of those tiny spheres had sought out every one of their vessels.

The small creatures had leeched onto the ships and they were consuming the fuselages. Neither the Ionians nor the Bardokians were to be spared. The propulsion systems, the armaments, the outer structures of the vessels were being scavenged by the Vargons. Finally, all that was left was the cockpit areas of the fighters. And when each Vargon was sufficiently energized, it opened itself and enveloped its chosen ship's pilot.

*****

Unaware of the course of the battle that had taken place above him, Kandar was pursuing three Bardokian fighters into earth's atmosphere. He had already used all of his on-board missiles. His only remaining offensive weapons were his pulse cannons, his mind and the *Dorius* itself.

He was gaining on the three fighters who were descending in a 'V' formation. He concentrated his cannons on the left wing-man and scored a direct hit to the Bardokian's propulsion system. The creature ejected while its ship spiraled down in flames.

The other two fighters split off in opposite directions. Kandar pursued the right wing-man, because he happened to be closer, but he knew full well that the other ship would attempt to flank him. Suddenly, his concentration was broken.

"Warning: incoming missiles," the *Dorius* intoned.

"Number and origin?" Kandar requested.

"Twenty-four missiles; originating from the planet."

Kandar pulled his ship upwards with full thrusters. He knew that earth's weapons were not known for either their elegance or their ability to differentiate between combatants. If the missiles happened to lock onto a Bardokian, he might have one less target to worry about, but he couldn't trust the accuracy, the intentions or the intelligence of the earth's military.

Kandar was certain that a typical earth weapon would run out of fuel long before it could catch the *Dorius*. In his ascent, he was amazed to find that there was no evidence of the battle that should have been taking place, so he rotated his cabin one hundred eighty degrees to see what became of the missiles.

Just as he'd expected, they had missed both Bardokians. Kandar rotated his thruster rings and plummeted down through the upper atmosphere. Now he had two Bardokian fighters to worry about and he had to deal with this new problem, as well.

"*Dorius,* is there any question as to the intended target of the earth-launched missiles?"

"Eight missiles launched from each of three locations, trajectories converging on previous location of the *Dorius:* 99.9% probability this ship was targeted," the onboard computer replied.

"Can you access the navigational functions of the earth missiles?"

"Archaic hexadecimal systems. Functions accessed."

"Display the eastern coastline of the continent below us."

A hologram of North America's Atlantic coast appeared in front of the Ionian. He gestured toward one particular point. "One hundred times magnification."

The specified area was enlarged and Kandar designated two points with his fingertip.

"*Dorius*, reprogram all twenty-four earth-launched missiles to pass over this first indicated point at an altitude of one-half kilometer with impact at second specified point."

"Reprogramming complete."

"Execute!" the Ionian ordered and the missiles veered east.

"*Dorius*, search data files for the voice-print of the Grand Regent of the kingdom directly below us. He is known as the President of the United States. Then allow me access to the communications grid in the previously designated area. Execute connection on match."

*****

Four men in dark suits burst into the Oval Office.

"Gentlemen, what is the meaning of this intrusion?" the President shouted.

"Mr. President, I'm sorry, but we don't have time for formalities. You have to come with us right now!" Mr. Jacobs insisted. "You are in imminent danger."

"Jacobs, I demand an explanation!"

"Mr. President, there's no time!"

Suddenly, all three phones rang on the President's desk — along with every other phone in Washington, D.C. The President grabbed the red phone from its cradle: "Vladimir, I don't have t—.""

As soon as he spoke, all of the other phones immediately fell silent. Then, the whole building began to vibrate.

"Mr. President, look out of your window," a strange voice commanded and the call ended.

The Leader of the Free World dropped the phone on his desk and walked over to the window just in time to see a phalanx of eight missiles thunder overhead.

"Holy Mother of—" the President muttered.

A few seconds later, another squadron of eight missiles roared past and then a third formation of eight very shortly thereafter.

"Launch everything we have at whoever fired those missiles!" the President ordered.

"I really don't think that would be wise, Mr. President," Jacobs whispered.

"Nobody launches missiles at Washington, D.C., and gets away with it!" the POTUS screamed.

"Those were *our* missiles, Sir!" Jacobs explained. "We fired all of those nukes at that alien ship and, apparently, he sent them right back at us as a demonstration of his power. He fired one right across your bow, Sir."

"What's that supposed to mean?"

"Mr. President, it was a warning shot — and, judging by what we've just seen, it's a warning that would be well-heeded."

A phone rang on the desk. The CIA agent picked it up: "Yes. This is Jacobs." He listened for a moment and ended the call with a curt, "Thanks."

"Mr. President, according to radar and satellite imaging, all twenty-four missiles should impact the Atlantic Ocean roughly two hundred miles off shore."

"Is that going to be a problem?" the elected official inquired.

"Actually, Sir, those were tactical nukes and they would have made one hell of a mess if they had detonated over their original target area. I'd say this alien just did you a really big favor."

The trembling Commander-in-Chief walked back to the window mumbling: "There's more coming. I can feel the vibrations!"

"That was the last of them, Mr. President," Jacobs assured him. "I'm sorry, Sir, but the only thing still shaking now is you."

*****

"Warning! Incoming missiles!" the *Dorius* intoned.

"Point of origin?" Kandar asked as he took evasive action.

"Bardokian fighters," the ship responded.

Kandar had been so preoccupied with the earth-launched missiles that he neglected to track the two enemy ships. They were rapidly coming up behind him. Kandar redirected his thrusters towards the area where the battle had commenced.

He knew that he could outrun the missiles, but he was bewildered by the complete void that lay ahead. While increasing his lead on them, he spun the cabin within its thruster rings and fired his pulse cannons at the incoming weapons — readily destroying both of them. The two Bardokian fighters veered off in opposite directions, so Kandar followed the nearest one.

Even in pursuit of the Bardokian, Kandar was amazed at the emptiness all around him. There was no battle, no wreckage — nothing. He fired his pulse cannons at the enemy fighter and disabled its thrusters. And, while he was preoccupied with crippling that ship, the other one came up from the opposite direction.

It was a suicide run. The last Bardokian was completely intent on killing the last Ionian in earth orbit. Kandar reacted quickly and minimized the damage to the *Dorius,* but the Bardokian was successful in one regard: he managed to die on impact as the edge of the *Dorius* sliced off the canopy and the tail of his ship.

*****

Daniel knelt to pick up Jessie. As he leaned forward to put his arm around her, she held up her right palm.

"Wait! I — I think I can get up on my own," she said.

The boy stood and offered her his hand instead. She grasped it and, in one quick motion, Jessie was on her feet.

"What are these things?" she asked, pointing at the creature.

"They're aliens from a planet called Bardok," he replied.

"I can't believe you just…*murdered*…that…*thing!*"

"I didn't have much of a choice," he answered. "It was either him or us — and there's absolutely no way that I was going to let him hurt you."

"Why are they here?" she persisted.

"They seem to be looking for Kandar. He's doing his best to save our planet from them," Daniel responded. "And, so far: we're still here."

The boy could once again hear sporadic gunfire in the distance and suddenly there was the unmistakable noise of helicopters —

several of them.

"It sounds like the cavalry has arrived!" the boy joked.

"Then, let's try not to get shot by friendly fire," Jessie replied sternly. She was exhausted, confused and in no mood to be joking about their situation.

"If you're feeling strong enough, I want to try taking the stairs back up to the main floor," Daniel suggested. "I need to make sure that Maxine and the rest of the staff made it out of there alive."

"Are you crazy? You want to go back in there?" Jessie asked in amazement.

"It's not really a matter of 'want.' I *need* to go back in there to make sure that my people are okay, but I can't leave you out here by yourself. So, if you don't want to go, I'll stay with you and try to get you home," the boy answered.

"Now you're trying to make me feel guilty," Jessie whined as she pulled herself close to him. "Daniel, I'm really scared. I've never been so scared in my whole life. I'm afraid to go anywhere. I'm afraid to close my eyes — even for a second!"

"I'll protect you. Whether we go back upstairs or walk straight out of the parking garage, I won't let anything hurt you," the boy said quietly, stroking her hair.

"I really want to believe you, Daniel, but I don't know what to believe anymore. This has been such a horrendous nightmare!" she said as tears welled up in her eyes. "I'll go wherever you take me, but please don't leave me."

"Come on, Jessie! You're strong. Everything is going to be alright. I promise you," Daniel told her, while holding her tightly. "We'll take a quick look to make sure the office staff got out okay."

"But there is one thing I'll need to do first. You keep an eye on

154

the elevator for just one second," he told her as he turned her away from the alien's body. He rolled the creature over and retrieved his Pa's knife. He wiped the blade on the Bardokian's uniform before he tucked the knife back under his belt.

On closer inspection, he noticed the stereoscopic lenses on the alien's helmet. It was apparent that they were being observed. He quickly disconnected the wires to the antenna.

"Okay, ready?" Daniel asked Jessie, just as the methane in the sub-basement exploded. A ball of flame shot up from the elevator.

"No, not really. I just want to get this over with," she whimpered. The explosion went practically unnoticed. She had been lost in thought, trying to concentrate on the elevator while blocking out whatever Daniel had been doing behind her. Whatever it was that he didn't want her to see, she didn't want to know anything about it.

He led her to the stairway entrance and motioned for her to stand to one side. He opened it quickly while brandishing the alien weapon. The stairway was dimly lit by the emergency lighting system and there was no one on the lowest level. He quietly gestured for her to follow him up the stairs. There was some broken glass and paint chips on the stairs, but no major barriers.

They slowly ascended to the first floor. Daniel looked cautiously up the stairs toward the second floor and then peeked through the window in the door at the lobby level. He concentrated for a second to see if he could hear anyone's thoughts, but all he could sense was confusion. He motioned for Jessie to lean against the wall behind him as he slowly opened the door.

He could see the door to Jonathan's office just down the hallway. The glass was shattered and blood-stained. He sensed that Maxine was alive in her office directly across from him. As he stepped through the doorway, he suddenly felt a madness washing over him. He threw himself to the floor, just as Walters swung a fire-axe into the door frame. The man screamed in frustration.

"Walters! It's me, Daniel!" the boy yelled as he lunged at the axe-handle. The dazed man wrestled for control of his weapon for a second, while the words slowly sank in.

"Daniel?" Walters asked, bewildered.

"It's okay. Everything is going to be okay. Just calm down," the boy assured him as he straightened up. "My friend Jessie is right behind me, so please don't hurt her."

"In the lab — they're all dead," the man muttered with a vacant stare.

"I'm sorry, Walters. We're going to get you help," the boy said calmly. He led Jessie cautiously across the hall into the secretary's office.

"Maxine, are you okay?" he whispered. "It's me: Daniel."

"Mr. Johnstone? Is that really you?" she asked, trembling.

The young woman was still hiding under her desk. Daniel had no idea how much horror she had witnessed, but he was determined to get her home safely.

"It's okay, you can come out now. You're with friends," he assured her.

Slowly, she crawled out from under the desk. She was visibly shaking as he bent down to help her up.

"Those things — I think they got Mr. Marx," she sobbed.

"Maxine, this is my friend Jessie. I want you two to hold onto each other. We're all getting out of here," Daniel promised.

"Walters, if you feel comfortable holding that axe, I'm not going to tell you to put it down, but be careful with it. I don't want anybody else getting hurt in here," the boy warned the terrified lab assistant.

*****

The red phone rang on the General's desk and he immediately lifted it from its perch.

"Yes, Mr. President, this is General Bascombe," he said.

"Bascombe, check all of your files! I want to know everything that you have on two aliens known as 'Kandar' and 'Vargon' and their ship. I want both of them taken into custody or terminated, if necessary. I do not want any alien presence on this planet instigating any more of these attacks, do you understand me?" the President demanded.

"Yes, Sir. I understand you completely, Sir!" the General responded.

"I want that ship; I want it intact; and I want it pronto! Kill everyone associated with it. We can figure the thing out without them," the President added.

"Mr. President, this alien, who seems to be defending us, apparently means us no harm and neither do his human companions—" Bascombe protested.

"General, we won't be safe until they're all dead. If you can't handle that, I will relieve you of your command," the President interrupted.

"Yes, Sir!" Bascombe answered and the call abruptly ended.

The General sat there for a moment fidgeting with his pen. He picked up his primary phone and called the nearest airbase for transport. A helicopter was already on standby awaiting his order.

*****

Daniel heard a soft tone emanating from his pocket. He

carefully retrieved the communicator and held it to his ear.

"Uncle Danny, get out of there now. You and Kandar are being targeted by the military and they want the *Dorius*."

Before the boy could respond, the call ended. He slipped the device back into his pocket. He knew that the main entrance would look like a battlefield so he directed his small group of survivors towards a nearby fire exit.

He pointed Walters, still wielding his axe, towards the left of the exit, while he held Jessie and Maxine toward the right. Daniel kicked the door open, while holding his hand at the ready above his holster. As the door banged against the outside wall, he could see a U.S. Marine, kneeling just a few feet beyond the door, with his weapon aimed directly at him. Daniel immediately raised his hands.

"Don't shoot! We just work here!" the boy shouted.

"Come out here slowly, where I can see you, and stand up against the wall!" the leatherneck screamed.

Daniel came out first, with his hands held high.

"There are a couple of young ladies and another man right behind me," the boy informed the Marine.

"Jake, I need help over here. Now!" the Marine yelled and two of his companions joined him, all with guns aimed at Daniel and the open doorway.

"Drop your weapons!" they yelled almost in unison.

The boy unbuckled the holster with one hand and dropped it to the ground. His Pa's knife fell out as well.

"Face the wall and put your hands up against it!" the first Marine ordered.

Daniel stood against the wall in complete compliance.

"Ladies, you can come out next!" the Marine bellowed.

Jessie entered the doorway holding onto Maxine who was clearly terrified. They both stepped out into view and down to ground level.

"Turn around!" one of the Marines ordered.

The two young women turned slowly, so that it was fairly obvious that neither of them was armed.

"Alright, you two, stand against the wall next to him!" the first Marine barked.

"If anybody else is in there, throw out your weapons and come out right now!" Jake ordered.

Walters stood in the doorway with the axe firmly in his grip.

"Drop the weapon! — Now!" the first Marine yelled.

The addled man stood there for a moment, unresponsive. Daniel watched them all closely and concentrated on the three Marines. Walters took one step down to ground level and the Marines began to squeeze the triggers of their weapons. Before they could fire, their fingers froze. The uniformed trio looked at their automatic rifles in disbelief. As they stood back a step to distance themselves from the distraught man, Daniel spun around and hurled himself at the back of Walters' knees, dropping him to the ground. On impact, he dislodged the axe from the lab assistant's hands. The man fought for control of the weapon, but Daniel managed to grab it and throw it back inside the doorway. As he straddled Walters and focused on the three Marines, two of their weapons fired wildly in the air, startling everyone.

"Well, I'll be!" exclaimed the Marine named Jake. "What are the odds that all three of 'em would jam at the same time?"

"Don't hurt him, this man isn't well!" Daniel pleaded.

A lieutenant came from behind the Marines and asked them

what was going on. After a brief conversation, he barked: "Private Jacobson, cuff that man and get him back to the ambulance. Sergeant Carter, escort the two young ladies back behind our lines and make sure that they're all right. Stivack, bring that kid here."

"Daniel?" Jessie whined, looking back.

"Go on with them, they'll take good care of you," the boy responded. "I'll catch up with you as soon as I can. I promise!"

As Jacobson and Carter followed their orders, Lance Corporal Stivack led Daniel to the young lieutenant.

"I saw what you did over there and you probably saved your friend's life," the Lieutenant began. "Maybe you can help me, too."

"What can I do for you, Sir?" Daniel asked.

"We're looking for a Mr. Johnstone, the guy who runs this place. According to my information, he should be in his sixties or seventies. Do you happen to know who he is or where we might find him?" the Lieutenant asked.

"I think the guy who ran this place is lying on the floor in his office. I'm not one hundred percent sure, but I believe he may be dead," Daniel replied.

"Are any of those alien creatures in there?" asked the officer.

"I saw a few dead ones, but I don't know if any survived."

"You're a pretty sharp kid. Ever think about joining the Marine Corps?" the Lieutenant commented. "You handle yourself pretty well and I think you'd have a great future in the military!"

"No, Sir, I really don't believe in killing things."

"Well, if you ever change your mind...," the Lieutenant began, as a blast cut through his torso. The young officer slumped down to his knees. As Daniel spun around, he saw a Bardokian taking aim at him from a second-floor window. The boy grasped at the air between himself and the creature and pulled the alien headlong through the broken glass. The Bardokian hit the ground hard and the pistol dropped from its hand.

Daniel was furious. The Lieutenant seemed to be a decent human being, but this thing had no regard for human life. As the Bardokian groped for its blaster, the boy walked over to it and kicked the weapon away. The alien looked up at him and smiled maliciously. The boy extended his palm toward the creature and concentrated his energy there. The smile slowly left its face as it began to gasp for breath. Daniel could easily have crushed the Bardokian into the concrete, but he wasn't a murderer and this alien was no longer an armed threat.

"You aren't worth my soul," the boy whispered as he turned his back to the thing.

Before Daniel could take another step, the Bardokian got up and lunged at him with its claws exposed. Lance Corporal Stivack instinctively squeezed off two rounds into the beast. The creature stood there for a moment, towering over the boy. Yellow fluid oozed from its wounds as it staggered in its place. It reached behind its back and pulled out a large curved dagger.

"Enough!" the boy said with disgust as he slammed his foot into the alien's groin. The Bardokian looked puzzled for a moment and then it raised the blade high above the boy's head. Daniel shielded himself with his open palm and all of the energy that he could focus there. The alien marine began to hobble backwards toward the building. Daniel advanced towards it in lockstep until the creature stood plastered against the wall. While the boy concentrated all of his mental energy on the alien's weapon, the creature began to slide up the side of the building, fighting hard to keep the blade a safe distance from its own body. Daniel closed his eyes as he forced the weapon through the Bardokian's chest. He left the creature pinned to the wall a full eight feet above ground level. It writhed for a moment and then it went limp.

Stivack stood there with his mouth agape. Realizing what the man had just witnessed, Daniel slowly walked over toward him. The Lance Corporal automatically raised his rifle in self-defense.

"You don't want to harm me. I am no threat to you," the boy intoned calmly.

The young Marine stopped raising his weapon, but his face was filled with fear.

"You didn't see anything alarming. Calm down. We're going to work together to see if we can save your lieutenant. Do you understand me, Young Man?" Daniel asked.

"Yes, Sir," Stivack answered in a quiet monotone. "The Lieutenant needs help."

"I will do my best to stop the bleeding, but you have to get a Medic. Now — Run!" the boy added with emphasis.

The Lance Corporal immediately snapped back to reality and ran for help while Daniel bent over the gravely-wounded officer. The alien's weapon had burned a hole clean through the young man's right lung. He was just barely alive and the boy was no doctor. He reached behind the Lieutenant to apply pressure to the back of the wound while doing the same to the front. He concentrated on the young man's blood pressure and pulse rate to moderate them as much as he possibly could without losing him.

Within a minute, an army ambulance pulled up and two medics jumped out of the back with a stretcher. They placed it next to the wounded officer and relieved the boy of his responsibility. Stivack jumped out of the passenger side of the vehicle. He looked at Daniel as if there was something important that he needed to remember about the boy, but the thought escaped him.

While Stivack helped the medics with the Lieutenant, Daniel stood there quietly. He lowered his right hand with his palm facing the building. The alien holster and pistol, that he had dropped earlier, slowly dragged across the concrete towards him. It gained momentum as it approached him from behind and leapt up into his hand. He fastened the belt so that the holster hung behind his back. Then he extended his right hand out from his side and Pa's knife hurtled into it. He slipped it into the back of his belt and pulled his shirt out over the weapons as he nonchalantly walked away from the scene.

Helicopters were descending on all sides of the main building. Soldiers and marines were disembarking to stage a coordinated attack. A squad of eight rushed in through the fire exit that Daniel had left open, while two others trained their rifles on the creature that was still pinned to the wall. The same scene was playing out all around the Rev-Tech complex: a massive military deployment to eliminate the alien invaders and rescue whatever surviving civilians they managed to encounter.

There were more marines and soldiers towards the front of the building, but the boy silently ambled past them as if he belonged there. Amazingly enough, his Jeep was still parked in his "reserved" spot and relatively undamaged by the battle. There was broken glass everywhere. He could see the smoldering, blackened sentry post where Jenkins had been on duty. There were still small fires around the Rev-Tech campus and the facade of the main office was essentially blown away.

Daniel and Job

Guards were posted all around the alien troop transport. That area seemed to be secured from the Bardokian intruders. Daniel picked up Job's blanket from the back seat of his Jeep and he held it close for a moment. His eyes began to glaze over as he thought of his lifelong friend. Then, he folded the blanket carefully and put it back on the rear seat. As an afterthought, he discretely removed the holster and Pa's knife and placed them under the blanket. He rummaged through his tool box until he found a snow-brush, which he used to whisk away the broken glass from the driver's seat and the dashboard. He dug his keys out of his pocket and sat in the vehicle. It wasn't until he started the engine that anyone took notice of him.

"Hey, kid! What do you think you're doing?" a soldier yelled.

"I have to get home. I was held captive by those creatures and I'm sure that my parents are worried sick about me!" Daniel yelled back.

"Are you sure you're okay? Maybe we should have the medics check you out?" the soldier responded.

"I'm just a little shaky and anxious to get home. They didn't harm me physically, but I'm really shaken up. I need to get away from this place as soon as possible. I want to be with my family!" he replied with a quiver in his voice. Job *was* his family and the thought of life without him brought real tears to his eyes.

"Well, wait here just a minute and I'll see if it's okay for you to leave!" the soldier told him before hurrying off towards the make-shift command post.

But, as soon as the soldier left, Daniel slipped the Jeep into reverse and turned the vehicle towards the gate. The volume of his engine never bothered him before, but now he was very self-conscious of it as he headed towards the exit. He wiped the tears from his eyes

164

as he approached the two armed guards standing near the opening. He stopped his Jeep between them.

"Gentlemen, I was told to follow the two young ladies who left the compound a few minutes ago. Could you tell me which way they were taken?" Daniel asked with obvious self-confidence.

"There's a field hospital set up about half a mile up the highway. You can't miss it," one of them replied, while gesturing down the road.

"Thanks a lot! You've been a great help," the boy told them as he drove out onto the main road. Just as he pulled out, Daniel could barely hear a soldier yelling: "Wait, Kid! The Captain wants to talk to you!" But, he had no intention of going back. He had to find Jessie and Maxine to make sure that they were both safe.

Chapter 8

Reunions

The *Dorius* held its orbit high above the earth. Kandar scanned for other ships and found nothing. There were no signs of the battle that he assumed had taken place. The Ionian was totally perplexed. He sat in his cockpit debating his next course of action. He wondered if he would ever see his friend the Vargon again. He also worried about Daniel and wondered if the boy could ever accept him as the friend and companion that he had always truly been.

He scanned the communication channels emanating from the planet below. There was no evidence that any major cities were attacked. It seemed as though the Bardokians had concentrated all of their efforts on the Rev-Tech campus. Kandar wondered if they were following the trail of the tracking device or if they were pursuing something else entirely.

The Ionian was amazed that the Bardokians hadn't launched a planet-wide attack. The "brutes of Bardok" were not known for their restraint — or for their strategic planning. He could only assume that they feared a major confrontation with a primitive culture that still used such dirty and self-destructive weaponry. Plus, the earth's oxygen-rich atmosphere made it virtually uninhabitable by Bardokian standards; and, modifying its content was far more work than a self-respecting Bardokian would endeavor to pursue.

"Apparently they were looking for the Vargon, the *Dorius* — and me," Kandar mumbled to himself, "so, to where have they all run off?"

He was hesitant to return to earth, so he leaned back in his chair for a moment.

"Continue scanning for life-forms between lunar orbit and low-earth orbit," the Ionian ordered the *Dorius*. He closed his eyes and stretched his large frame. This body was exhausted. He had fought a tense battle and hadn't rested for a moment since he exited the restoration chamber. He was thirsty and feeling a bit hungry as well. He thought of how strange the earth food seemed to him when he first encountered it through the bodies of Daniel and Job. He wasn't sure if this body could digest a plate of fried catfish, but right now he would do just about anything to try.

"Life-forms detected," the *Dorius* intoned.

"Positions and numbers?" Kandar asked excitedly. His eyes were now wide open.

"Advancing on this position from all directions; eight hundred seventy-three and counting," the *Dorius* responded.

Kandar was not one to fear anything, but he was startled by this response. He stood in the cockpit and looked out in all directions. At first, he saw nothing. Then he realized that hundreds of small spheres were converging within one hundred meters of his ship, like so many shooting stars. As they collided together, they shone nearly as brightly as a nova and he could almost feel the heat generated by the growing, glowing sphere.

"My dear, beautiful Friend!" the Ionian exclaimed as the Vargon stabilized at its normal size and its myriad colors swirled over it.

"What has become of the Bardokians and my comrades in arms?" Kandar asked.

"*They have all been returned from whence they came,*" the Vargon responded. "*I have returned to transport you as well. Where you choose to belong is your decision.*"

*****

Daniel spotted the temporary field hospital and pulled up to the guard post.

"Two young women were just brought in here from the Rev-Tech complex. One of them is my sister. Can you help me find them?" he asked the sentry.

"Kid, they're probably in that tent down on the right," the guard responded.

"Thanks a lot, Corporal!" Daniel replied, noting his two stripes.

"And, take it slow down there! We've got a lot of pedestrians!" the guard added.

"Sure thing!" the boy answered. "We really don't need anybody else getting hurt around here."

Daniel turned right and continued slowly toward the hospital tent. He parked as close as he could without impeding his exit. He wasn't sure how he was going to get his friends out of the military's "protective custody," but he was determined to do so.

He walked up to the tent and pushed the flap to the side. There were three rows of cots running the length of the tent. Many of the bodies were covered with bloodied sheets and medical personnel were attending to the injured survivors.

"This can't be the right one," Daniel whispered.

He walked across the grassy lot to a smaller tent and peeked inside. There were officers conducting interviews with some of his employees. He heard the name "Mr. Johnstone" mentioned repeatedly. He dared not go in, but he knew that in all likelihood Jessie and Maxine were there.

Daniel stood away from the tent and focused his mind on his young friends.

"Jessie Drake, you need to excuse yourself, so you can go to the washroom. If she's there, ask Maxine to go with you!" the boy thought. He kept repeating the message with his mind. Within a couple of minutes, a soldier emerged from the end of the tent, holding the canvas door for the people behind him.

"It's just down that way, Ladies," the guard gestured as two young ladies followed him out. It was Jessie and Maxine. Daniel took a roundabout path, so he could meet the two of them at the latrines.

Jessie spotted the boy immediately: "You can't be here. Somebody's going to see you and turn you over to the authorities!"

"Mr. Johnstone, they're all looking for you! They really want to talk to you," Maxine chimed in, and, turning back toward the tent, she started to yell: "Hey, he's over here! Mr. John—"

"Stop!" the boy commanded.

Jessie had been in the process of bending down to take her shoe off. Both women froze mid-thought. Daniel cupped his hand over Maxine's mouth and picked her up.

"You are not to mention my name," he told her as he deposited her behind the portable toilets. "I'm just Jessie's brother 'Danny'; do you understand?"

"Yes, Danny," Maxine responded entranced.

"Now you can go about your normal business and use the washroom, if you wish," the boy instructed her.

"Oh, I'm sorry, Danny! You'll have to excuse me. I need to use the washroom," Maxine replied.

While she walked around to the front of the latrines, Daniel returned for Jessie, who was still balancing on one foot.

"Okay, Jessie — as you were," the boy whispered in her ear.

Jessie removed her shoe and looked around for her intended

target. "Where'd she go?" she asked Daniel.

"Don't worry about Maxine; she isn't going to say anything to anybody," he replied. Jessie grabbed his arm to steady herself as she put her shoe back on.

"Have you ever considered anger management classes?" Daniel laughed.

"Hey, do you really think I'm going to stand idly by and let them vivisect you?" the girl retorted, as she headed back towards the latrines.

"So, where are you going now?" he asked.

"I've got to pee!" she snapped back.

"No, you don't. I just put that thought in your head to get you out of there," he replied with a smile.

"Well, you can't expect to put that thought in a girl's mind and not expect her to act on it. You made me feel like I have to go and now I've got to go!" she responded.

"And, by the way, who gave you permission to start messing around with my biology?" Jessie asked with some annoyance. Then, suddenly, in deference to her urgent need, she added: "Remind me where I left off. This can't wait!"

She ran into the nearest portable toilet and slammed the door behind her.

Daniel stood there grinning for a second, but the smile quickly left his face. He began to feel somewhat dizzy and his head was throbbing. He suddenly felt weak in the knees, so he leaned against the back of the portable toilet that Jessie had entered.

Maxine found the boy first.

"Danny, are you okay?" she asked.

"I just need a minute. I'll be fine," he replied

"Your nose is bleeding," she informed him. "Are you sure you're okay?"

"I'm sorry, I hadn't realized," the boy answered, hurrying to find his handkerchief.

"What did you do to him?" Jessie barked as she rounded the corner.

"Nothing, Jessie! It's just a nosebleed," Daniel said. "I've probably been straining myself and overdoing things a little bit. I'm sure it will stop in a minute."

"Maybe we should get you home," Maxine suggested.

"At the very least, let's get out of here," Daniel countered as he struggled to get back on his feet. Maxine grabbed his left arm and Jessie grabbed his right to help him up.

"Thanks a lot, but I think I can walk just fine," he told them, standing shakily.

"You're looking a little pale," Maxine noted.

"My Jeep is across the way, near the other tent. We'd better take the long way around," Daniel suggested. "Hopefully, no one will pay much attention to us."

The boy led the way, holding Jessie's hand, while Maxine trailed a few steps behind them.

"You sure don't act like a brother and sister!" she told them.

"What?" Jessie gasped.

"Never mind that," Daniel whispered to Jessie. "I'll explain later."

"If I didn't know better, I'd think you two were a 'couple'!" Maxine added with a sly smile.

It only took them a couple of minutes to arrive at the Jeep. It was just as Daniel had left it. He helped Maxine to get into the back seat and then he assisted Jessie on the passenger side. As soon as he sat in the driver's seat, he started the vehicle.

"Maxine, where do you live, so I know where to drop you off?" Daniel asked.

"Turn left on the main highway and go to the second light," the young woman replied. "That's Mapleton. Make a right turn there. I live in the third house down."

"You've been through quite an ordeal, so I'm sure you'll be happy to get home and be with your family," the boy said.

"Actually, I live alone, Danny," she replied coyly. "If your sister doesn't mind, you're welcome to come in and stay as long as you like!"

Jessie was not amused. "What's with this 'sister' stuff?" she began, while Daniel reached his hand out and tried to cup it over her mouth. She pushed his hand away.

"What is *wrong* with you?" she barked at Daniel — more than a bit perturbed.

He put his finger to his lips and shushed her just as they were pulling up to the sentry post.

"I see you found your sister and her friend," the guard said, remembering the boy.

"Is the whole world going crazy or is it just me?" Jessie muttered.

"Yes, I have permission to drive them both home," Daniel addressed the Corporal while ignoring Jessie's comment.

"Can I see your paperwork?" the guard asked.

"They didn't give me actual copies of the papers, but General

Bascombe approved them," the boy replied.

"You spoke directly with the General?" the sentry inquired.

"Actually, no, but the Lieutenant told us that a General Bascombe had approved everything." Then Daniel added: "Why else would I know that name?"

"I guess you've got a point," the guard conceded. "I wasn't even aware that General Bascombe had arrived yet."

"Go ahead," the Corporal added as he waved them through.

Daniel made a quick left as he pulled out onto the main road.

"Who's General Bascombe?" Maxine asked.

"An old friend of our family," the boy answered as he gestured toward Jessie.

"Your 'family' is going to throw you out of your freaking Jeep, if you don't explain what this 'sister-brother' stuff is all about!" Jessie threatened.

"Please, just give me another minute," Daniel answered quietly.

He turned his vehicle down Mapleton and pulled over to the curb in front of the third house. "I think this is your stop, Maxine," Daniel announced.

"Would you mind coming in with me to make sure it's safe?" Maxine asked.

"I can walk you to your door, if you don't feel comfortable going by yourself," the young man offered.

"Good grief!" an exasperated Jessie muttered.

Daniel hopped out of the Jeep and helped Maxine get out on his side. As he walked her towards her door, she grabbed onto his arm, pulling herself close to him.

"Jessie isn't really your sister, is she?" an overly-affectionate Maxine asked as they stopped at the door. She bent to retrieve a key from under the mat and opened the front door. "Either way," she began, "you're always welcome to come back and visit!"

"That's so nice of you: I'll keep that in mind," the boy answered, quite flattered.

"I can be *very* interesting company!" she whispered, pulling him by his collar into her foyer. She stretched up and kissed him gently.

"Uh, thank you very much, but I think I'll have to take a rain-check," Daniel told her as he backed out of the doorway.

"See ya!" he added, while beating a hasty retreat.

"Bye-bye, Danny!" Maxine whispered flirtatiously. "I hope to see you soon!"

She closed the door and leaned her back against it.

"There's something *so familiar* about that sexy young hunk!" she sang aloud.

*****

Daniel walked around to the driver's side of the Jeep and sat down.

"Could you two have been any more obvious?" Jessie huffed at the boy.

"What do you mean?" he asked feigning innocence.

"You know what I mean!" she snapped. "All of a sudden I'm your 'sister' so you can get cozy with her? Am I supposed to be blind?"

"No, *I* was supposed to be blind. Remember?" he joked as he adjusted his shades.

"Do you think you're funny?" Jessie asked, obviously not in a mood for levity.

"Okay, I had to convince the guard that I was closely related to one of you, so he'd let me enter the compound," Daniel explained. "Then when Maxine started to scream my name near the latrines, I had to suggest to her that I was just your brother 'Danny' rather than her boss 'Mister Johnstone.'"

She looked at him somewhat indulgently for a moment.

"So, why didn't you say that *she* was your sister?" Jessie asked.

"I didn't think that she would believe that even under hypnosis," Daniel replied after a brief pause. "She doesn't know you and she really doesn't know me that well either, so I just assumed that a familial relationship between us would be more plausible."

"Did you just happen to think that up right now?" she asked sarcastically.

"Look, I had already told the guard that I was looking for my sister," he explained. "I didn't dare change the story with her. I just couldn't allow her to keep calling me 'Mr. Johnstone.' I heard them asking about me back at that tent where you were being held."

"Well, that part is true. They really seem to want to get their hands on you in the worst way," Jessie admitted. "I'm a little afraid of what they're going to do with you when they find you."

"We'll just have to make sure that they don't!" Daniel said as he started the Jeep.

He made a U-turn and got back to the main highway.

"Do you still want me to take you home?" he asked the young woman.

"Not on your life!" she replied. "This story is going to make me a star reporter!"

"That's good, because we may have to live off your salary for a while!" the boy teased as he pointed the vehicle back towards his own place.

"What?" Jessie mocked. "What happened to Mr. Big Shot who was going to make sure that I was 'never *ever*' going to have to work again?"

"Well," Daniel began, "it looks like Rev-Tech is currently 'under renovation' and I may not be able to get my hands on my assets for quite some time!"

Jessie folded her arms in a dramatic pout for a moment.

"I'm sorry, Jessie," the boy told her.

"So, you're *not* going to 'hire someone to throw my shoes at you'?" she asked in her best impersonation of the boy's voice.

"Really, Jessie — I'm sorry!" he replied earnestly. "I'll make it all up to you, I just need a little time to see what I can salvage."

"You men are all the same!" she dead-panned and then she burst out laughing.

"You are really something!" she giggled.

"So, you're not really mad?" Daniel asked hesitantly.

"You are *soooo* naïve!" she laughed.

The boy turned his vehicle down the private road to his residence. He brought the Jeep to a halt and, looking at Jessie in all earnestness, asked: "Jessie, do you like me?"

There was an uncomfortable silence as they made eye contact.

"Not at all?" Daniel asked, presuming her answer.

The young lady looked away for a moment and sighed.

"Of course, I like you," she replied, smiling. "I just liked you a whole lot more when you weren't a wanted fugitive!"

"I hadn't really thought about that much," he admitted, then he pressed the accelerator and continued up his private road.

*****

When they arrived at his house, Daniel was shocked to see the place still standing. He got out of the vehicle, walked around to the passenger side and scooped Jessie up.

"Hey, Big Guy!" she said laughing. "I can walk!"

"I know," he whispered, "I just wanted an excuse to hold you."

His face suddenly turned somber as he held Jessie tightly.

"We're not alone," he muttered.

"Freeze!" a voice screamed from the trees. "You're surrounded, Johnstone!"

The boy stood there holding the woman he loved, as a dozen camouflaged troops emerged from the woods with their weapons aimed straight at him. Jessie could see the red laser dots flitting across the boy's head and chest as the soldiers moved in.

"I'm not armed!" he yelled at them. "Please, don't hurt the girl!"

The soldiers slowly converged on the boy, encircling him and Jessie.

"Put the girl down — slowly!" an officer yelled at him.

Daniel lowered his right arm and bent slightly until Jessie's feet reached the ground. He raised his right hand in surrender and, when the young woman got her bearings, he raised his left arm as well.

"Step to your right and away from the girl!" the officer barked at him.

"I'll do anything you say," the boy replied. "Just, please: don't hurt her."

*****

"Sergeant, take the girl back to the compound for questioning," the Lieutenant ordered. One of the soldiers shouldered his rifle and stepped forward to lead the young woman back down the path that led toward her car.

"Am I under arrest?" she asked them.

"Let's call it 'protective custody,' Ma'am," the young officer replied.

"Just come this way, Young Lady," the Sergeant requested, as he offered Jessie his arm. "I won't let anything bad happen to you."

The young NCO was trying his best to be polite, so Jessie cooperated with him. She took a few steps toward the path through the trees, then she paused for a moment. She looked over her shoulder at Daniel and the only thought in her mind was: "Take good care of yourself, Mr. Rev-Tech. — I love you." She couldn't actually bring herself to say it aloud, but, as she turned around and proceeded down the path, she heard the words: "I love you too, Jessie!" resonating in her head.

"Hey! Did you just say something?" she asked the Sergeant accusingly.

"No, Ma'am, I didn't say anything and I didn't hear anything either," he replied. "Let's just move along."

She looked back over her shoulder at a smiling Daniel.

The soldiers had closed the circle around him and they were securing his hands behind his back. He didn't need to cooperate, but these were "our" guys: the good guys. He didn't want to hurt these soldiers who were doing their best to conquer their fears and to serve their country in the only way that they knew how: by following their orders.

*****

"What's your name, Sergeant?" Jessie asked the young NCO.

"Nelson," he replied without thinking.

178

"Is that your first name or your last name?" she persisted.

"I'm sorry, I shouldn't be telling you anything," he answered. "Just call me either 'Sergeant' or 'Nelson.' I'll answer to either."

Jessie could see the creek where Daniel liked to fish and they were nearing the cave where Job had saved him from Ol' Bob. It was getting late. The overhanging trees made the path and the surrounding woods seem a lot darker than it should have been. But, if it hadn't been so dark, she might not have seen the shaft of light that projected from the entrance to the cave. Nelson suddenly let go of Jessie's arm and grasped at his chest. He dropped to his knees as his rifle slid down from his shoulder.

"Run, Lady!" the young man cried, as he tried to lift his weapon to aim it.

A second beam of light cut through the soldier as he fired once at the ground. He dropped face first into the dirt. Jessie screamed. Before she could turn and run, an alien marine lumbered out of the cave. She screamed again and then turned around, but before she could take another step, the alien fired its weapon at a low-hanging branch which crashed down in front of her — blocking the path back to Daniel.

She felt something snag her hair. She strained to see the creature standing behind her, gripping her dark tresses in its talons. It could have killed her as easily as it had just killed the soldier. It was obvious to Jessie that it had other plans.

*****

"Jessie!" Daniel yelled when he heard the screams.

"You two: hold him!" the Lieutenant ordered the soldiers who flanked the boy. "The rest of you: hightail it down there and find out what's happening!"

"Yes, Sir!" several of the soldiers replied while running down the path.

"Spread out and keep low!" one of them yelled to the others as they disappeared from sight.

"I can help them," Daniel said anxiously.

"No, you can't, Johnstone," the officer informed him. "You're not going anywhere."

"She's my friend. I have to help her!" the boy pleaded.

"Kid, Sergeant Nelson is one of our top marksmen," the Lieutenant responded. "You heard that rifle shot. You can bet everything you own that whatever scared that young lady is lying dead in those woods!"

Daniel closed his eyes and listened for Jessie's thoughts. He knew that she was terrified and that the Sergeant was dead. He also saw the image of the alien near the cave.

"Your sergeant is dead and my friend is in trouble," Daniel told them. "You have to let me go. There's an alien loose in those woods."

"Settle down, Johnstone!" the officer yelled. "My men are trained to deal with any sort of situation!"

But Daniel was not about to "settle down." With his eyes closed, he concentrated on the plastic restraints that secured his wrists behind him. They fell to the ground like so much dust. As he stood with his back to the Jeep, he opened his right palm towards it and the alien pistol launched itself, from under Job's blanket in the back seat, straight into his waiting hand.

"Drop your weapons!" he ordered them as he brandished the blaster pistol.

"No arguments. Drop them. Now!" he repeated, with

emphasis.

"How'd he get that?" one of his erstwhile guards muttered as the three uniformed men backed away and dropped their weapons.

"I want all of you face down on the ground!" Daniel yelled.

As the officer and his two soldiers complied, Daniel secured the alien holster around his waist and slipped his Pa's knife under the back of his belt. Another drop of blood trickled down from the boy's nose.

"I have no quarrel with you and I don't care if you follow me, but let me save my friend before you shoot me!" the boy told them. Then he turned and ran down the path.

There was an awkward pause as the two soldiers looked across the dirt at their commander. "So, what are you waiting for?" the Lieutenant yelled. "Grab your guns and get after that kid!"

*****

Daniel could hear more gunfire up ahead as he ran. An army helicopter flew just above the trees on a course for his house. He didn't want to hurt any of the soldiers, but he wasn't about to let anyone or any *thing* keep him from saving Jessie.

As he got closer to the creek, he could see that soldiers had taken up positions behind boulders and trees that surrounded the cave. Most of them weren't moving much. He could see blood on some of their uniforms, but the most telling sign, that things had gone badly, was the sudden silence.

The one thing that he absolutely knew was that Jessie was still alive. He didn't have time to worry about the soldiers. All that he cared about was saving *his Jessie* from those creatures. He had a feeling that he was being watched as he approached the cave, so he slowed his pace slightly and opened his mind to the thoughts in the air.

He could feel the agony of several of the soldiers who were dying from their wounds. He also sensed that there was more than one alien in the area. He could see an image of himself as viewed from above his right flank. He turned to his left and walked a few steps until he could envision the alien raising its weapon behind him. Then, Daniel spun quickly, pointing his blaster up into the tree, and fired. There was a loud screech as the treetop burst into flame sending the nesting birds into a panic. The Bardokian fell towards the ground only to be caught by its ankle in the fork of a large branch. It hung there swinging and smoldering until its methane tank exploded.

Daniel was dazed for a second and he instinctively fell to the ground. He felt his left arm stinging just as he heard a gunshot. One of his former captors had grazed him. The boy looked up at the soldier in time to see him incinerated by an alien positioned above the cave entrance. Daniel rolled over and fired cleanly through the Bardokian's helmet. The creature fell head-first off the ledge and rolled down towards the bank of the creek. Two aliens were dead and there was still no sign of Jessie.

*****

The young officer shielded his face from the flying debris as the military chopper descended into the open area in front of Daniel's cabin. He stood there with his head bent down waiting for the helicopter's blades to slow to a halt. While they were still turning, an older and much more-decorated officer slowly lowered himself from the chopper. The younger officer saluted.

"At ease, Lieutenant," the disembarking officer yelled above the roar of the chopper after returning his salute.

"General Bascombe, it's good to see you again," the young man began, trying to make the meeting as pleasant as possible.

"Where's Johnstone?" Bascombe asked, ignoring the pleasantry.

"Well, Sir, we had him and, unfortunately, then he got away," the Lieutenant responded. "My men are right on his tail."

There was a loud "bang" off towards the front of the house. Both soldiers spun around to see the screen-door swinging back and forth in the wind, while instinctively drawing their sidearms. The Lieutenant raised his pistol, but before he could fire it, the General pushed the barrel down.

"You don't shoot something unless you know what you're shooting at!" the older officer chided. Bascombe thought he had glimpsed a shadow bolting through the high weeds. There was something so familiar about that moment — as though he'd seen it all played out before. They both holstered their pistols and the General glanced back at the house before gazing off into the woods.

"Nope," he muttered to himself. "Couldn't be!"

*****

Daniel held his left arm and watched the blood oozing between his fingers. He was not accustomed to pain, but he had to ignore it and get himself up again. He rose to his feet. Then he bent over to pick up the blaster with his left hand while he tried to staunch the stream from his wound with his right.

"Drop it, Johnstone!" the second soldier screamed at the boy.

"Get down!" Daniel yelled back.

The soldier dropped to one knee and took careful aim at the boy.

"Drop your weapon now!" the soldier repeated. "I don't want to shoot a kid, but I've got my orders."

183

"My friend is still alive!" Daniel pleaded. "We need to help her!"

"Well, it looks like most of *my* friends are dead," the soldier replied. "What makes your friend so special?"

While the soldier surveyed the dead bodies, the boy bolted towards the cave.

"Damn you, Kid!" the soldier screamed as he squeezed off two rounds.

Daniel's leg gave out from under him as he slid down the slight grade in front of the cave. He dropped his blaster into the weeds when the first bullet hit him in his thigh. He could hear the rustle of the soldier running towards him through the brush.

"Stop, Kid!" the soldier warned. "I don't want to have to kill you, but I can't think of one good reason why I shouldn't!"

The young Private was so focused on Daniel that he failed to notice the large figure emerging from the cave. The tall Bardokian officer held Jessie almost horizontally under its left arm while raising its right arm to aim a blaster-pistol at the soldier.

"Look out!" Daniel screamed at the young man.

The soldier glanced slightly to his left just in time to see the beam that burned through him. His rifle fell out of his hands and he looked helplessly at the young woman in the grip of the creature. The soldier slumped forward, straining to see what the alien would do with her. He couldn't do anything to help her except perhaps pray, while he was still alive and conscious, that God might intervene on her behalf.

The alien had no apparent interest in the soldier. It stood in front of the cave staring down at Daniel. The boy hadn't paid much attention to it before, but he could hear that familiar beeping sound again. It was emanating from the device on the alien's belt. The huge creature holstered its pistol and unclipped the small box from its waist-band. When the Bardokian pointed it towards the soldier, the signal diminished, but as soon as the alien aimed it at Daniel, the beeping increased in both volume and speed of repetition.

The creature snapped the device back onto its belt. It seemed to smile and then it made a loud, strange noise. It appeared to be laughing at the boy. It raised its left arm and lifted Jessie vertically against its body. She was already exhausted from struggling with the alien. There was almost no fight left in her.

"Don't hurt her. — Please!" the boy begged.

"Kan-DARssss," it hissed in its best imitation of Ionian while pointing at Daniel. Then it reached over its shoulder and slowly drew a curved blade from a sheath on its back. The creature held the blade to Jessie's throat and added: "et Shah-LAY-Ahssss!"

The Bardokian made the horrible laughing sound again and repeated the whole sequence menacingly. It pointed the blade at the boy as it spoke Kandar's name and then it held the blade to Jessie's throat as it hissed: "et Shah-LAY-Ahssss!"

"No, please don't!" Daniel pleaded; his eyes welled up with tears. "Not again! Please, not again!"

The wounded Private was doing his best to reach for his rifle. Tears were running down his cheeks too, as he watched the creature threatening the young woman with the huge blade. Then he heard a rustle in the high brush and he saw just a trace of movement.

"Now! Do it! Take the shot!" he whispered hoarsely. There was no response. No shot was fired.

The creature let Jessie's feet slide to the ground as it grasped her beautiful dark hair with its left claws. The boy was trying to summon all of the energy he had, to save his precious Jessie, but he was bleeding badly and barely conscious. He held his palm up and tried to focus his powers at the alien, but there was nothing left. He had never felt so helpless in all of his many days on earth. There was nothing he could do to save the woman that he loved.

"Let her go. Just kill me!" Daniel implored the alien.

The Bardokian marine lifted its left arm slightly, so as not to harm itself with the fatal blow. It raised the blade slowly and menacingly while it stared deeply into the boy's eyes. It obviously wanted to enjoy the absolute horror on his helpless, hopeless face.

Just as the blade reached the alien's eye-level, it noticed a low growling sound coming from behind. The Bardokian froze for a second as the growling increased in its horrifying volume. It was not at all familiar with the wild animals of this planet and so it slowly rotated its eyes to the right and then turned its head slightly in that direction in an effort to see what could possibly be making such a threatening sound.

For just a split second, the alien looked straight into the blazing eyes of the feral beast that leapt from the small ridge above the cave. The animal dug its claws into the Bardokian's back and sank its fangs deep into his throat. It was as though the ghost of Ol' Bob had come back to protect his territory. The alien dropped both Jessie and the knife in an instinctive attempt to defend itself against the wild creature. Jessie rolled slightly down the grade. The Bardokian flailed at the beast, but its own breathing apparatus prevented contact. The giant staggering alien couldn't dislodge this *thing* that locked its powerful jaws so tenaciously around his throat. The Bardokian was gushing yellow fluid and its methane hose was completely severed. The sound of its breathing was replaced by a disgusting "gurgling."

Daniel strained to reach behind his back and pulled his Pa's knife from his belt. With all of the strength that he could muster, he hurled the knife into the alien's torso. The alien dropped to its knees and then forward on its face. The boy crawled slowly across the dirt towards Jessie as the wild animal continued to tear the alien to shreds. The terrified young woman opened her eyes and pushed herself away from the battle that was being waged so dangerously nearby. Daniel continued to drag himself straight for her and he sheltered her with his body. She was quite visibly shaking with fear.

The boy looked at the large animal still ripping into the alien's body and smiled. Tears of joy ran down his cheeks. He uttered one word before he lost consciousness.

"Job!"

And so it was that the great Kandar — known to some as the "Demon of Mundago" and to others as the "God of the Savages" — returned to this earth and took the form of a dog, for the love of his only chosen son.

*****

General Bascombe, the Lieutenant and the helicopter crew arrived only moments later. The dog was still tearing at the dead Bardokian. The young Lieutenant pulled his weapon to dispatch the wild animal.

"No, Sir. You can't!" the bleeding Private begged. "That big dog just saved the girl's life."

"Leave the dog alone, Lieutenant," Bascombe ordered. "Apparently, he knows how to recognize our *real* enemies — and he also knows how to deal with them."

187

"Yes, Sir," the Lieutenant replied, while easing his pistol back into its holster.

Jessie pushed Daniel's body off of her, rolling him over on his back. She wasn't seriously injured, but tears streaked down her face when she finally noticed the blood all over the unconscious boy. Blood streamed from his nose, his left arm and his right thigh.

Job strode defiantly across the Bardokian's carcass and lay down next to Daniel. The dog nuzzled the boy's face and rested his head on Daniel's chest. He looked across at Jessie, who was still struggling to catch her breath and regain her composure.

"Good Job!" she whispered as she reached over to pet him.

"Lieutenant, get that soldier and this young lady to the hospital. NOW!" the General barked. "As for the rest of you: there are a lot of wounded soldiers lying around here who need to be evacuated. Save the ones you can and bring in another team for your fallen comrades!"

"That's Johnstone, Sir!" the Lieutenant insisted, pointing at the boy.

"Young Man, that may be *A* 'Johnstone,' but he isn't *THE* 'Johnstone' that we're looking for!" the General replied. "I *knew* Daniel Johnstone and he would have to be in his seventies by now!"

"But, this one pulled a gun on us!" the Lieutenant insisted.

"Well, unless you want to see that happen to you twice in one day, you'd better follow your orders, Young Man!" Bascombe threatened.

"Yes, Sir!" the Lieutenant snapped to attention and saluted.

"Move it!" the General barked as he hurriedly returned the salute.

The Lieutenant helped Jessie to her feet while two men from the helicopter crew threw together a makeshift stretcher to carry the wounded Private. Other crew members checked the remaining soldiers for any signs of life. A corporal stood guard over the scene just in case there were any more aliens lurking about.

"You'll have to come with me, Young Lady," the Lieutenant ordered Jessie, while grabbing her arm.

"Is this what you call 'protective custody'?" she asked him, gesturing with her free arm at the carnage. "I'm going to have nightmares for the rest of my freaking life!"

"And, you can keep your hands to yourself!" she yelled, pushing the Lieutenant away. Then, she kicked him in the shin — just for good measure.

She looked at the General.

"I don't know you, but you'd better take good care of that kid or I'm coming back for you, too!" she threatened before stomping off with the Lieutenant.

Bascombe watched the two of them walking off together. She was still yelling at the young officer, gesticulating wildly and occasionally stopping to kick dirt at the man.

"That has *got* to be Jessie!" the General muttered to himself, with just a hint of a grin. "She sure is a feisty little thing!"

Daniel opened his eyes and raised his hands to the dog's head.

"You are *such* a good boy, Job!" he whispered.

The General knelt down next to them and glanced at the boy's wounds.

*****

"Uncle Danny, the good news is: you're going to live," Bascombe whispered as soon as his men got beyond hearing range.

"Your wounds aren't life-threatening, but we really need to get you to a hospital."

He tried to lift the boy by his arm, but Daniel winced in pain and the dog growled menacingly. The General lowered the boy's arm gently and backed away.

"That *can't* be Job!" he remarked incredulously.

"Jerry, I thought I'd seen the last of him myself," the boy replied. "But, sure enough, that's my Job! — And, I've never been happier to see anyone in my whole life."

"We still have to get you to a hospital," the General urged.

"Just give us a second," Daniel said as he looked into the dog's eyes and held him close to his chest. "I really missed you, Boy!"

"Uncle Danny, you're bleeding," Bascombe reminded him. "You don't have time for this right now."

"I *always* have time for Job," the boy insisted.

Job lowered his head onto Daniel's right thigh.

"Your dog's covered with dirt and alien blood. You're going to get an infection!" the General warned.

"Leave him be, Jerry," the boy said, wincing from the pain. "I trust him."

The dog remained there motionless for nearly a minute and then he rested his head on the wound on Daniel's left arm.

Bascombe knelt down next to his old friend once again. He pulled a clean handkerchief from his pocket and tried to clean up the wound on the boy's right thigh.

"It looks like the bleeding's stopped," the General noted as he stuffed the handkerchief into his jacket pocket.

"It's still going to be plenty sore for a while!" Daniel said.

190

Job raised his head from the boy's arm and looked up at the General.

"I just don't understand any of this," Bascombe said. "You and Job look exactly the way I remembered you — the way you looked back in the early Sixties!"

"Yeah! It just goes to show you that if you don't smoke, you eat right and you take good care of yourself: you might just live forever!" the boy joked.

*****

Jessie and the Lieutenant arrived at his camp not far from where she had left her vehicle just a few days earlier.

"Sergeant! Escort this young lady to that ambulance — and stay right with her!" the Lieutenant ordered the nearest NCO. "And, be careful: she's a fighter!"

"Yes, Sir, Lieutenant!" the Sergeant replied. And then, looking at Jessie, he added: "You'd better be good, Young Lady, because I don't have any problem with hitting a woman!"

"I'm sure you don't — unless she's bigger than you!" Jessie sassed back.

She walked up to the ambulance with the Sergeant following a step or two behind. She knocked on the side of the vehicle until a Medic stuck his head out of the door.

"I'm a reporter. I was sent here to get the real story behind all of these strange sightings," Jessie began.

The Sergeant grinned and shook his head slowly from side to side.

"No, she's just another nut-case. Put her in a jacket!" he told the Medic.

Before she could turn to run, the Medic grabbed her by her left

191

arm and injected her. Jesse struggled for a few seconds as the campsite began to spin around her. She made one desperate attempt to reach down for her shoe, before she collapsed into the Medic's arms. The Sergeant assisted him, lifting her into the ambulance.

"That should keep her quiet for a good, long time," the Medic assured the Sergeant.

They sat the young woman on a gurney, slipped her arms through a strait-jacket and secured it behind her. Then they lifted her legs onto the gurney and rolled her over on her side.

"Now that she's quiet, she doesn't look half-bad!" the Sergeant remarked as he leered at the unconscious woman.

The Medic pointed at two small video cameras in opposite corners of the vehicle and cautioned him: "Don't you even think about it!"

The disappointed NCO stepped down from the ambulance and slammed the door behind him. Jessie's eyes rolled open briefly from the impact and, just as quickly, she resumed her induced nap.

*****

"Do you think you can stand?" Bascombe asked the boy.

"You wouldn't happen to have any food on you, would you?" Daniel asked.

The General began to check his pockets.

"I might have a small bag of peanuts somewhere," he replied, as he continued his search. "Here it is. I brought them with me on the flight from Washington!" He tore the bag open and sat next to the boy. "Be my guest."

"Thanks," the boy answered as he grabbed the bag. He had only shelled a few peanuts and filled his mouth when he noticed Job

192

staring at him.

"You *can't* be hungry!" Daniel told the dog, but Job just whined at him.

"You practically ate a whole Bardokian officer and you're still hungry?" the boy asked him in disbelief. There was a silent pause, then Daniel started to laugh.

"What's so funny?" asked the General.

"Job said that he chewed, but he didn't swallow!" the boy explained with a giggle. "Apparently, they taste as bad as they smell!"

The General grinned and looked at the two of them in amazement.

"He also said that he and Kandar are both starving," the boy continued. "Neither one of them have eaten a thing since this whole battle began."

"Kandar? So, where *is* this 'starving' Kandar?" Bascombe asked excitedly.

Daniel looked at the General and slowly pointed his finger in Job's direction.

"You won't tell anyone?" the boy asked.

"Absolutely not, Uncle Danny," Bascombe swore. He raised two fingers and added: "Scout's honor!"

*****

More soldiers came tramping up the path from the nearby camp. The very few wounded soldiers had already been evacuated. These troops were coming to remove the bodies of the less fortunate ones.

"Do you think you can walk, Uncle Danny?" the General asked the boy.

"If you can help me up, I think I can make it," he replied, as he offered Job the remaining peanuts in his hand.

The General stood and extended his hand down towards Daniel. A young Private spotted the elderly officer and hurried over.

"Allow me, Sir!" the soldier interrupted, as he offered his hand to the boy.

With very little effort, he had the boy up on his feet and Job immediately stood at his side. The General looked for the nearest commanding officer. Spotting another lieutenant, he yelled: "This soldier is with me!"

Then, with Bascombe on his left arm and the Private on his right, Daniel shuffled back up the path to his house. Job squeezed just a few feet ahead of them to lead the way. He would walk a few steps with his tail wagging wildly and then he would wait for the men to catch up. It only took them a few minutes to get back to the clearing in front of their home.

*****

"Where's Jessie?" Daniel asked.

"She was escorted back to the field hospital — just to make sure she's okay," the General replied. "She's got a lot of spirit!"

"Indeed, she does!" the boy said with a smile. "Can you take me to her?"

"Now isn't a good time," Bascombe responded and, gesturing towards the old picnic table, he added: "Let's have a seat."

"Private, you've been a great help. I thank you very much, but you should head on back to your camp now. You're dismissed!" the General told the young soldier.

"Yes, Sir," the private answered with a snappy salute.

The General returned the salute and waited for the Private to turn and leave. The boy sat on the picnic bench and the old officer sat next to him.

"There are too many people who know you around here," Bascombe whispered to the boy. "You and Job are going to have to disappear."

"Disappear?" the boy asked.

"Look, Danny, the President wants the *Dorius*. He wants Kandar and all of his accomplices—" Bascombe hesitated, waving his finger at Daniel and Job. With some reluctance, he finished the sentence: "Dead."

"You're going to be in trouble, if we get away," the boy said matter-of-factly.

"Not necessarily," the General continued. "I haven't heard that the *Dorius* has been sighted or picked up on radar, so I can explain to the President that Kandar took his ship and went back home. As for the two of you, I couldn't be faulted for not recognizing a man of your age who looks like a teenager."

Daniel rubbed his left shoulder and winced.

"Dare I ask: how old are you anyway?" Bascombe leaned in.

"Somewhat shy of two hundred years," the boy replied. "And Job's probably a good ten years younger."

"My word!" the General's jaw dropped. He shook his head slowly and asked, "And where is the *Dorius*?"

Daniel looked at Job for a moment and connected with Kandar's thoughts.

"The Vargon put it back exactly where it was," the boy answered. "Right behind the house."

"Well that has *definitely* got to be gone before my chopper lifts off," Bascombe told them. "When we landed here, there was nothing but a big hole behind that house and I'm sure that someone's going to notice if there's suddenly a flying saucer back there!"

"Do you have any idea how to fly it?" the General asked.

"We could probably manage to get it off the ground, but where are we supposed to go with it? This is my home. It's all I've ever known," Daniel protested.

"Once that thing is airborne, every radar on earth is going to be tracking it. If you leave earth, you can't come back!" Bascombe advised him.

"What if we could leave without the radar tracking us? Can you suggest any place where we could go?" Daniel asked his old friend. Then he remembered: "Do you still own your Dad's old ranch?"

"Actually, I do. It's been sitting empty since Dad died," the General replied. "I'd planned on retiring and moving there in a year or two."

He paused and mulled the possibility for a moment, then he added: "If you can get that ship to the ranch without it lighting up the radar, you're most welcome to stay there. I know you guys and it would be ideal for you. There are acres of land, good fishing and a huge barn where you can store the *Dorius*!"

"Are you sure you want to take the risk?" Daniel asked the old man.

"You are the closest thing to my Dad that I have left," Bascombe told him. "I'm honored to offer you the accommodation and absolutely overwhelmed at the possibility of learning all that you can teach me."

"Then, it's a deal!" Daniel said, offering his hand.

The General clasped the boy's hand firmly. As they stood up,

Daniel noticed a squad of soldiers approaching from down the path.

"We had better go, Jerome!" the boy said. "Do you still have the communicator?"

The General tapped his breast pocket.

"Right here!" he said, adding: "Good luck, Uncle Danny! Keep in touch."

"Will do, Jerry!" the boy yelled back as he and the dog ran through the front door of the old cabin. Daniel locked the door behind him and set a kitchen chair up under the doorknob.

"Job, do you really think we can pull this off?" he asked the dog.

*****

"General, drop your holster! We have orders to take you and that boy into custody," the Lieutenant yelled.

"Whose orders?" Bascombe challenged.

"The President's orders, Sir!" the young officer replied.

The General unhitched his holster and let it slide to the ground.

"Okay, so my gun's on the ground and you've got me in custody, now what?" the elderly officer asked, with a slight grin.

"Get the kid!" the Lieutenant yelled at his troops.

The soldiers ran towards the house, shooting at the windows and doors, as if they were expecting return fire. One of them held the screen-door back, while two others rammed against the door. On their second try, the door frame shattered and they fell over the chair as they entered the cabin. Red dots were dancing across the walls of the darkened house as snipers pointed their rifles through the broken windows.

The General stood there grinning at the sullen-faced Lieutenant.

"What's so amusing, General Bascombe?" the officer began.

"You could easily be facing court-martial."

As the rest of the soldiers charged through the front door, the older officer looked at the young man and asked: "Do you know what's behind that old cabin?"

"No, Sir, I do not!" the Lieutenant snapped back.

The sound of the soldiers ramming into the back door echoed through the house. There was one loud bang, followed by a second — and then a blood-curdling scream.

"One big ol' crater!" the General laughed.

*****

Daniel had asked the Vargon to put the *Dorius* in the barn on Albert's old ranch and the Vargon had complied. It was late and the boy needed to rest, so he lay back in the pilot's seat and stretched himself out with Job reclining at his side.

"Job, I really missed you," he told the dog. He reached down to stroke the dog's head and added, "Thank you, Kandar. Thank you ever so much! And, thanks to you, Vargon, as well."

Chapter 9

Aftermath

In what seemed like a long, horrible nightmare, Commander Korbay could clearly remember seeing the Vargons consuming all of the ships around him. When he realized that his fighter was being attacked as well, he had ejected himself into open space. From that vantage point, he could see the terrified faces of both his enemies and his fellow Ionians as they were swallowed by the merciless Vargons. Reacting to the silent screams of his countrymen, he had pulled out his sidearm in a futile attempt to save one of his pilots. Suddenly, a shadow rose up and engulfed him from behind.

He closed his eyes for just a moment to adjust to the darkness. When he reopened them, he was still buckled into his pilot's seat and his weapon was still in his hand, but he was no longer in the space above the planet earth. He was seated — devoid of his fighter — on the tarmac of his airbase on Ionus. He removed his helmet and released himself from his harness. He stood in the silence of his home world and surveyed the area. A cool breeze wafted through the Commander's thin hair.

All of his pilots, who had survived the battle with the Bardokians, were lined up in neat rows on either side of him. Most of them were seated in their ejector seats; some of them were still enclosed by portions of their cockpits. They had all been returned to their base alive and he could only assume that the same scenario had played out for their Bardokian counterparts.

*****

The Lieutenant escorted the General back to his chopper.

"Sir, have you got anything on you that might be used as a weapon?" the younger officer asked respectfully.

"I've got my car keys, some change, my wallet, a couple of

pens, my handkerchief and a small electronic game, Lieutenant," Bascombe replied. "If you'd like to frisk me, you can go right ahead."

"No, Sir, I will take you at your word," the young man answered. "I have the greatest respect for you and the service you've given our country. And, I really don't want to make this any more unpleasant for you than is absolutely necessary."

"Thank you kindly, Young Man," the General said with all sincerity. "I truly appreciate your attitude and your consideration."

"Can you at least show me the game, Sir?" the Lieutenant asked politely.

The General dug the alien communicator out of his pocket and handed it over to the young officer.

"Be careful with it," Bascombe implored him. "My grandson was playing with it right before I left and he gave it to me for safe keeping."

"How do you play it?" the Lieutenant asked.

"It's just a controller device for a game console. Without the rest of the system, it doesn't do much of anything," the General told him.

"Thank you, Sir," the young man responded as he handed the device back to the older officer. "I think you have enough problems already. I don't want to get you into any trouble with your grandson."

After climbing into the helicopter, the two officers secured themselves to their seats. The pilot looked back at them for his orders.

"Proceed back to base," the General told him without thinking.

The Lieutenant looked at the pilot and nodded in assent.

As the chopper rose above Daniel's property, Bascombe looked down at the crater behind the house and smiled. He knew that the boy and his very special dog were safe for now. The helicopter continued to climb and headed east.

*****

After sleeping for a couple of hours, Daniel opened the hatch to the airlock and then the exterior one. He walked straight out into Bascombe's barn with Job at his heels. He was still quite sore from the two bullet wounds, but they were heeling quickly from the inside out. Job had done an excellent job of repairing the damage, although the boy was still somewhat weak from blood loss. A good meal was in order.

"Job, how'd you like to go fishing?" he asked the dog.

Job looked up at him in anticipation of a much-needed meal. Daniel examined the interior of the barn closely. He would have to cover a few windows to keep people from seeing in, but, otherwise, it seemed to be the perfect hiding place for the *Dorius*.

The Vargon had deposited the ship in the best possible place within the confines of the large barn. It was the only way that they could transport it without being seen or tracked on radar. Daniel owed the Vargon — and the General — a huge favor.

The boy walked back up the ramp into the ship with Job close at his side. He knelt down to examine the contents of the box that he had thrown together as he ran through his cabin. He managed to save his fishing pole and creel, the four leather-bound booklets, his book of songs, his guitar, his cell-phone, his banking information and the padre's beads. He still didn't know what to do with those beads, but he'd had them for so long that he felt some attachment to them. A quick glance around the cockpit of the ship revealed a protuberance on the instrument cluster. Daniel hung the rosary there, suddenly realizing that he had seen people do much the same thing in their cars.

"Job, now all we need is some fuzzy dice!" he joked.

He picked up his fishing pole and basket on his way back down the ramp.

"We'd better find that fish pond before it gets too dark," he told Job.

*****

When the General arrived at the base, he was escorted toward his office.

"Sir, if there's anything that you'd like to lock up in your desk before we take you to a holding cell, this will be your only opportunity to do it," the Lieutenant advised him.

"Thank you very much for extending me that courtesy, Lieutenant, but I'd like to use the washroom first," Bascombe answered.

The Lieutenant looked inside the washroom. There were no windows big enough to accommodate an escape. He held the door for the elderly officer and nodded.

"Sir, I'll be waiting right out here when you've finished," the Lieutenant said.

"Thanks again," the General replied.

He closed the door behind him and quietly twisted the lock, then he walked to the farthest stall. He pulled the communicator out of his pocket, turned the dial and pressed the triangular icon. When he realized that Daniel wasn't answering, he tried the boy's personal icon.

"Jerry?" the boy responded.

"Uncle Danny, I'm being held in custody for right now. I'm going to have to lock the communicator in my desk drawer, so be careful what you say if it should ring again," the General advised him.

"I'll be very careful not to say anything that might incriminate you, Jerry," the boy answered. "Good luck in dealing with your superiors."

"Thanks, Danny, but I don't think they have much of a case against me. I'll try to contact you as soon as I'm released," Bascombe sighed. "I'm getting too old for this."

"Are you sure you don't want me to get you out of there?" the boy asked.

"I'll be fine," the General smiled. "I've been in tighter spots than this before."

"If there's anything that I can do, just let me know," Daniel offered.

"Well, there is one thing actually," the man began. "If the world is ever threatened by any danger that our military can't handle, will you promise me that you'll put Kandar and the *Dorius* back to work?"

"Absolutely! You can count on me, Jerry," Daniel assured him.

"If I need to use it, that promise might be the bargaining chip that will get me free and take the government off your back," the General replied. "Thanks again, Danny. It was great seeing you and Job again."

"Likewise," the boy answered, adding: "I'm sure it won't be for the last time."

The General heard the doorknob twist back and forth. Then there was a hurried knock on the door. He stuffed the communicator back into his pocket.

"General, is everything okay in there?" the Lieutenant asked anxiously.

"I'm fine! I'll be out in a minute! Things just take a little longer when you get old!" the General yelled back.

*****

Daniel put his communicator back into his pants pocket.

"Job, we've really made a mess of things," he told the dog. "Jerome is in custody and we don't even know where they took Jessie. As soon as we get some food, we need to secure this area. Then we'll have to start figuring out how to put things right."

He opened the barn door and looked outside. He hadn't been on Bascombe's ranch in decades, but he still had many fond memories of fishing with Albert at the pond. It was just over the hill to the north.

It was a short leisurely walk. The sun was already low in the sky and he didn't have any bait. He squatted down near the water's edge.

"Are you as hungry as I am?" he asked the dog.

Job whined in obvious agreement. The boy flipped the lid of the creel open. Then he focused on the surface of the water and held his hand above the open basket. A large catfish leapt from the pond into the basket and Daniel flipped the lid back down.

"I know that's cheating, but we *do* want to eat today, don't we?" the boy joked. "It's too bad I can't get him to clean and gut himself!"

The boy stood up and Job followed him back to the barn. Daniel opened his mind to his surroundings and sensed that there was no cognizant entity for at least a couple of miles in any direction. He was certain that he could cook his feast without anyone being alerted to their presence on the ranch.

*****

The Lieutenant was a little upset with the General for locking the door and taking so long in the washroom, but he had promised him the opportunity to stop at his office. It was right across the hall and it would have seemed rude to deny him access at this point. The General pulled out his keys and fingered through them until he found the right one.

"I'll just be a minute, Lieutenant," Bascombe said.

"Sir, with all due respect, I'm going in there with you," the young officer insisted.

"Of course," the General acknowledged, as he unlocked the door.

He walked around and sat behind his desk. He looked at the sequence of numbers on the lock and carefully unlocked the desk drawer. The General began to pull it open.

"Stop right there, Sir!" the Lieutenant barked, while pulling his weapon.

"Young Man, you know there's a gun in here and I know there's a gun in here," the General began calmly: "I have no intention of touching it, okay?"

He raised his hands and stood slowly, pushing his chair back with his legs. As he backed away from the desk, the drawer rolled open to reveal an old military-issue Colt .45 semi-automatic pistol. There were also a couple of boxes of ammunition and three extra clips. The General pulled his wallet out of his back pants pocket and dropped it into the open drawer.

"Wallet," he said quietly; and, as he dropped his car keys and the communicator into the drawer, he added: "Car keys and my grandkid's toy."

He held his hands out above the desk while he slid the drawer back in with his lower body. He reached down to spin the dials of the combination lock.

"Thank you for allowing me to secure my valuables, Lieutenant," Bascombe said.

"Sir, we really should be going now," the young man reminded him.

"Of course," the General mumbled. "Of course."

*****

The government had been controlling all news broadcasts for days. Some of the local meteorologists had called attention to the lights in the night sky and, with that particular cat out of the bag, it took some real arm-twisting to persuade the media to initially broadcast the "news" that it was nothing more than a bizarre meteor shower. As soon as the military determined that the focal point of the attack would be the Rev-Tech facility located just outside of the tiny town of Apple Creek, a whole division of military vehicles and agents was dispatched to that area.

If there had been sufficient lead time, the residents of the town would all have been evacuated, but, lacking that advantage, the military deployed trucks with megaphones. All area residents were ordered to take shelter in their basements prior to the attack. And, for the most part, the townspeople complied.

There were very few witnesses to the alien invasion who had survived the experience. The majority of the people, who were close enough to the Bardokians to actually see them, had been killed by them. But, anyone, who had seen anything amiss and survived, was detained and interrogated by the military. And, those few were committed to a government-owned facility — at least for the time being. The bureaucrats had no plans for providing long-term "mental health" care, but neither did they have the stomach to authorize the executions of honest, tax-paying American citizens. The government had to invent a story to account for the dead and the missing. So, the alien invasion had suddenly become another successful "terrorist attack," primarily perpetrated by persons unknown, save for one.

*****

The television was turned on in the home of Wilbur Drake on the very day of the attack, when the Washington spin-doctors released their initial broadcast: *"Just a few hours ago, a young man believed to be Daniel Johnstone, the owner of the Rev-Tech Bionics company, entered his facility near Apple Creek, Colorado, and detonated a series of explosive devices that he had allegedly placed in the lower levels of the buildings. It is not known whether he is among the hundreds of casualties or whether he survived the explosions. This is a composite sketch of Johnstone, based on eyewitness accounts by Rev-Tech employees. Please notify your local authorities, if you see this man. He should be considered armed and extremely dangerous."*

Wilbur lowered the volume of the TV and walked into the kitchen.

"Sophie, wasn't Jessie supposed to get a job at this here Rev-Tech place?" Wilbur asked his wife.

"She already has a job at the newspaper, why would she want another one?" his "better half" answered with a touch of sarcasm.

"I know that, Woman! But didn't she say something about 'going undercover' or some such nonsense at this Rev-Tech company?" he insisted.

"I don't know, Wilbur. That girl is always making something out of nothing. I don't even listen to her anymore!" Sophie prattled on. "Like that nonsense about how many boys she says she's dated since high school!"

"That's officially eighty-nine, last count. Of course we haven't heard from her in a week or two, so she might be into triple digits by now," Jessie's father replied.

"Do you think she just invents these stories about guys, so we don't suspect she's a Lebanese?" Sophie asked with some concern.

"She's not a Lebanese, Woman! The word is 'liberal,' and I don't think she's that either!" Wilbur muttered. "I think she just exaggerates her experiences a bit."

The old man stood at the window, lighting his pipe.

"I don't rightly know what's wrong with her. She's really not all that rough on the eyes," he mumbled, as he puffed away. "I think maybe she's just a little shy around boys — like her Ma was," he added as he pinched Sophie's backside.

"Now, Wilbur!" she snapped back, with a titter.

*****

"General Bascombe, it's good to see you. Won't you take a seat?" the President began. "Your young Lieutenant has been advising me that you conspired with the enemy in Apple Creek."

"Mr. President, I think there's a lot of confusion about who the 'enemy' is in this case," the officer replied.

"General, the enemy is precisely whoever your President tells you he is. I told you quite explicitly what I wanted and you failed to produce!" the President stood to say.

"You said you wanted the two aliens known as Kandar and the Vargon. And you wanted me to capture their ship called the *Dorius*. Truth be told, Mr. President, I would love to be able to present their heads on a silver platter, and the ship as well, but your own radar indicates that the ship went into orbit and vanished without ever returning to Earth," the General laid out his argument.

208

"And the Johnstone boy?" the President insisted as he sat down again.

"He can't possibly be the guy we're looking for," the old officer countered. "I met the Daniel Johnstone who was associated with Rev-Tech when I was a kid. That was nearly sixty years ago. Now, if I'm over sixty and he was a teenager at the time, doesn't logic dictate that he'd still be older than me?"

"What if he isn't human?" the POTUS hypothesized.

"Well, there you go — if he isn't human, then maybe we can't capture or kill him. Maybe he's on the *Dorius*? For that matter, maybe he's invisible and right here in this very room! In fact, I think I just saw the curtain move behind you!" Bascombe suggested.

The President jumped back out of his chair and spun around to look. The old officer chuckled for a second and immediately silenced himself when the President's eyes came back to focus on him.

"Do you think this is funny, Old Man?" the President sneered. "Does spending the rest of your life in the brig sound funny to you?"

"No Sir, Mr. President," Bascombe replied. "Does getting your butt laughed out of office appeal to you?"

The Leader of the Free World grabbed a pen off his desk and threw it angrily at the old uniformed man: "Are you threatening me? I can have you taken out of this office and shot. You're a disgrace to that uniform!"

Without even flinching, the General quietly replied: "Mr. President, I served my country for forty-plus years. I've put bullets through the eyes of our enemies for pennies a day, while guys with half my IQ make millions of dollars putting a ball through a dang metal hoop. You can threaten me all you want. Sure, you can have me taken out and shot, if that's what you really want to do. But, bear in mind that if I had thrown this pen at you with any intention of hurting you, it would have taken a crack team of doctors to extricate it from that tiny brain of yours!"

The General stood up and placed the pen back on the desk. Then he turned and walked towards the door.

"Don't you dare walk out on me, Bascombe! I'm not through with you yet!" the POTUS screamed.

"Yes, Sir, Mr. President. You sure as hell are," he replied as he reached for the door. "You really should learn to respect your elders!"

"I'll have you court-martialed!" the President yelled back.

The General turned around and slowly walked towards the politician. The young man backed away from the approaching officer and fumbled blindly with his left hand for the intercom button on his desk.

"You don't need that. I'm not going to hurt you," Bascombe told him. "Maybe you inhaled when you were in college, but I'm going to try to explain something to you in terms that even a weed-smoking, snow-snorting punk like yourself can understand."

"How dare you!" the President hissed.

"Shut up and be enlightened," the General snapped back. "You saw what that ship can do. That one ship, called the *Dorius,* took on a whole armada of alien fighters and our best aircraft was no match for even the losers! If you believe that I'm in cahoots with Johnstone or those aliens, then I could have them come and rescue me and, you know full well that, that one amazing ship could reduce all of Washington D.C. to ashes."

"Is that a threat?" the President asked angrily.

"No, Mr. President: that's an indisputable fact!" Bascombe

replied with a slight grin. "If I were you, I think I'd want to be really nice to my old pal the General, because either he didn't do anything wrong. Or, he's holding all the aces."

"Get out of here!" the President screamed.

"Yes *Sir*, Mr. President. It's always nice talking to you, too, Sir!" Bascombe replied with a slight chuckle, then he added: "And, by the way, if the earth ever finds itself in really serious trouble, the boy said he's on our side and Kandar would be glad to help. So, you leave all of us alone and you've got that in reserve."

The General twisted the knob and stepped through the doorway. He looked back at the seething politician and added: "Otherwise — God help you!"

*****

Jessie woke up in a darkened room. She tried to get out of bed, but something held her wrist. She groped at it and quickly recognized the cold feel of a metal wrist band and a short chain leading to a second one. She was handcuffed to the bed rail.

"Hey!" she screamed. "Is anybody here?"

The door opened just a crack. The light from the corridor was almost blinding, but she could barely discern a uniformed guard looking in at her.

"Nurse! She's awake!" the guard yelled down the hall and closed the door.

A few moments later, there was a light tapping on the door.

"If you're expecting me to get up and open that, you're pretty darned stupid!" Jessie bellowed while shaking her chain.

The door opened slowly and a nurse walked in. She switched the lights on and Jessie shielded her eyes from the glare.

"Why am I handcuffed?" she snarled.

"You're Jessica Drake?" the nurse began, while glancing at the medical chart.

"Yes," Jessie nodded in agreement.

"I'm sure that was just a precaution. I'll see if we can get that removed as soon as possible," the nurse continued.

"Why am I here?" Jessie asked. "And where *is* 'here'?"

"You're in the psychiatric ward of a military hospital," the nurse advised her. "It appears that you were in close contact with those terrorists who attacked us and our staff of doctors is making sure that they didn't do anything to harm you."

"I'm fine," Jessie insisted. "Can I go now?"

"You've been unconscious for nearly two days and the doctors have had time to scan and examine you for obvious injuries," the nurse replied. "But, now that you're awake, you still need a very thorough psychological examination."

"So, you think I'm crazy?" Jessie scoffed.

"It doesn't matter what I think," the nurse responded. "A lot of tough soldiers come back from combat with serious mental and emotional issues. You've been through quite a lot. The doctors need to know exactly what you saw and how it's influenced you."

"Well, aren't they all so considerate!" the girl sassed. "Where was all of this help when an alien was holding me up by my hair?"

"That's exactly my point!" the nurse replied. "You've been through a war and we need to know everything that you experienced, so we can figure out what we can do to help you to put all of this behind you."

"If you would just unlock this cuff, I'd be more than happy to put all of this behind me," Jessie answered. "I want to go home!"

"Just be patient, Young Lady!" the nurse replied with a smile. "I'm sure the doctor will be here shortly and, as soon as you can convince him that you're okay, you can be on your way."

The nurse dimmed the lights and closed the door quietly behind her.

*****

"General Bascombe, can I impose upon you for a moment of your time?" a familiar voice asked. The General turned around to see who was addressing him.

"Mr. Vice-President?" he asked, immediately recognizing his face. "Perhaps you should ask my guards."

"Lieutenant. Sergeant. You are both dismissed. We are assuming protective custody of the General," the Vice-President commanded.

"Excuse me, Sir, but our orders—" the officer interjected.

"Have been rescinded, Lieutenant!" the young statesman insisted. "You are both officially dismissed. Now report back to your base."

"Yes, Sir!" the Lieutenant replied, as he and the NCO snapped to attention and saluted. They wheeled around and headed down the corridor.

"Now, what can I do for you, Mr. Vice-President?" Bascombe asked, as the two soldiers found their exit.

"You can call me 'Jim,'" the young man replied. "I'd like you to meet a couple of associates of mine. You see, not all of us agree with the President's decision regarding the Johnstone boy and his friends. Some of us place a very high value on the well-being of our alien allies. And also on the well-being of those who can keep us connected with said 'allies'!"

"I'm not sure I understand," Bascombe bluffed.

"This is Mr. Jacobs, our CIA insider, and young Ben here is Special Ops," the Vice-President continued. "We would like you to work directly with us. I promise you that we can assure your safety and the safety of your comrades, who, by the way, seem to be staying at your ranch out west. But it would probably be best if you disappeared off the grid, too."

"Disappeared?" the General asked.

"Yes, 'disappeared' — as in 'Arlington National,'" Mr. Jacobs explained.

*****

Jessie had nearly fallen asleep when there was a light rap on the door.

"Yes?" she answered with a hint of exasperation.

The door opened and a young doctor stepped in.

"Is it all right if I come in and chat for a minute?" the young man began.

"You're already in. And it's not like I have anything to say about it!" she barked.

"I can come back some other time—" the man stuck one foot back outside.

"No. Look, you're here. The sooner you decide that I'm okay, the sooner I get to go home!" Jessie replied, as the doctor approached her bed.

"Would you like to go home?" he began while scanning her chart.

"Of course I'd like to go home! Who likes to stay handcuffed to a bed in a hospital!" she yelled. Then she lowered her voice to add:

"I'm sorry. I've had a really rough couple of days and I don't mean to yell at you, but I — want — to — go — home. Got it?"

"I think we have that fact established," the doctor smiled. "Have you been having any nightmares?"

"Do you mean when I was sleeping or while I'm awake?" she grumbled.

"Sleeping," he answered curtly.

"I don't remember. A Medic injected me with something and I was out for quite some time. I don't even know if I dreamt. Then I was about to actually *fall* asleep and a doctor came tapping on the door!" she sassed back.

"I see!" he remarked.

"No, you don't see at all! I'm a decent, law-abiding, tax-paying American citizen. I haven't done anything wrong and I'm being held here against my will!" she continued impatiently.

The doctor clicked his flashlight on and bent down towards her.

"Open your eyes wide and look up here," he said, gesturing with his finger.

She looked at his finger and widened her eyes.

"Hmmm," the young doctor intoned.

"What's wrong?" Jessie asked worriedly.

"Young Lady, you have the most gorgeous eyes!" he smiled.

She tried to pull away from the flirtatious young man, but she was still chained to the bed rail. "Don't you dare try anything!" she snarled at him.

"I'm sorry, I really didn't mean to say anything to upset you, but you just have the kind of eyes that a man can get lost in," the doctor said matter-of-factly.

"Here, let me take care of that nasty bracelet you're wearing,"

215

he offered, while reaching into his pocket for a key ring. He peeled through the various keys on the ring until he found the right one.

"This should do it!" he remarked as he slipped the key into the lock on her cuff.

With hardly a sound, the handcuff fell open. Jessie immediately drew her left wrist towards her torso and rubbed it with her right hand.

"Does it hurt?" the doctor asked. "Is there an abrasion?"

The doctor walked towards the light switch and raised the intensity of the lighting within the room. He walked back towards the bed.

"Let me see it. I don't want you getting an infection," the young man continued.

She stuck her wrist out for him to examine.

"Oh, that's fine! You're just a big baby — that shouldn't even hurt!" he chided.

Jessie smiled at the man. The handcuff hadn't been tight, but it was definitely an inconvenience. At least now it was off, she thought.

"What's your name?" she asked the doctor.

"I'm Cha Ming," he replied.

"Aren't you supposed to be a Prince?" she asked, with a laugh.

"Maybe in another life," he said.

"Where are my glasses?" she wondered aloud.

"Let's see — they should be — here on the nightstand," he answered. He picked up her eyeglasses and placed them over her nose. A feeling of déjà vu washed over the girl and she suddenly thought of Daniel. She strained to read the doctor's name tag.

"Chen!?!" she exclaimed. "Your name isn't 'Charming,' it's Chen!"

"Look closely: Doctor Cha Ming Chen," he replied while leaning forward to display the badge.

"Oh! My mistake," Jessie apologized disingenuously. "Now can I go home?"

"How does 'tomorrow' sound to you?" the doctor asked.

"Promise?" she responded hopefully.

"Sure," he replied. "We haven't found anything physically wrong with you and you really don't seem to be exhibiting any alarmingly unexpected behavior, so I'll have you checked out of here first thing tomorrow. But, you have to promise me: if you have any nightmares or if you just don't feel right, I want you to notify me immediately!"

"Fine!" she said curtly.

"No. You have to promise!" he repeated.

"Okay! Sure, Doctor Chen, I promise," she answered.

"Okay, then!" he replied, as he turned to leave the room.

"Have a good night, Miss Drake," he said as he dimmed the lights and closed the door behind him.

*****

Doctor Chen approached the Desk Sergeant at the nurse's station.

"Is all of the electronic surveillance a 'go' for the Drake apartment?" he asked.

"Yes, Sir, Doctor Chen. We have a wiretap, cameras, microphones, snipers and guards all around the place. Nothing could possibly get in or out without us knowing all about it," the Sergeant replied.

"Great!" the doctor answered. "She's to be released first thing tomorrow. If she knows how to contact Johnstone, she'll do it and we'll be right on it."

"Or if he tries to contact her," the Sergeant added.

"Exactly!" Chen replied. "We're going to nail this guy one way or the other."

*****

"General Bascombe, we're going to need your uniform, your wallet and some of your personal belongings," Ben suggested.

"How do I know I can trust you guys?" the officer asked.

"You just told the President that you're 'holding all the aces,' didn't you? Are you losing your confidence?" the Vice-President asked with a slight chuckle.

"You heard all that?" Bascombe asked in amazement. "You mean: you guys actually bugged the Oval Office?"

"Hey, I just told you that Jacobs here is CIA. Now what do you think?" the young politician laughed.

"Well, if I'm going to throw in with you guys, I'll need to stop at my office and pick up a few things," the old officer said.

"That's no problem. We can swing by there so you can get whatever you need, but make sure you take everything, General," the Special Ops officer interjected. "It's highly unlikely that you'll ever be going back there again."

*****

The young man named Ben drove General Bascombe back to his office and waited for him outside. Bascombe walked casually and unhurriedly to his door. He had left the door unlocked, because his keys were secured inside his desk drawer.

218

The old man opened the door and quietly surveyed his office. He sat behind his desk and dialed the combination for the long drawer. As the drawer rolled out toward him, he grabbed his wallet, his keys, the communicator and his old Colt, which he placed on the desktop. He put the boxes of ammunition and the extra clips there, as well; then he stood up and opened a file cabinet. He removed his uniform waistcoat and ripped a slit through the right-hand pocket of his civilian jacket. Then, he slipped his arms through the shoulder holster that was in the top drawer.

The General opened the boxes of ammo and quickly loaded the empty magazines. He slid the pistol into the holster and put his jacket on over it. He distributed the extra clips among his remaining jacket pockets, then he opened a closet door and removed a complete set of civilian clothes. It seemed as though his days in the military were about to come to an abrupt and unceremonious end.

*****

Jessie was still sleeping when there was a tap on the door. She opened one eye cautiously and scanned the room in the dim light that filtered through the closed blinds. It was morning and it suddenly occurred to her that she would be going home.

"Come in!" she yelled.

The door opened slightly.

"Miss Drake, are you decent?" a male voice inquired.

"Actually, I'd say I'm way above average!" she snapped back sarcastically.

A young lieutenant stuck his head into the room.

"Oh, you're not even up yet," the Lieutenant noticed. "I'm supposed to take you to the doctor's office for a brief visit. If all goes well, I'll be taking you home later."

"Give me five minutes!" she answered anxiously.

The Lieutenant stood there expectantly.

"Out! Get out and let me get ready!" she insisted loudly.

The young officer stepped out and closed the door quietly behind him. Jessie threw back the sheets and dashed towards the washroom. She hurriedly used the toilet and took a quick shower. Her hair was wet and there was no dryer, so she toweled it dry as best she could. When she exited the bathroom, she rifled through the drawers of the chest and searched the closet for her clothing. She found the mismatched, bloodied and dirty attire that she had been wearing when they drugged her.

"Ugh!" she groaned as she reluctantly pulled the soiled clothes on.

The Lieutenant knocked on the door again.

"Almost there!" she yelled back at the door. She finished tying the shoes and looked up as the door slowly opened.

"I'm sorry, but we were supposed to be at the doctor's office by now," the young officer informed her.

"Well, then, you should have woke me up sooner; shouldn't you have?" Jessie snarled back. "Guys are so stupid!" she muttered to herself.

"Miss Drake, you could have gone there in your hospital gown. There was no need to dress," he insisted.

"And wouldn't you have enjoyed that?" she barked back. "Me with my butt sticking out!"

"I was just supposed to wheel you down there in this," he replied as he guided the wheelchair into the room.

"Great!" Jessie muttered: "Miss Drake, your chariot awaits!"

She shuffled slowly across the room and plopped into the chair.

"Take me to your leader!" Jessie ordered with a hint of resignation.

*****

It was just a short trip down the hall to Doctor Chen's office. The Lieutenant knocked on the half-open door to announce their arrival.

"Come in, please," a familiar voice intoned.

The Lieutenant pushed the door fully open and guided the wheelchair into the doctor's office. He moved a chair to one side and slid the wheelchair into its place. He turned and walked back toward the door.

"She's all yours, Dr. Chen," the Lieutenant said. "Have a good day, Miss Drake."

"Thanks for the ride, Soldier!" Jessie smiled back at him, and turning toward the desk she added: "And how are you today, Prince Charming?"

"Quite well, thank you, Miss Drake," he replied. "So, you remember me?"

"Let's see: I got maybe four hours of sleep since I saw you last? Did you think I would forget you so soon?" she inquired.

He looked down at her chart and made some notations with his pen.

"I mean — really? Are you going to write down everything that I say?" she asked.

"It isn't what you're saying specifically. I'm just making sure that you are fully aware of your surroundings and that your memory is sharp and clear. Did you have any dreams last night?" the Doctor began, while glancing up from his notes.

221

"Not that I can recall," she answered. "Did you? — and was I in them?"

"I can't say, but I can assure you that Mrs. Chen wouldn't approve," he replied.

"Oh, so I have competition?" she asked sexily.

Doctor Chen turned a photograph around on his desk. It was apparently a picture of him, his wife and their two children. Jessie leaned forward in the chair to get a better look.

"Cute kids!" she offered curtly. She enjoyed flirting with guys — especially with guys who had some authority over her. Whether it was a traffic cop trying to give her a ticket or a military doctor who had the power to set her free, she always had great success in reversing their roles.

"Miss Drake, you were seen with a young man named Daniel Johnstone," the Doctor resumed. "Is there anything particularly special about him? Anything that you'd like to tell me?"

"There you go again," Jessie laughed, "another cute kid! Apparently, either the world is full of them or we're just too darned polite to talk about the bow-wows!"

"This is important, Miss Drake," Chen continued. "What relationship does this 'Daniel Johnstone' boy have with the aliens?"

"The only thing that I can tell you is that he's darned good at killing them!" she replied. "I'd be dead several times over, if it wasn't for his quick thinking. I mean that young man is as sweet as can be, but you *really* don't want to get him angry!"

"So, you would say he's 'dangerous'?" the Doctor prodded.

"Absolutely not! He's just my guardian angel when bad things want to hurt me!" she responded. "Wouldn't you do anything within your power to protect your wife?"

"Of course, I would," Chen answered. "So you have an emotional, or perhaps a sexual, relationship with this young man?"

"Well, I like him, but we haven't done anything!" Jessie sassed back. "He's just a kid! I mean, what is he — like sixteen or something? I think he may have a crush on me, but I'm twenty-two and I'm not doing jail time for anything like that!"

"Does he act like any normal sixteen-year-old that you've ever known before?" the Doctor pressed on. "Wouldn't you say there's something a little unusual about him?"

"I've only know him for a few days. I don't know what you're trying to make me say. All I want to do is go home!" she answered desperately. "Tell me whatever it is you want me to say and I'll say it."

"I have a prepared statement here, that I'd like you to sign," Doctor Chen began. "Read through it very carefully. If you don't agree with something, just put a line through it, and, when you're finished, sign and date it on the bottom."

He handed the paper to Jessie over the desk. She leaned forward slightly to reach it, then she skimmed it over quickly.

"Who makes this stuff up?" she asked with disgust.

"Just read it and sign the statement," he insisted.

"Give me a pen!" she barked, and he slid one across the desk.

"You think that kid is some kind of an alien?" she laughed and began lining through the paragraphs.

"You think that he has his own flying saucer?" she continued.

"And, you really think that sweet kid is a threat to the United States of America?" she snorted with a flare of anger. "That kid is no terrorist! He saved me and a whole lot of other people from evil aliens from outer space! Whose side are you supposed to be on anyway?"

She finished with the paper, signed and dated it, and tossed it across the desk. The doctor quickly scanned down the page.

"I, the undersigned, Jessica Drake, do hereby testify...signed Jessica Drake!" the Doctor read. "You've lined-out the entire statement!"

"I gave you exactly what you asked for," she insisted. "You told me I could line-out anything that wasn't true and that's exactly what I did. Danny isn't an alien; he isn't a threat to this country and he doesn't want to hurt anybody. He's just a sweet kid who—"

Jessie burst into tears.

"He's just an ordinary kid. He likes music and he goes fishing with his dog," she wept. "Can't you just let me go and leave all of us alone?"

"Your Mr. Johnstone is a terrorist, Miss Drake," the Doctor insisted. "He is a threat to the security of these United States and we are going to find him: with or without your help. Do you have any idea where he is?"

"No, I don't," she continued to sob. "He was hurt really badly. He lost a lot of blood and I don't know if he could've even survived."

"Well, we have it on good authority that he did survive his wounds and that one of our own officers aided in his escape," Chen admitted.

"Then, good for Danny!" Jessie interjected. "I hope you guys never find him!"

"Miss Drake, I'm sure you must realize that your attitude is drastically diminishing the chance that you'll be leaving this facility any time soon," the Doctor threatened.

"Fine, then I'll go right back to my room!" she hissed back. "But, we both know that isn't going to happen, don't we? Because I'm the 'bait' and you think that I'm going to lead you to Danny, don't you?"

Doctor Chen fidgeted with a pencil, trying to control his anger. Then he threw it solidly into the cork-board near the door. He glared at Jessie and pointed his finger at her.

"Someday that smart mouth of yours is going to get you into a lot of trouble!" he growled.

"Maybe, but today isn't going to be that day!" she replied sarcastically.

"Lieutenant! Take Miss Drake back to her room so she can collect her things," Chen yelled towards the door.

The young officer, who had been waiting just outside, re-entered the room. The Doctor pointed at Jessie and, with the same hand, gestured towards the door. The soldier gripped the handles of the wheelchair and backed her out through the doorway.

"By the way, Miss Drake," the Doctor added. "You might want to consider taking some sessions on 'anger management'!"

"Hey! *I* didn't throw the pencil!" she yelled in response, as the officer wheeled her back to her room.

*****

Daniel had spent a couple of days covering the windows of the barn and securing the immediate area. There was a lot of open land around the structure, so anyone approaching on foot would be spotted immediately. Unfortunately, there wasn't much that Daniel could do to prevent an all-out aerial assault on the Bascombe ranch. He just hoped that it wouldn't happen.

He hadn't heard anything from the General since his detention and he was now beginning to worry that, sometime soon, government agents might investigate all of the properties associated with the Bascombe family. His only recourse would be to launch the *Dorius* and escape. With Job's assistance, there was no doubt in his mind that he could do just that.

He had already tapped into his off-shore cash reserve and transferred it to another account. There was a chance that he could buy a large property in another area where he could conceal the ship, but he had fond memories of this place and he was quite reluctant to leave it. He, Job and Albert, and even a very young Jerry, had fished, barbecued and played music on this ranch. It wasn't until he came back to it that he realized how dear it was to his heart. Job seemed to love the place, too. Perhaps, it was just a yearning for simpler times, but something was still missing. Daniel needed to see Jessie again.

He had his cell-phone in his hand and he was just about to try to contact her, when his communicator sounded. He snapped his phone shut and removed the activated communicator from his shirt pocket. He turned the dial to the flashing icon and very quietly intoned: "Daniel here."

"I only have a second, Daniel," the voice replied. "Just stay put and don't believe everything you hear on the news. I'll be in touch with you as soon as I get a chance."

The icon went dark and the boy put the communicator back into his pocket.

"Job, that sure sounded like Jerry, but he seemed awfully stressed out!"

*****

When Jessie arrived at her apartment, she stopped at her

mailbox to extract a huge wad of bills and junk mail from it. The Lieutenant, who escorted her up to her door, carried a small canvas bag. It wasn't until she realized that she didn't have her keys, that the young man handed her the sack.

"These are your things, Ms. Drake," he told her politely. "Your purse, your keys, your wallet, some articles of clothing — essentially everything that we managed to retrieve from the Johnstone cabin."

"Thank you very much! I thought I was going to need to get a new driver's license and everything!" she commented, quite elated at this turn of events. "This is so much better than having to break a window to get into my own flat!"

She found the right key and unlocked the bolt. The door wouldn't open. She thought for a moment and then she inserted another key into the doorknob. The door unlocked easily and she smiled at the young officer.

"Thanks again, Soldier! I can take it from here," she said cheerfully.

"By the way, I was told that your vehicle is parked in your assigned spot out back," the young Lieutenant added.

The soldier smiled and took a step backward. He tipped his hat to the young woman before he turned to leave. Jessie entered her small apartment and pushed the door closed with her back. Then, she spun the bolt lock and looked down at the doorknob.

"I never lock the knob. Somebody's been in here!" she muttered to herself.

She looked around the room as casually as possible, poking through her artificial flower arrangements and "accidentally" slamming cabinet doors as she put things away in places where they couldn't possibly belong. She eyed each room quite suspiciously and turned her entertainment system up as loud as she could bear to hear it.

"I don't know where they are or how they're doing it, but somebody is spying on me!" she mumbled.

She turned the light on in the bathroom and closed the door behind her. She stood on the rim of the tub and looked around the entire enclosure with a flashlight. She stepped up on the toilet seat and peeked above the medicine cabinet. Then she glared up at the fan in the ceiling fixture. She hadn't found any evidence yet, but she just *knew* it had to be there.

Jessie reopened the bathroom door and marched to the linen closet. She grabbed a couple of heavy blankets and brought them back to the bathroom. She found some duct tape and secured one edge of the blanket to the top of the shower rod, then she taped the second blanket to the edge of the first and draped it over the toilet.

*****

"What's she doing?" asked the younger FBI agent in the unmarked van.

"I think she's making a privacy tent," older agent Banks replied.

"Do you think she knows that we're watching her?" the first one asked.

"I don't think she's found anything yet, but she sure suspects something!" the older agent answered. "I guess you'd call that a wee-wee tepee!"

Both agents snickered at that. It was going to be a long night and very likely the first of many long nights of reconnaissance outside the Drake apartment.

"Is that going to be a problem?" young agent Beckert asked.

"Not unless she figures out a way to escape through the plumbing!" Banks replied, adding: "All we really want to do is listen to the phone conversations and make sure that nobody gets in or out of that apartment."

"You mean this Danny Johnstone guy?" Beckert ascertained.

"Him or any of his alien pals, Kid!" Banks yelled. "You *were* briefed on this assignment, weren't you?"

"Yes, Sir, Agent Banks!" the young man replied with mock seriousness.

"Well, then, next time — pay closer attention to what's being said!" Banks yelled.

*****

Jessie had been pacing from one end of her apartment to the other and over nearly every square inch in between. She switched on her television set. The national news was already in progress.

"In our top story tonight, the four men who suddenly appeared naked in the streets of downtown Baghdad last Tuesday have finally been released to the American Embassy. The American Ambassador is withholding the names of the four men, all of whom claim to be employees of the recently-destroyed Rev-Tech Bionics complex in Apple Creek, Colorado."

A somewhat-bored Jessie instinctively hit the mute button as she began to walk away from the set. Suddenly, her mouth dropped wide open as the realization set in. She turned around to view the screen and hit the mute button again. It was too late. They had already moved on to the next story, but another vaguely familiar face filled the screen. She boosted the volume.

"In a shocking development, an elderly man believed to be General Jerome Bascombe was killed in a one-vehicle accident last

night outside of Washington, D.C. There were no witnesses to the accident, but police are speculating that the General may have been intoxicated when his car hit the tree."

"That's the guy!" Jessie screamed, gesticulating wildly. "Oh, my God! That's the guy I left Daniel with!"

"Oh, dear God! If he's dead, what did they do to Danny?" she sobbed, as she dropped to her knees in front of the television.

*****

"Are you getting all of that?" Banks asked.

"Everything seems to be recording just fine," Beckert replied.

"I'll bet she phones somebody," the older agent ventured.

"Like Johnstone, maybe?" Beckert suggested.

"Wouldn't that be nice?" Banks replied. "That would be *too* easy! 'Cause, then I could pack this crate up and go home to my family. But, with this nutty broad, there's no telling what she's going to do next!"

"Did you catch the name of the guy on the TV?" the young agent asked.

"General Bascombe. He's a real straight shooter," Banks remarked. "I served under him in Desert Storm. There's no way that he could possibly be connected with any of this garbage. Nobody loves this country more than General Bascombe."

"Well, according to the story they just ran on the news, your friend, the General, is dead!" Beckert reiterated.

"I don't believe a word of it!" the older agent snapped back. "It would take a good army to kill that old soldier. And, besides that, the General doesn't even drink!"

*****

Jessie was still weeping when she picked up her phone. She hit a speed-dial button and held the phone to her ear.

"Hello? Jessie?" a woman answered.

"Yes, Mom, it's me," she sobbed.

"What's wrong, Dear?" Mrs. Drake asked sympathetically.

"I don't know where to start. So much has happened!" Jessie blurted.

"Is it about a boy?" her mother asked.

In the background, Jessie heard her father ask: "What's that girl's problem now?"

"Hush, Wilbur!" Mrs. Drake insisted while covering the wrong end of the phone with the palm of her hand. "Our poor misguided daughter's in tears over some boy and she's calling her Mommy for support!"

"Mom, you *do* know that I can hear you, don't you?" Jessie wondered aloud.

"What's that, Dear?" Mrs. Drake asked.

"You always do that. You talk to Dad and you put your hand over the earpiece so I'm not supposed to hear it!" the young woman sniffled.

"So, who's the boy this time?" Sophie continued. "Oh wait, I'll put you on the speaker so your Daddy can hear you, too. Say 'hello' to Daddy."

"No! Wait, Mom! Don't!" Jessie implored her, knowing full well that it was already way too late. "Hello, Daddy!" she added in exasperation.

"Hello, Jessie! Now you just tell me this boy's name and I'll hunt the slimy little bugger down!" Wilbur barked at the speakerphone.

"No, Daddy, it's not like that at all!" Jessie pleaded. "I love this boy and I haven't heard from him. He was hurt really badly and I need to find him!"

"Well, is he a *nice* boy?" Sophie asked indulgently.

"Mom, he's so sweet — and honest — and innocent — and wonderful. He's just so unbelievable!" Jessie answered between sobs.

"How did you meet him?" her Mom inquired.

"Well, these four guys were chasing me and I saw a blind boy and a big dog right before they knocked me out!" Jessie began.

"Somebody knocked you unconscious?" Wilbur yelled.

"Yes, Daddy, but Daniel saved me from them," Jessie continued.

"So, this boy Daniel is blind?" Sophie asked incredulously.

"No, he's not really blind. It just makes it easier for him to keep his dog with him if people think he's blind," Jessie replied.

"So, this sweet, honest boy Daniel is really just a liar?" Wilbur barked.

"No, he doesn't actually lie, so much as he—" Jessie began.

"As he just doesn't tell the truth," Wilbur interrupted. "Now, you go right ahead and tell your story while I put my boots on!"

"So, did you meet this Daniel when you woke up in the hospital?" Mom asked.

"No, actually I woke up in his bed the next day," Jessie responded.

"I'm getting my shotgun!" Wilbur screamed from the background as he stomped over towards the closet. He reached behind the coats and pulled the weapon out.

"No, Daddy! Nothing happened! I swear to God! Nothing!"

Jessie sobbed.

"You woke up in some strange guy's bed and nothing happened?" Wilbur yelled as he injected shells into his pump-action shotgun.

"Nothing, Daddy! I still had my clothes on and everything!" the young woman went on. "In fact, I didn't even know he could see until I took *my* clothes off and started to put *his* clothes on!"

"What?" Wilbur yelled as he dropped his gun butt-first on the floor. Poor Sophie screamed as the shotgun discharged into the ceiling and chunks of plaster showered down.

"Mom? Dad? What was that?" Jessie screeched into the phone.

"Don't worry, Dear. Your Daddy just had a little accident and I nearly had one, too!" Mrs. Drake exclaimed as she punched her husband angrily on the arm. "Now, why were you in bed with this Daniel?"

"Mom, I wasn't in bed with him. I was just *in* his bed," Jessie explained.

"Well, that's your business, Dear. After all, you've told us that you've gone out with *how* many guys since high school?" Sophie asked as her tears welled up.

"Ninety-one, Mom," Jessie sighed in exasperation.

"Well, if you've slept with ninety-one guys, what's one more?" Sophie sobbed.

"Mom, you don't understand! I've gone out with ninety-one guys, because I *don't* go to bed with them. If you don't 'put out' after one or two dates, they don't call you back again!" the young woman blubbered.

"Hmm," Wilbur intoned, "now that almost makes some weird kind of sense!"

"Then you haven't slept with *any* of those boys?" Jessie's Mom asked.

"No, Mom. You always told me to 'save something for the honeymoon,' so I've been saving!" the girl replied, fanning herself and muttering. "I've *really* been saving!"

"So, what's this Daniel's last name?" Mom asked politely.

"His name is Daniel Johnstone. He's only a teenager and he owns his own company," Jessie assured her.

"Johnstone?" Wilbur yelled. "Johnstone's the crazy maniac who blew up that whole Rev-Tech complex!"

"No, Daddy!" Jessie yelled back. "We were being invaded by evil aliens, so Daniel and his big dog Job and their alien friends helped save all of us!"

There was a long pause as Jessie's parents stood gaping at each other.

"Girl, have you been smoking those funny-smelling cigarettes?" Wilbur asked suspiciously.

"No, Daddy! I swear to God. Daniel and his dog Job have this alien presence in them. See? And they've got a flying saucer called the *Dorius* and they saved us from the evil Bardokians!" Jessie blurted.

Wilbur and Sophie looked at each other for quite a long while: each motioning the other towards the phone to speak and both shaking their heads from side to side.

"Mom? — Dad?" Jessie pleaded. "Are you still there?"

"Yes, Dear," Sophie finally sat down to say. "And this boy's just a teenager?"

"Well, actually he's much older, but he could easily pass for sixteen," her daughter responded.

"How — *much* — older?" Sophie asked cautiously.

"He said he was born in 1838, but you can't tell at all by looking at him," Jessie replied.

"So, he's as old as your Grampa?" her Mom asked reluctantly.

"No, Woman! That would be *19-38*! She said *18*-38. This boy's older than dirt!" Wilbur corrected her, then he added: "Jessie, if you're at home, you stay right where you are. I'll be there as soon as I can and we'll get you all the help that you need."

"Daddy, I'm not crazy!" Jessie laughed.

"Honey, nobody's calling you 'crazy.' You just need some help. There's no shame in that. Everybody needs a little help sometimes," her father said solemnly.

"But, Daddy, I know I'm not crazy. They just let me out of the psychiatric unit of the army hospital! Now, they wouldn't have let me out if I were crazy, would they?" Jessie insisted.

Wilbur folded his arms on the table in front of him and burst into tears. He dropped his head down in his arms. Sophie stroked his hair as she picked up the phone.

"Jessie, you made your Daddy cry!" she wept.

"I'm sorry, Mommy!" Jessie bawled. "Tell Daddy I'm sorry, too!"

Wilbur raised his head slowly and sobbed: "You just hang on tight, Sweetie! We're coming to help you. We're going to get you all the help that you need. And I'm going to make that horrible monster pay for every terrible thing that he's done to you!"

Sophie and Wilbur could only hear a dull thud on the line as Jessie's phone bounced off her shoes.

*****

"It's going down now. Hit it!" Banks screamed.

Two separate teams rushed to the doors of Jessie's apartment. She had wedged a chair under the doorknob in the kitchen, so the team that broke through the back door had to ram it three times before it gave way. By the time they got to the living room, the first team was already standing there.

"Hello? Hello, Jessie?" Sophie continued to plead on the phone. "Please, answer me. What's happening, Jessie? Is anybody there?"

Banks spotted the phone resting on Jessie's clothes. He picked it up and stared at it for just a moment. Then, he barked: "Sorry, Lady! Wrong number." He hung up.

"No sign of her anywhere, Agent Banks," Beckert announced.

"No sign of her anywhere, Agent Banks!" the senior agent mimicked the young man, then he screamed: "Now tell me something that I *don't* already know!"

Banks hurled Jessie's phone wildly and smashed it against the wall.

*****

Daniel held the blanket up with the top edge above his eye level.

"Job, are you sure she's going to materialize right here in front of me?" he asked.

The dog looked up at him and sighed.

Suddenly, there was a high-pitched scream.

"You *MORON!*" Jessie yelled while fumbling to cover her naked body with her hands. "Daniel Johnstone, you are an *ABSOLUTE MORON!*"

The voice was coming from behind the boy. Daniel gazed ashamedly down at his feet, then he closed his eyes and shook his head slowly from side to side.

"And don't you *dare* turn around!" she added threateningly.

"Jessie, I'm sorry! You were supposed to materialize on the other side of this blanket!" Daniel protested, while maintaining his posture.

"Don't turn around. Don't you dare move one muscle! Just hand me that blanket over your head," she screamed angrily.

He swung the blanket behind him and felt it snatched viciously out of his hand. She immediately wrapped herself in the heavy blanket.

"You're sorry. You're always sorry. 'Sorry, sorry, sorry!' I'm so sick of 'you're sorry.' That's all I ever hear!" she muttered.

"Okay, now give me your shoe!" Jessie demanded furiously.

Without turning around, the boy apprehensively raised his right foot high enough to remove his shoe. He dropped it onto the deck of the ship and slid it back towards the girl with his right foot. Jessie reached down and picked it up. With one quick toss, she bounced it off his head.

"Ow!" he yelped. "That *hurt*, Jessie!" The boy held his ear to allay the stinging.

"Okay, now the other one!" she barked angrily.

"Alright, but try not to hit my ear this time," he replied. He carefully balanced on his right foot and removed his left shoe. He very reluctantly propelled that shoe backwards, as well, but this time he braced himself: shielding both of his ears with his hands.

The young woman walked up behind him and swatted him sharply across the backside with his shoe.

"Hey! That really smarts!" the boy cried out in pain. "Can I turn around yet?"

"Not yet. So whose idea is it to transport people willy-nilly through the universe without their clothes on?" Jessie asked angrily.

"Now, wait a minute! That's not my fault!" Daniel protested.

"I'm listening!" the girl snapped back.

"Kandar is a very proud, educated, aristocratic Ionian. He is embarrassed to death to have to do his 'business' in public and walk around naked in the body of Job. He could probably transport people with their clothes on, too, but it's his little way of evening up the score for the lot that he's had to endure," the boy explained.

"Well, Mr. Kandar, I guess I owe you one, too, then!" she screamed as she threw the shoe at the dog.

Job yawned as the shoe froze mid-air. When the dog finally released it, it dropped straight to the floor having lost all forward momentum.

"Yeah, that Job — he's a really hard target to hit!" Daniel remarked with a laugh.

"Are you laughing at me, Mr. Rev-Tech? Do you think this is at all funny?" she screamed at the boy.

"No, Jessie, I'm not laughing. Honest, I'm not!" he snickered.

"Well, you better not be, because I'm not done with you yet!" Jessie barked back. "Now give me your socks!"

"Okay, my socks," the boy muttered, while reluctantly bending over slightly to remove them in compliance. He threw both socks over his head in the girl's general direction. The girl balled them up together and bounced them off his head.

"Aren't you getting tired of this?" Daniel asked impatiently.

"Not at all, Mr. Johnstone. Take off your shirt!" she barked.

The boy sighed and unbuttoned his shirt. He pulled the shirttail out of his pants and quickly slid his arms out. As soon as he freed himself from the shirt, he tossed it back over his head.

"Okay. So, are you happy yet?" the boy asked with a hint of annoyance.

"Pants!" Jessie snapped back.

"You've *got* to be kidding me!" Daniel exclaimed as he began to turn around.

"Freeze, Mr. Rev-Tech! You do *NOT* turn around until I tell you to! Do you understand me?" she screamed.

There was no immediate answer.

"*DO - YOU – UN – DER - STAND - ME?*" Jessie bellowed at the top of her lungs.

"Okay! *Yes*, I understand you! I understand you!" the boy said in exasperation.

Then, she repeated her demand: "Pants!"

"Jeez!" the boy muttered as he leaned forward to remove his pants. He slowly unzipped and unbuckled his trousers, then he stepped out of them: one leg at a time. He held them up in front of himself and folded them neatly in half. Finally, with an obvious sigh of resignation, he tossed them back over his head.

"Jessie! I mean it, I'm really sorry. You were supposed to materialize in front of the blanket and I wouldn't have seen you. *We were supposed to be happy!*" he pleaded.

"Underpants!" she demanded.

"No way!" the boy protested as he again began to turn around.

"Freeze right there!" Jessie screamed. "You do *NOT* turn around until I tell you to; or I am walking right out of here and you will *never* see me again! Never, *EVER!* Do you understand me?"

"Okay, I'm not moving, but I'm not taking my underwear off

either," Daniel replied adamantly.

"You mean you don't want to snuggle under this nice cozy blanket?" she cooed.

The boy stopped for just a moment to ponder that question.

"I hope you're ready, Jessie, 'cause here they go!" he said playfully as he bent slightly and dropped his briefs to the floor. He stood there naked with his back to her and kicked his underwear off to the side.

"Can I turn around now?" he asked, smiling.

"Yes, Dear. Come snuggle in this nice, soft, cozy blanket," she teased, coyly holding the blanket up in front of her body.

He turned around to look at her. She stood about twelve feet away holding the blanket up under her chin.

"Ta-*DAAA!*" she intoned, just as she dropped the corner of the blanket from her left hand and held it out towards him with her right,

There was an awkward silence as Daniel's jaw dropped.

"That's not fair!" the boy protested. "You're wearing my clothes!"

She grinned victoriously and, having second thoughts about the blanket, tossed it back over her head — and well out of Daniel's reach.

"My mother told me that I should always 'save something for the honeymoon'!" she snapped back, before she focused on the young man's nakedness.

"Wow!" Jessie exclaimed, finally looking at Daniel's perfect, muscular, teenage body. She had seen lots of pictures of men's naked bodies in her twenty-two years, but she had never seen anyone who could compare with Daniel — and certainly not up close and personal!

"I'm sorry," Daniel began, totally mortified. "Like you said once before: it's nearly two hundred years of pent-up teenage hormones!"

Jessie's vengeful attempt to humiliate the boy had suddenly taken an unexpected turn.

"I mean: Wow!" Jessie repeated. "No. Don't apologize. No, no, no. We can fix this. We can make this right. I mean *that* is amazing! We *have* to make this right," she rambled as she unbuttoned the neck of the shirt. "What do we do now, Mr. Rev-Tech?"

"Well, you did say 'honeymoon' before, didn't you? You *definitely* said you were 'saving something for the honeymoon,'" Daniel insisted. And then he wondered aloud: "I mean, would you actually marry me?"

"Yes!" she replied with her eyes beaming. "Yes, I'll marry you! I thought you'd never ask!" She bit her lip anxiously.

"Okay, give me a second! Let me think about this. As the captain of the *Dorius*, I can officiate at weddings!" the boy rationalized hurriedly. Jessie unbuckled the pants.

"Do you, Jessica Drake, take me, Daniel Johnstone, to be your lawfully wedded husband?" he stammered, as she fumbled with the zipper.

"What?" she asked, transfixed by his naked, flexing body.

"Do you, Jessica Drake, take me, Daniel Johnstone, to be your lawfully wedded husband?" he repeated more slowly and patiently.

"Uh, yes! I will. I mean, I do—" she hesitated briefly.

"I mean: I — will — do — *any*-thing!" she vamped sexily.

"And I, Daniel Johnstone, do take you, Jessica Drake, to be my lawfully wedded wife," he added quickly.

She dropped the pants and tripped slightly, as she approached the boy. His shirt still covered her body nearly to her knees.

"Is there anyone present who duly objects to this couple being bonded in holy matrimony?" Daniel added offhandedly. They both looked at Job. The dog sighed and lay down with his paws crossed over his head.

"By the power vested in me by the planet Ionus, I hereby pronounce us man and wife!" the boy rattled the words out as fast as they would come. "I may now kiss the bride!" he added, extending his arms out expectantly.

"Ionus?" Jessica asked, pausing, but undoing another button. "Is this even legal?"

"As Job is my witness!" he replied solemnly with his left hand on his heart and his right palm raised in testimony.

"Well, I, for one, would trust Job with my life!" she said softly. Suddenly, she stopped mid-stride and thought for a moment.

"In fact, come to think of it, I should be *marrying* Job, because *he's the one who saved my life!*" she yelled defiantly, as the realization set in.

"Hey! I had to escape from those soldiers. I killed three Bardokians and took two bullets trying to rescue you!" Daniel protested.

"You took two bullets for me?" she cooed, releasing another button.

"Yes, don't you remember? One in the arm and one in the thigh?" he replied.

"Does Danny want me to kiss them and make them better?" she asked in a babyish tone. He held his left arm out and pointed to the nearly invisible mark that was once a bullet wound.

"That's it?" she blurted in amazement, while undoing another

242

button.

"Oh, well," she added and kissed the tiny mark.

"And, where else?" she inquired, looking up into his eyes.

"Right thigh," he mumbled.

With just the bottom button left secured, she let the shirt slide back off her arms and down around her ankles. She locked her fingers behind his neck and gently pulled his face down towards hers.

"I'll get there," she whispered, as she kissed him passionately. "Eventually—"

Chapter 10

Revelations

Only four days had passed since Jessie and Daniel's onboard wedding. The fishing was good on Bascombe's ranch; Daniel was an excellent provider; and, they were both greatly enjoying married life. They had covered the windows of the barn where the *Dorius* rested, but they were still uneasy about the present state of affairs. Daniel was quite understandably concerned about the reports of the General's death. Not only was Jerome an old friend, but it was only a matter of time before somebody would come to investigate his real estate holdings — including this ranch. It was just past seven when Daniel noticed that Job sat up with his ears at alert.

"What is it, Job?" the boy asked.

Within a second or two, Daniel could hear it clearly for himself: a vehicle moving at a high rate of speed. He dropped his fishing rod and jumped up.

"Jessie, let's get back to the barn. Somebody's coming!" he informed her.

"Nobody knows we're here," she protested.

"It doesn't matter what we think we know. There's a car coming and we have to get back to the ship," Daniel insisted. "Right now!"

"Okay, already! I'm coming!" Jessie said with exasperation.

He grasped her by the hand and practically pulled her off the ground.

"Hey, Big Guy! I said, I'm coming!" she repeated, slightly annoyed.

The boy was not about to wait for Jessie to get her legs in gear. He lifted her into his arms and ran up the hill towards the barn. Job ran just ahead of them. As they reached the top of the grassy mound, they could see a trail of dust rising from the roadway beyond the barn. It was going to be a close race.

"Okay, I see it! We can all run faster if you'd just put me down!" Jessie exclaimed.

Daniel lowered her to her feet and then grasped her hand. Together they dashed towards the back of Bascombe's barn. Suddenly Job bolted out ahead and waited at the door. As soon as Daniel arrived there, he unlatched it and they all rushed into the old wooden structure. The boy secured the door behind them.

"Jessie, get on the *Dorius*," he insisted.

"We're in this together, Sweetie. Whatever happens to you affects me, too," she responded, with just a hint of trepidation.

"Please, Jessie, get on the *Dorius*. I have a bad feeling about this!" he pleaded.

"Yes, Master!" she answered sarcastically. "If this is the way it's going to be, I might just file for a divorce!"

"Well, under Ionian law, marriage is for life. So, you're going to need a really good Ionian lawyer, a dowry for your replacement and, of course, you'll have to pay for your own execution," Daniel deadpanned.

"Under American law, I'm not even sure that we're married!" she sassed back.

Reluctantly, Jessie walked up the ramp onto the ship and waited just inside the airlock. Daniel stood near the window with the best view of the dirt road that accessed the ranch and he peeked from behind the makeshift curtains. A small black sedan came to an abrupt halt near the door to the barn.

The boy didn't immediately recognize the lone occupant of the vehicle until he passed within twenty feet of the window. It was

General Bascombe, but he was in mufti. Daniel ran to open the door, quite obviously overjoyed to see the old man.

"Jerry, it's great to see you. I was so worried about you!" the boy greeted him and immediately extended his hand. The General clasped his hand and wrapped his left arm around the boy's shoulder.

"I didn't know if I'd be able to come here, Danny," the old man replied. "I'm honestly not sure if I did the right thing, but I put in with this elite group that claims they want to side with you against the 'powers that be.'"

Daniel looked at the General, apparently at a loss.

"We heard that you were dead!" the boy exclaimed.

"Yeah, well — that could still happen at any moment, but now nobody would even miss me. My whole family thinks I'm already buried," Jerome intoned sadly.

"That isn't fair to anyone. We're going to have to fix that somehow," Daniel said.

"I don't know what can be done at this point. The President wouldn't listen to reason, so I joined up with this small cadre of CIA and Special Ops. They're telling me that they want me to be their liaison with you and Kandar, but I really suspect that they just want the ship," the General explained. "They faked my death to get the President off my back."

"Do you have any reason not to trust them?" the boy asked.

"I have *every* reason not to trust them!" the old man replied. "Like I said, they're Special Ops and CIA. They don't follow any rule books! I just wasn't sure what else I could do at the time."

"Well, now that you're here, you're safe with us," Daniel assured him.

Job nudged the boy's leg to get his attention.

"I may have spoken too soon," the boy added. Now he himself could hear the sound of at least one other vehicle approaching rapidly.

"They already seemed to know where you were, so it was just a matter of time before they'd show up here," the General muttered. "I honestly don't know if they're here to make friendly contact or if they have more sinister intentions."

"I guess we're about to find out," Daniel replied. "Maybe you should wait on the *Dorius,* Jerry."

"Ordinarily, I'd jump at the prospect of climbing aboard a flying saucer, but I'm not going to leave you here to deal with these buggers alone!" the old man insisted.

"Daniel, is that your friend the General?" Jessie asked from the airlock's ramp.

"Oh, Jessie, I'd like you to meet my dear friend: General Jerome Bascombe," Daniel began, gesturing with his left arm while keeping both of his eyes firmly focused on two approaching vehicles. "Jerry, this is my beautiful wife Jessie."

"Hello, I'm very pleased to meet you. I think we've already met — although under rather deplorable circumstances," the General smiled. "Congratulations to both of you!"

"Thank you!" Jessie and Daniel replied nearly in unison. Then the boy added: "Jessie, get back inside the ship! This is starting to look like trouble."

The first vehicle pulled up behind the General's sedan. The second one drove toward the back of the barn. The occupants of the first vehicle walked straight to the front door. Young Ben stood to one side while Mr. Jacobs knocked.

"I'd better get that!" the General insisted.

He unlocked the barn door with his left hand and waved them in. Then he stood there casually with his right hand in the pocket of his jacket. Daniel stood with Job only a few feet nearer to the entrance of the *Dorius*. The boy focused on the two new faces while the dog was keenly aware of the men approaching from behind the barn.

"This is a private party. I don't remember having invited either of you gentlemen!" the General announced. "But seeing that you're here, I'd like you to meet my young friend Daniel, whom I've told you about. Danny, this is Mr. Jacobs of the CIA and his associate Ben from Special Ops."

"I've heard about people restoring old cars in their barns, but don't this beat everything!" Mr. Jacobs joked. "How much do you want for her, Kid?"

"She's not for sale," Daniel said quietly.

"That's a shame. I thought we could be reasonable," Ben mumbled.

"Now, now. Let's not be too hasty," Jacobs admonished them. "I'm sure that we can still negotiate a deal that will satisfy all interested parties."

"This ship belongs to Kandar of Ionus," Daniel insisted. "I am its caretaker and it is not for sale."

"General Bascombe, perhaps you can appeal to your young friend's patriotism and broker a deal?" Jacobs asked with a somewhat devious smile. "It would be a shame if anybody got hurt here."

"Mr. Jacobs, I can assure you that nobody *that I care about* is going to get hurt," the General retorted. "The disposition of the ship is entirely up to Daniel."

"Well then, maybe I can change your perspective," Mr. Jacobs continued, while removing a small plastic bag from the pocket of his jacket. "Do you recognize this, General? We found it in your uniform waistcoat just before we put it on that unfortunate corpse." He walked two steps closer to the officer and held the bag out to him.

The General grabbed the bag with his left hand and glanced at the contents.

"If that came out of my jacket pocket, then I suppose it's my handkerchief," the old man replied. "How am I supposed to know for sure that it's the same one?"

"Well, you see, General, that's the interesting part. Of course, it's all dry now, but both that handkerchief and the inside of your pocket were covered in blood and tissue samples," Jacobs continued. "We didn't know where any of that came from, so we ran some tests on all of it."

"And?" Bascombe interjected.

"It isn't your blood, General," the CIA agent continued. "But when we tried to match the DNA with anyone in our database, yours was the closest match."

"That isn't possible," the old man replied, totally unimpressed by the obvious bluff. "There is no way on earth that I could be related to the source of those samples!"

"Here are the printouts," Jacobs insisted as he reached inside his jacket for them.

Job leaned against Daniel's leg for just a moment and the boy's face blanched from the sudden drain of energy. A drop of blood trickled from his nose and he placed his hand on the dog's head to steady himself, while the General scanned over the reports.

"Gentlemen, secure the area!" Mr. Jacobs commanded into his earpiece.

There was no response, so the CIA operative adjusted the electronic device.

"Gentlemen, secure the area!" he repeated.

"I hope your friends can swim," Daniel suggested.

The four naked agents had materialized in the middle of the fishing pond behind the barn. There were some barely-audible screams in the distance and a good deal of flailing and confusion there, as well.

"What did you do to my men?" Ben asked threateningly.

"They just decided to go skinny-dipping about a quarter mile behind this place," Daniel replied nonplussed.

"You know, Kid: I don't need their help to take you down!" Ben insisted as he reached inside his windbreaker.

"Young Man, were you thinking that I was just happy to see you?" the General asked as he fired his pistol through his jacket. The bullet hit Ben in the right leg just as he was grasping at his own weapon. He was thrown to the floor writhing in pain.

"Now, don't you even think about it!" Bascombe ordered Jacobs.

The CIA man raised his hands away from his torso.

"I hope you realize that none of you are getting out of here alive," he told them.

Job nudged Daniel as the approaching helicopters droned in the distance. Jessie ran out of the *Dorius* to see what was happening. She immediately saw Ben in agony and bleeding on the ground.

"Are you guys just going to stand around here killing each other?" she screamed at everyone present. "You have to do something to help that man!"

"Jessie, please stay out of this and get back on the ship!" Daniel ordered her.

"Nobody is dying here on *my* watch!" she screamed back. She walked straight to the nearest window and ripped the make-shift "curtain" down. Then she brought it over to Ben and wrapped it around his wounded leg. Suddenly, a beam of blinding light burst through the newly-uncovered window as the first helicopter landed just outside the barn.

"Everybody on the *Dorius*!" Daniel yelled as he and Job backed toward the ship.

Jerome freed his pistol from the constraints of his jacket and aimed it squarely at Mr. Jacobs: "Tell them to stand down!"

"Did you actually think you could keep that thing for yourselves?" Jacobs scoffed. "You just started a war that you can't possibly win! My men are under orders to secure this area, *and that ship,* regardless of what you do to me."

Bascombe edged over towards the ramp, still leveling his old .45 at the agent.

"Jessie, leave him be! You have to come with us. Now!" Daniel pleaded.

"This man needs help!" she screamed back in frustration.

Jerome and Job were both within the airlock when the boy started to run towards Jessie. Suddenly, bullets ripped through the exposed glass and the short distance separating the two lovers was filled with a stream of deadly flying lead.

"Jessie!" Daniel cried out, as he retreated into the ship.

The young woman tried to get up, but Ben grabbed her by the arm of her jacket. He held his gun to her head as the outer hatch of the *Dorius* sealed shut.

"Daniel!" she screamed with tears running down her cheeks.

"Don't leave me!"

"Job! Now!" Daniel ordered from within the airlock.

Jessie managed to rise to her feet with Ben in tow. He struggled to stand and maintained a firm grip on her jacket as he raised his pistol to her ear. Mr. Jacobs fired his gun until he emptied his clip at the hatch of the *Dorius* — with no effect.

"*DANIEL!*" Jessie shrieked as loudly as she could.

"You open your mouth one more time and I'm going to put a bullet through it!" Ben threatened. Then he screamed: "*Do you hear me?*"

Jessie jabbed him in the ribs with her elbow as hard as she could. Ben raised his pistol above her head and swung it down with all the strength that he could muster. The butt of his pistol sliced down through the empty jacket and hit him solidly in the groin.

"Ooh! Where the—?" Ben muttered just before he collapsed unconscious over Jessie's clothes.

*****

"*DANIEL!!!*" Jessie screeched as she realized what had happened. She immediately covered her body with her hands and arms as best she could, but the General stood gaping from across the cargo bay. He was as awe-stricken by her sudden appearance as he was shocked by her nakedness.

"*FINE! TAKE A GOOD LOOK!!!*" she bellowed. Daniel tossed the blanket over her just before she threw her arms out and splayed her legs. She pulled the blanket down from her face and managed to wrap it around herself.

"I'm going to kill you! — I'm going to divorce you!!" she muttered; and more emphatically added, "And *then I'm going to kill you again!!!"*

The General couldn't help but chuckle.

"Jerome, please don't laugh," Daniel whispered, but it was too late.

"So, you think this is funny, Old Man?" Jessie threatened. She started to reach for her shoe and suddenly realized she was barefoot. She plopped down on the floor and burst into tears.

"I'm never going to marry another spaceman again!" she bawled.

Neither Daniel nor the General could control themselves as they both burst into raucous laughter. Jessie huddled under the blanket and she couldn't help herself either. She began to laugh nearly as loudly as the two men, while her tears continued to flow.

There was a sudden impact on the hatch and then a second one.

"I think it's time for us to leave," the General posited. "Daniel, are you sure you can fly this thing?"

"We're about to find out," he replied as he walked towards the storage unit. "You probably should put this on." He handed Jerome the pressure suit that was hanging in Professor Markus' locker, then he brought Shahlaya's flight suit to Jessie.

"I think you're both going to find that these are a little big on you," Daniel said. "Ionians tend to be a rather tall race of people." He held the blanket in front of Jessie while she slipped Shahlaya's suit on. Then he handed her the helmet.

"General, you'll probably need your helmet, too," the boy advised. "You just slip it over your head and twist the collar a quarter turn to the right. I'll tell you when you need it." He opened the hatch to the crew's quarters on the side of the ship opposite the sickbay and led the way.

"Jerome, sit here and strap yourself in tight. I'm a student driver!"

Daniel warned.

He turned around to see Jessie in Shahlaya's suit. She was slightly hunched over with the arms of the suit nearly touching the ground. She waddled into the crew's quarters and Daniel directed her to her seat. He strapped her in and he was about to assist her with the helmet, when she held up her hand.

"Wait a minute! What if I get sick in here?" she asked.

"Then try to think of that visor as a kaleidoscope and enjoy the pretty colors!" he responded. He secured her helmet and he was about to walk back to the cargo bay, when she punched him solidly on the left arm.

Daniel walked up the steps to the cockpit and strapped himself in. Job climbed up there, as well, and sat between the boy's legs. The dog assured him that Kandar had overridden his 'my voice only' command and Daniel had already plugged his communicator into the computer's interface. The boy put on his dark sunglasses, closed his eyes tightly and opened his mind to Kandar's presence. He reached out blindly, but instinctively, at the controls and a low hum permeated the *Dorius*. He opened his eyes and looked through the canopy as the inside of the barn glowed with swirls of flashing multicolored lights. He barely touched the throttle and watched attentively as the underside of the barn roof slowly approached.

*****

Mr. Jacobs grabbed Ben by the arm and dragged him towards the door of the old farm building as the ship slowly rose. The lights emanating from the ship's thruster-rings were almost mesmerizing, but the older man focused on getting through that doorway as quickly as possible. Neither of them had the remotest idea of what a safe

254

distance from the ship's thrusters might be, but both assumed: the farther the better. Just as they cleared the doorway, a squad of Special Ops agents smashed their way into the barn.

"It's too late! Clear the area!" Jacobs screamed into his ear-piece. The agents stood around the *Dorius* transfixed by the spectacle of the dancing lights and the rising ship.

"Get out of there, you morons!" Jacobs bellowed. He could hear the agents emptying their weapons at the ship in cacophonous rapid fire. Then there was a momentary silence before he heard someone scream: "Run!" The barn windows exploded outward with the bodies of the agents fleeing the scene as the hum of the *Dorius* increased to an intolerable level.

*****

"General, make sure your helmet's secure!" Daniel yelled out as an afterthought.

He pulled the throttle a quarter-way back and the ship smashed through the roof of the barn. For just a second, the boy thought he saw a few military helicopters hovering around the old structure as the *Dorius* soared up toward the clouds. If they had fired at the ship, there was no impact felt nor was he aware of any sounds emanating from outside his vessel. He could see the moon and the stars clearer than he had ever seen them before. The ship was soon safely in a high orbit above the earth.

*****

"*Dorius,* maintain orbit," Daniel commanded.

"Good boy, Job!" the boy hugged his dog. "And, thank you, Kandar! Thank you ever so much! I couldn't have done any of this without you." Daniel was keenly aware of all that the Ionian had done to assist in their escape. It was obvious that Kandar was doing everything within his power to keep the boy and his friends safe.

"Now, let's go check on Jessie and the General," he suggested, and together they descended the few steps to the cargo bay.

The boy opened the hatch to the crew's quarters and he was somewhat surprised to see the two of them clutching the arms of their seats. He tapped on Jessie's helmet to get her attention. She looked up at him as he twisted her collar to remove her helmet.

"Aren't we supposed to be going somewhere?" she asked him.

"We're already there," he assured her, then he removed the General's helmet. The old man had just fallen sound asleep. Daniel released the harnesses from both of them. The General opened one eye.

"Did I miss anything?" he asked.

"Come and see for yourself," the boy insisted. He led them back through the cargo bay to the cockpit area and directed their attention to the stars.

"That sure doesn't look like that old barn roof!" Jerome exclaimed.

"I don't know if we'll ever get back there again, but I probably owe you a whole new roof," the boy apologized. "In fact, I *might* owe you a whole new barn!"

Jessie stood next to the boy looking at the stars through the canopy.

"Okay, I see stars. So, where are we?" she inquired.

"Follow me, Jessie," the young man suggested as he rose into the cockpit. She stooped down next to the pilot's seat and looked up through the canopy.

"*Dorius*, rotate slowly one hundred-eighty degrees on the

horizontal axis," the boy commanded. The ship began the slow rotation. First, a very large moon filled the canopy and then a distant mottled blue sphere of nearly the same dimensions.

"*Dorius,* stop rotation," Daniel intoned as the earth replaced the view of the moon.

"My Gawd!" Jessie's jaw dropped. "I'm going to be sick. I am *SO* afraid of heights!" The color drained from her face.

"No, Jessie, listen to me!" the boy ordered. "We're in space, so there's no 'up' or 'down.' There is no sense of 'height.' Do you understand me? We have artificial gravity to keep everything right where it belongs."

"I certainly hope you're right about keeping things where they belong, because I think I'm about to lose my cookies," she muttered.

"Don't even think that!" Daniel said with real concern. "Job, do we have anything onboard for motion sickness?"

The dog loped to the sickbay and came back with a vial of pills. Daniel took the container from the dog and stared at the Ionian label. He closed his eyes for a moment to approximate a translation, then he dumped a pill out into his hand and placed it in Jessie's open palm.

"Here, chew this," he advised her.

"What? Like your dog's suddenly a pharmacist?" she asked apprehensively.

"Kandar knows how much I love you and he wouldn't hurt you for the world," the boy whispered. "Just chew it and swallow it. You'll feel better."

"I hope so!" she snapped back. She put the pill in her mouth and slowly chewed it until she could swallow it. "At least it didn't taste bad. Have you got anything to drink?"

The boy walked across the cargo bay to a dispenser. "*Dorius,* the traditional cold beverage in a drinking glass, please." The dispenser produced a container filled with an orange fluid. The boy took a sip from the glass, before he handed it to Jessie.

"I think you'll like this," he postulated.

"Are you sure it's safe to drink?" she asked as she took a small sip. She closed her eyes and swirled the fluid around her mouth with her tongue before she swallowed it.

"Nice!" she exclaimed. "Now *that's* what I call a drink!"

"Jerome, would you like one?" the boy asked.

"I don't mind if I do," the old man replied. "It's been a long couple of days and I've been busier since I died than I was when I was still alive!"

"*Dorius*, two more drinks, same composition, please," Daniel commanded. The drinks appeared below the dispenser in quick succession. He handed one to the General and kept one for himself. The boy waved toward the wall of the cargo bay and a long couch rolled out of it. He gestured his two companions towards it and added: "I think we should all relax while we contemplate our next move."

"Do you have any idea what this stuff is?" Jessie asked.

"I know that it's a cold, refreshing Ionian beverage," the boy replied — knowing full well that it was the ceremonial Ionian nuptial wine.

"Another one of these and I'll be ready to join the 'mile high club'!" Jessie cooed.

"This stuff really works," Daniel mumbled.

"What?" she asked, only half-hearing the comment.

"Oh, nothing. Just thinking out loud," he assured her.

"You know, I'm not one to tipple, but I'd swear there's alcohol in this drink," the General guessed correctly. "In fact, if the stuff on earth tasted this good, I'd probably never sober up!" he laughed.

The old man leaned back on the cushion and suddenly realized: "You two 'love-birds' are supposed to be on your honeymoon. I'm really sorry to be an intrusion."

"That's quite all right, Jerry," Daniel replied. "It isn't your fault. Sometimes things just don't work out the way you expect."

"Tell me about it!" Jessie muttered to herself.

The General unzipped the flight suit and reached for the papers that Jacobs had given him. He opened them up and put on his reading glasses. As he slowly scanned the columns of data, he pulled out the plastic bag with the handkerchief.

"You're looking upset," Daniel addressed his old friend.

The General sat there for a moment uncomfortably trying to find the proper way to broach the subject.

"I really don't know any other way to ask you this," he began, "but just how close were you and my mother?"

The boy surmised where this conversation was heading.

"After Job here, your father was the best friend that I've ever had," Daniel replied. "I know what you're thinking, but you've got it all wrong."

"According to the analysis of the blood and tissue samples on my handkerchief — *your* blood — there is a 99.9% chance that you are my father!" Jerome exclaimed. "Now *you* tell *me:* what *exactly* do I have wrong?"

"Your Dad Albert was a brilliant physicist. He had the curiosity of a genius and the imagination to solve almost any problem he encountered," the boy began. "He also had cancer when I met him; and, there was no treatment on earth that could save his life."

"My Dad lived well into his nineties!" Bascombe interrupted.

"He wanted to examine the power source of the *Dorius*. I was afraid that neither of us would survive the exposure, but he insisted," Daniel continued. "He didn't want me to take the risk, so he entered the ship while I was at Rev-Tech. When I returned, I found him on the floor of the cargo bay. He had managed to put the shield back over the power source before he collapsed. That saved Job and myself from being exposed."

"So how does that explain this?" the old man asked, holding up the DNA analysis.

"The radiation neutralized all of the pathogens, and all of the cancer, in Albert's body," Daniel continued, "but it also left him sterile."

"So, my father wasn't really my father?" Jerome muttered.

"Don't ever say that! Albert was the best father that you, or anyone else, could ever have hoped for," the boy admonished him. "Your Mom was a brilliant surgeon and your Dad was an extraordinary scientist. They wanted a child and I explained to them that *in vitro* fertilization was not uncommon on Ionus. Albert begged me to provide the genetic material — and nothing more. Maybe he thought that you would inherit some of Kandar's abilities, but I kept telling him that Kandar is in my mind and in my soul, not in my DNA."

"So, *you're* my biological father?" the General asked.

"If you insist on putting it that way, I guess the short answer is: yes," the boy replied quietly. "Nobody was ever supposed to know. That was why your Dad stopped bringing you to visit me. It just wasn't fair to either of us to foster that type of attachment. He knew that I couldn't help but love you, as any father would. And, he was afraid that you would reciprocate."

"I honestly don't know what to say," Jerome said with tears in his eyes. "I had every reason to believe that my parents were both dead and now I have to reassess everything that I thought I knew."

"You mean you married me without even mentioning that you had a kid?" Jessie shrieked at Daniel in horror. "What *other* wonderful surprises are lurking in your two hundred year old alien closet?"

She punched him solidly on the arm before she took another sip from her glass.

"I am *not* changing any diapers! I'm telling you that right up front!" she added.

The General and the boy looked at each other and burst out laughing.

"Well, I'm not!" she insisted. "You guys can laugh all you want to, but when your sixteen year old husband springs his hundred-and-five year old son on you, you just have to draw the line somewhere!"

"Sixty-two!" the somewhat-insulted General insisted with a laugh.

"I know it's a lot to absorb, but I hope that neither of you will hate me for it," Daniel said quietly.

"Hate you?" Jerome asked. "I just don't know what to call you, Uncle Danny."

"Well, that's always worked for us before," the boy assured him.

"So, my stepson is almost three times my age? Where's a mirror? Oh, God, I think my hair is turning gray!" Jessie whimpered as her tears began to flow.

"Hey, Beautiful! I think you've had quite enough of this stuff!" Daniel told her as he reached for her glass.

"No way! Whatever this stuff is, I haven't had *nearly* enough!" she exclaimed. "In fact, get me another one before I find out that I have any *more* kids!"

"She's a 'keeper,' Uncle Danny!" the General roared with laughter.

"Yeah; that she is!" the boy smiled. "I think both of you should go back to the crew's quarters and get some sleep. Believe it or not, there is a washroom in there, if you should need to use it. With the artificial gravity of the *Dorius*, you don't need any special instructions. It's quite intuitive — and safe."

Jessie leaned back on the couch and closed her eyes for a moment. She quickly fell sound asleep. The boy picked her up and carried her into the crew's quarters. He gently lowered her onto the same reclining seat that she had used on take-off. By the time he returned to the cargo hold, the General had drifted off on the couch as well.

"Job, I think they've got the right idea," he told the dog. They walked back into the crew's quarters. Daniel stretched out on the seat next to Jessie and Job lay down between them. The boy reached over and brushed the dog's head lightly as he pondered their predicament and they both sought an appropriate solution.

*****

The boy woke up a couple of hours later with Job asleep at his feet. Daniel got up carefully to avoid stepping on the dog and walked back through the cargo hold. The General was still snoozing on the couch. Job opened his eyes and followed the boy to the pilot's station.

"Where should we go, Job?" the young man wondered aloud. He looked out of the canopy at the earth and then he glanced down at the console. The answer was clearly staring him back in the face.

"I guess we know where we're going. Now, don't we, Boy?" Daniel asked the dog. "Let's hope I can do this without disturbing anyone's sleep." He closed his eyes for just a second and grasped the controls of the ship, then he opened his eyes and interlocked his fingers over his chest. He decided that it might be best if the ship piloted itself.

"*Dorius,* display an image of the nearest planet, please," he ordered; and, a holographic image of the earth appeared before him.

"Magnify only this area: one hundred times," Daniel added as he pointed at the display. "Again, repeat magnification on this specific area."

Satisfied that he had found a safe harbor, he commanded: "*Dorius*, set a course and land precisely where I've indicated. I want the time of arrival to coincide with dawn at the landing site." The ship began a gradual descent into the earth's atmosphere. He rose from the pilot's seat and started toward the steps, when Job looked back at the flight console.

"Good idea, Job! I'm on it," the boy replied as he reached for the object.

"*Dorius,* how much time do I have until arrival under the specified parameters?" he inquired quietly.

"Approximately three hours seventeen minutes by common earth standards," the ship intoned.

"They're going to be expecting a spaceman, so I had better look the part," Daniel told the dog. He walked down the steps to the cargo bay and opened the storage lockers. He knew that Kandar was wearing his own suit, but he also realized that there had to be at least one "backup" in the event of an emergency. He unlatched the door of the fourth locker and there it was.

*****

The ship descended slowly and quietly into the empty square just before the sun rose over the city. There were a number of workmen with push-brooms cleaning both the street and the wide open area that Daniel had chosen for his landing site. He nudged the General's arm as he walked towards the airlock. The old man opened one eye cautiously and sat up, yawning.

"Uncle Danny, do you need help with something?" he asked.

"Maybe," the boy responded. "Let's see how this goes."

"I've got your back," the General assured him as he pulled out his pistol and checked the clip.

"Keep that thing hidden away," Daniel insisted. "That's the one thing that might throw a monkey wrench into the works!" He turned toward the old man with a wide smile and added: "We come in peace."

"Gotcha!" the old man grinned.

"Stay here, Job," he addressed the dog. "I'll be right back."

Daniel opened the inner hatch of the airlock and walked down the ramp towards the outer one. He put the helmet on, but didn't bother to secure the collar. Then he opened the outer hatch.

*****

There was both excitement and confusion as the boy reached the end of the ramp. Two uniformed guards crossed their halberds to block his path. He cautiously removed his helmet to allay their fears, then he reached into his pocket and held his "gift" out towards the guard on his right. The uniformed man extended his open palm to the boy and Daniel lowered the object into his hand. The boy commanded the guard: "Please, give this to your superiors."

Daniel wasn't one hundred percent sure that they completely

understood what he told them, but he had no doubt that the item would soon make its way into the proper hands. He bowed slightly toward the men and turned to walk back up the ramp. As soon as he was safely within the airlock, he closed the outer hatch. He walked into the cargo bay and closed the inner one as well. The General gave him a quizzical look.

"I think it went well," the boy told him. "With any luck, they'll offer us asylum."

He put the helmet back inside the locker and opened the crew's quarters to check on Jessie. She was still sound asleep. He stood there staring at the young woman for a moment and smiled. He walked back out to the cargo hold.

"She's really a thing of beauty!" he told the General.

"That she is!" the old man agreed.

"We'll probably be getting company shortly, so we'd better be prepared," Daniel suggested. "I'm going to write up a shopping list of things that we need, so, if you have any ideas, be sure to let me know."

"Will do," Jerome replied.

*****

It didn't take long before the guards returned with their master, plus an entourage of news-people and photographers. Daniel decided not to wake Jessie, as he was certain that she wouldn't want to be seen in the baggy spacesuit or without serious primping. He opened the airlock's hatches and walked down the ramp with Job and the General trailing close behind. He stopped at the end of the ramp.

"My name is Daniel Johnstone. This is my son Jerome Bascombe and that is my dear friend Job. We have done nothing wrong. We have harmed no one, except in self-defense; but we are being hunted by greedy, power-hungry men," he addressed the crowd. "So, we seek sanctuary here."

"I am Monsignor Buonarroti," the apparent leader began with a slight Italian accent, "Welcome to Vatican City." He extended his hands, palms up, and bowed slightly before his guests in a clear gesture of welcoming. "If that is-a your son, I must advise you that we do things-a differently on this-a planet."

"Uncle Danny, I think he's a little confused by our age difference," interjected the General. "That really *is* a bit hard to explain."

"So, your son is-a your nephew, too?" the holy man asked.

"It's complicated," the boy smiled. "I hope you don't mind our imposing upon you, but there are a few necessities that we really need: including some clothing for my beautiful young wife. And, we would like a clergyman to bless our marriage."

The Monsignor accepted the list, smiling and nodding.

"You gave-a the Guardsman the holy rosary of-a our Blessed Guglielmo Ricchi," the Monsignor began. "How did-a you come by that?"

"He left it behind when we accidentally teleported him to a fountain here in Rome," the boy answered apologetically. "That was around 1850 or so."

"So much-a for the only substantiated miracle of Padre Ricchi!" the old cleric muttered to the priests behind him.

*****

Jessie finally woke up and walked out to the cargo bay. She was slightly hung-over and holding her head with both hands. She looked up towards the cockpit area for Daniel and she lowered her arms to her sides. The sleeves of the flight suit immediately dropped to the floor. She bent over, with her back to the airlock, trying to reach the cuffs of her sleeves to no avail.

"Look! A big-a chimpanzee! Is that-a you space-monkey?" the Monsignor asked loudly while pointing at the figure within the ship. Jessie was still bent over, looking down between her legs at the open airlock, when she heard the comment. She reached for her empty wine glass.

"SPACE MONKEY?!?" she screamed as she spun around and hurled the glass at the apparent speaker. The drinking vessel bounced wildly down the ramp.

"DOES THIS LOOK LIKE A SPACE MONKEY?!?" she bellowed as she unzipped the front of the pressure suit. *"JESUS CHRIST!!!"* she yelled in disgust.

"Close, but no cigar, Jessie! He's only a monsignor!" Daniel yelled back over his shoulder without paying much attention to her appearance.

"Well, maybe a little cigar!" the General mumbled with a grin.

"Say 'hello' to Monsignor Buonarroti, Jessie!" the boy introduced the man as he turned toward his wife and finally realized that she had half-unzipped her flight-suit.

Jessie took a good look at the Monsignor before she looked down at her half-exposed body. She managed to say: "Hell-?" before her eyes rolled up into her head and she passed out, falling backwards onto the couch.

"Yeah, she's a keeper!" the General smiled.

"I'm-a so sorry!" the Monsignor insisted while he repeatedly signed himself with the symbol of the Cross. "Please, please-a forgive me!"

"It's okay, Monsignor!" Daniel assured him. "My wife is quite demonstrative."

"I'm-a so sorry!" the clergyman implored him, while still staring past the boy at Jessie. "Please-a forgive me!"

"It would be easier for me to forgive you, Monsignor, if you could take your eyes off of my wife!" Daniel asserted with a hint of anger. He moved slightly to his right to block the cleric's view of the interior of the ship, but the Monsignor continued to crane his neck in that direction.

"I'm-a so sorry!" the cleric repeated while still leaning to his left.

"Monsignor, I don't speak-a good Italian," Daniel began mocking the man's accent and raising his fist, "but-a my fist is-a gonna meet-a you face, capish?"

"Please, forgive me!" the Monsignor begged, covering his eyes with both of his hands. "I just can't help-a myself. Your wife, she's-a so beautiful!"

Daniel gestured towards the blanket and telekinetically dropped it over Jessie's partially-exposed torso. Then he put his hands on the Monsignor's shoulders and turned him one hundred-eighty degrees, commanding: "List! — That way. — Go!"

"I'm-a go to confession," the Monsignor continued to mutter: "I'm-a so sorry!" He kept peeking over his shoulder even as he ran off towards his chauffeured vehicle.

*****

Wilbur and Sophie Drake were quietly watching television while the broadcast of the spaceship's landing in Saint Peter's Square continued to interrupt all programming.

"Was that Jessie?" Sophie asked, leaning forward.

"Yup!" Wilbur intoned.

"Was I seeing things or did she just 'flash' the Pope?" Jessie's Mom asked.

"I think they said he was a Monsignor 'Boner-something,'" her husband replied.

"So, it wasn't the Pope?" she asked.

"Nope," he assured her. "Just a Monsignor."

"That's better," she smiled.

Wilbur got up and grabbed a cardboard box that was sitting in the corner. He quietly walked around the room, picking up things and putting them in the box.

"What are you doing, Wilbur?" his wife asked him.

"Packing," he replied.

"Are we moving?" she wondered aloud.

"Yup," he answered curtly.

"But Jessie won't know where to find us!" Sophie exclaimed.

"Nope!" Wilbur replied.

*****

Daniel, Job and Jerome had re-entered the ship and sealed the hatches, waiting for the return of the Monsignor and the items on their list. The boy looked at Jessie who was still passed-out on the couch. He reached under the blanket and carefully zipped up her pressure-suit.

"With any luck, she won't remember a thing," he whispered to the General. Then he walked over to the dispenser. "Do you have anything like 'coffee': a hot caffeinated beverage in a mug?" the boy asked the machine. The dispenser produced a mug of hot, dark liquid. Daniel carefully grabbed it by the handle and took a sip.

"I guess I've tasted worse," the boy commented. "But, then, I'm not a coffee-drinker."

"Jerome, would you like one?" he asked.

"Why not?" the old man answered.

"Another 'coffee in a mug,'" Daniel ordered the dispenser. He removed it from the machine and walked it over to the General. Then he lifted Jessie to a seated position and sat down with his arm around her. She opened her eyes briefly.

"Here, have a sip of coffee," he offered.

"Have I got a headache!" she moaned, then she poked him with her elbow. "You got me drunk! You didn't tell me there was alcohol in that drink!"

"Aside from the headache, are you feeling okay?" the boy asked.

"Well, I'm still afraid of heights, if that's what you mean!" she complained.

"You don't have to be. We've landed. The *Dorius* is back on the ground," he assured her.

"Whew! That's a relief!" she gasped. "You know I had the weirdest dream a little while ago — in fact, actually it was more like my worst nightmare!"

"Don't even think about it!" he hushed her. "Everything is going to be fine."

*****

It wasn't long before the Swiss Guards returned with the Monsignor and several boxes. Daniel walked down the ramp to meet them; and, the waiting crowd of people cheered at the sight of the "spaceman" emerging from the flying saucer. He waved at them, but he wasn't sure that he appreciated all of the attention. He had always tried to maintain a low profile.

"I hope that this is-a what you need," the Monsignor began, while covering his eyes with his hands.

"Thank you very much. I'm sure that this will do fine," the boy replied, then he quietly added: "By the way, it's safe to look now!"

The Monsignor uncovered his eyes and cautiously looked up into the ship.

"Young Man, His Holiness is anxious to meet-a you and-a you friends," the cleric continued. "Would it be alright if-a he come here to see-a the flying saucer?"

"Of course. We would be quite honored," Daniel replied. "He's welcome here any time."

"Grazie!" the Monsignor replied with a smile. "Thank you so muchly!"

He turned to walk past the Swiss Guards and paused briefly to wave.

"A-bye-bye!" he added smiling, before he ran to his vehicle.

Daniel ascended the ramp with his arms full of packages and closed the hatches behind him. As he eyed the parcels, he whispered, "Jessie, I hope these clothes will fit you."

*****

The boy set the boxes on the couch. He had ordered fast food for the four of them along with some basic groceries. One box was marked 'requested clothing.' Daniel handed that one to Jessie.

"That's for me?" the young woman smiled.

"I hope you don't mind," the boy said. "I told them that we wanted to have our marriage blessed and that you didn't have anything white to wear for the ceremony."

"That's so sweet!" she gushed. She stood up, threw her arms around the boy and kissed him, saying: "I'm finally going to have my dream wedding!"

"Well, I don't know what was wrong with the wedding that we had," Daniel smirked. "I realize that my memory isn't the best, but I don't remember hearing any complaints about the way we were dressed at the time!"

"You!" she muttered as she pushed him away.

The General just sat there eating, totally bewildered by the conversation. He looked at Daniel and shrugged his shoulders slightly.

"I'll tell you about it sometime," the boy assured him.

"Over my dead body!" Jessie barked. "Haven't you embarrassed me enough already?" She lifted the cover off the box and spread the folds of white tissue paper apart. She could see that it was definitely smooth white material folded neatly in the cardboard carton.

"I know I'm going to love it!" she exclaimed in anticipation. "It's going to be gorgeous!" She lifted the gown out of the box and held it against herself. She had been expecting something a lot lighter in weight — and considerably more sheer and revealing.

"Is that the veil?" she asked Daniel.

He lifted the cover from the inner box and covered his mouth with his hand.

"What's wrong?" she inquired as he began to convulse with laughter.

"Actually, I think it's called a 'wimple,'" he snickered.

"What does a veil have to do with the guy who sells toilet paper?" she wondered aloud. She lifted the white material out of the box and let out a horrified scream.

"*I'm not wearing that!*" she bellowed. "Do you think this is funny, Young Man? I am *not* putting that thing on! NO WAY!!!"

The boy and the General were both doubled over with laughter. She threw the gown at them. Then she hurled the cartons at them for good measure.

"Haven't you embarrassed me enough already?" she screamed between her tears. "You teleported me *naked* to a Cub Scout camp! You teleported me *naked* in front of this Old Goat! And now you want me to go to my wedding in a *nun's habit*?"

"Hey, you 'flashed' the Monsignor all by yourself!" Daniel protested without thinking.

"I...*what*...?" she muttered with rising intensity.

"Never mind," the boy mumbled.

"Oh—my—Gawd! It wasn't a nightmare!" she gasped. "*Oh, my God!* You got me drunk and I wasn't responsible for my actions! I didn't even know it *was* alcohol. *It's all your fault, Daniel Johnstone!*"

She collapsed into a seated position on the floor. She had never *ever* been so humiliated in all of her short life. She stared at the two men and her tears dried as quickly as her anger intensified.

"I want a divorce *or I am going to kill myself!* I can't live like this," she muttered as she picked herself up off the floor. She strode past them, walked into the crew's quarters and slammed the hatch loudly behind her.

"I don't think the Pope's going to bless *that* for you guys!" Jerome opined.

"Jerry, this isn't my fault! I just told them that I needed a white dress for my young wife. I didn't expect anything like this," he protested.

"Well, you *did* know that even nuns have a wedding ceremony, didn't you?" the General asked.

"You've *got* to be kidding me. I had no idea!" the boy admitted.

273

He turned to the dog and confessed, "Job, I love her with all my heart. What can I do to fix this?"

The dog looked at the boy sympathetically. The General got up to stretch his legs, just as he heard a scream coming from the crew's quarters. He ran and tried the hatch, but it was locked from the inside.

*****

"You scared the Hell out of me!" Jessie screamed at the boy.

"I'm sorry! I didn't mean to. Honest, I wasn't expecting this myself!" Daniel apologized profusely. "I told Job that I just *had* to tell you how sorry I am — and how much I love you."

"Well, save it! I'm never going to believe another word that comes out of your mouth!" she exclaimed.

Jessie looked at the boy's horribly pained expression and realized that just perhaps it wasn't all his fault. She started to grin, but she didn't want him to see it, so she raised her hand to her face. "You *do* know that you're stark naked, don't you?" she giggled.

"I've opened my heart and my soul to you. Why should I care?" he answered. "I swear: I didn't ask them for a nun's habit. I guess something got lost in the translation."

"I don't know why, but it's really difficult for me to stay angry with you, when you're dressed like that!" she vamped. "But I'm *still* not wearing that *thing* to my wedding!"

"You don't have to," Daniel assured her. "If it'll make you happy, you can wear *my* clothes and *I'll* wear the dress! So long as you marry me, I'll do whatever you want."

She unzipped her pressure-suit and let it fall. "You know that dog of yours would make a pretty good marriage counselor!" she whispered as she put her arms around him.

*****

The General was about to pound on the hatch, when he noticed Daniel's clothes on the couch. He smiled and thought better of it: "Job, you are really something!"

The dog climbed up on the couch and foraged through the rest of the fast food. The old man considered chastising him, but he immediately changed his mind. He preferred to be right where he was — and with his clothes on. Job was obviously not a force to be trifled with!

*****

"I want that ship! I don't care how you get it. Whatever you have to do. Whether you kill them and steal it or whether you negotiate a deal!" the President screamed. "Just do it and do it now!"

"Excuse me, Mr. President, but have you ever considered offering them amnesty and inviting them to come back home?" Agent Banks suggested.

"I don't like dealing with people that I can't control," the POTUS responded.

"Perhaps you should make an exception in this case?" Banks requested.

"And why would I do that?" the President asked.

"First of all, whether he's an alien or not, this Johnstone guy has been supplying the government with hi-tech equipment for decades and never given us any problems," the agent began. "Secondly, that was clearly the 'late' General Jerome Bascombe standing on the ramp of that ship in the TV broadcast."

"Bascombe's alive?" the President fumed.

"Apparently so," Agent Banks answered. "He's a good man. One of the best, most-loyal soldiers I've ever known. He's one of the few people on this planet whom I would trust with my life."

"Bascombe is nothing but a pompous, outspoken pain in my backside!" the Leader of the Free World declared. "I was about to have him court-martialed for disobeying my direct orders, but then he turned up 'dead.'"

"Well, Mr. President, obviously, there's still some life in the Old Bird and I think you should appeal to his patriotic nature," Banks replied. "That man would do anything for his country."

"Okay. Contact them. Offer them amnesty," the President agreed. "But do it now before some other country beats us to it!"

"Yes, Sir, Mr. President!" Banks assured him.

*****

Daniel and his companions remained on the *Dorius* awaiting the return of the Monsignor. The boy wasn't sure how long they would be welcome in Vatican City and he never dreamt that there would be throngs of people gathered around the ship, waiting for any signs of the "spacemen" on board. So far, he was not aware of any open displays of hostility towards them.

He was standing in the cockpit, eyeing the crowd, when he noticed a motorcade approaching. Security guards parted the crowd to allow the vehicles access to the area around the ship. He leapt down to the cargo bay with Job close behind him.

"It looks like we're getting visitors," he alerted his companions.

"Uncle Danny, I love you like my own father, but I can't do this!" the General protested.

"Jerry, I keep seeing the *Dorius*!" the boy responded.

"Of course, you're seeing the *Dorius* — you're *on* the Dorius!"

"You don't understand. I'm seeing it from the *outside*," Daniel explained. "Those agents that we teleported from behind the barn are out there somewhere, and I've seen your two 'buddies,' too!"

"Well, that can't be good," the old man replied.

"Consider yourself 'undercover'!" the boy advised him.

Daniel walked down the ramp wearing the pressure-suit, with his helmet tucked firmly under his arm. Job followed closely and stood at his side. Jessie waited just at the edge of the cargo-bay. Her hair was pulled back neatly in a bun and she was wearing a man's shirt and pants. The General waited well-within the *Dorius*.

The Monsignor waved to the young man as he led the procession. Daniel knelt on one knee at the end of the ramp with his head bowed down. He didn't know the proper protocol for his current situation.

"Greetings from Earth!" the Pope addressed him.

"Greetings from Kandar of Ionus," the boy responded.

"You do not appear as I would have imagined," the old man opined.

"Actually, Your Holiness, my name is Daniel Johnstone and I was born here on earth," Daniel assured him. "The ship is from a planet called Ionus and the essence — the soul — of its pilot is shared between Job and myself."

"The dog is called Job?" the Pontiff asked.

"Yes, Your Holiness, like the man in the Bible," the boy replied.

"Can I make contact with this alien creature?" the Pope inquired.

"Yes, but actually there are two *different* species of aliens whom you may wish to meet," Daniel suggested. "Kandar was a humanoid, but the Vargon is multidimensional. If you wish to meet Kandar, you need only touch Job."

The old man dropped to one knee in front of the dog and placed his hands on Job's head. He closed his eyes and opened his mind to

Kandar's thoughts. The old man wasn't telepathic, but the Ionian allowed him to understand. The Pope could see images from the entire span of Kandar's life: snapshots from across the universe as well as earthly remembrances from the past two centuries.

"Your dog is the most loving and loyal creature I've ever met," the Pontiff rose slowly and addressed the boy.

"I know, Your Holiness," Daniel agreed. "Whether you realize it or not, Kandar just saved this planet."

"I could see that quite clearly," the Pope assured him. "But what touches my heart most deeply is the sacrifice that he made for you. He has taken this specific form to be the friend that you've always loved."

"I understand that, too," the boy replied quietly.

"The Monsignor has told me that you would like your marriage blessed," the Bishop of Rome suggested in an attempt to lighten the mood.

"Yes, Your Holiness, please come with me and I will introduce you to my beautiful young bride," Daniel responded as he stood up. He led the old man up the ramp and onto the *Dorius*.

*****

"No! I cannot do this. This is not America!" the Pope insisted with agitation as he spotted the person wearing the nun's habit. "The Church will not marry two men!"

"Your Holiness, he's my son, not my bride!" Daniel corrected him. Then he directed the Pontiff's attention to Jessie: "This is my beautiful bride!"

"This old man is your son?" the Pope inquired. "And she's your bride?"

278

"Yes, Your Holiness," the boy assured him. "She's my bride. He's my son. No, forget that I even said that he's my son. Let's just deal with one thing at a time here."

The old cleric laughed: "Life must be very complicated in your world!"

"Your Holiness, you don't know the half of it!" the boy replied.

"Lovely Lady, and what may I ask is your name?" the Pope inquired.

Jessie stood there awe-stricken for a moment.

"Her name is Jessica Drake, but she answers to 'Jessie,'" Daniel insisted.

The Pontiff shook his finger at her and said, "I think I may have seen you on TV."

"Oh — my — Gawd!" she mumbled.

"Much closer, but still no cigar!" the General wisecracked.

"I'm so sorry, Your Majesty! I was drinking something and I didn't know it had alcohol in it and I probably drank too much of it and it's all Daniel's fault and I wasn't responsible for my actions and—" she prattled on in obvious embarrassment.

"It's alright, Young Lady. I'm not here to judge you. I'm here to marry you," the Pope calmly advised her.

"You'll have to wait your turn, Your Holiness, because she's already married to my Uncle Danny!" the General joked.

"So your son is also your nephew?" the Pontiff asked the boy.

"Technically, no. He's my son, but he's called me 'Uncle Danny' since he was a child. Actually, he was raised by his mother and his *other* father. — Do we really have time for all of this?" Daniel asked with a hint of frustration.

"I have time for whatever I can learn from you and these alien creatures," the Pope replied. "If in God's wisdom He has chosen to put intelligent life on other planets, then I need to know of these things and to embrace this knowledge. I need to reconcile what we learn to be true with all that I have taken on faith."

"Then, I will not waste your time with trifles," the boy replied. "Your Holiness, I think I should introduce you to the 'choir of souls.'"

The Bishop of Rome looked at the boy with intense curiosity.

"Vargon, if it pleases you, manifest yourself," Daniel intoned quietly. Job walked over to the boy's side and sat there. Jessie stood behind them somewhat afraid of what might appear. The boy closed his eyes and rested his right hand on the dog's head. He extended his left palm and an infinitesimal speck appeared to float there. Within seconds, the speck became an orb and, as the orb grew to nearly a meter in diameter, Daniel lowered his left arm to his side. The Vargon levitated before the awe-stricken cleric. The creature's myriad colors swirled over it like microcosmic hurricanes.

"Your Holiness, if you wish, you may place your hands on it," Daniel suggested.

The Pope was hesitant at first, but he placed his hands lightly on the creature and, feeling no adverse effects, he then kissed it and placed his face against the shining orb. His countenance became beatific. A few minutes passed and tears began to trickle down the old man's cheeks.

"I feel as though I've seen Heaven, but I'm not allowed to stay," the Pontiff told them through his tears.

"Jessie. Jerry. If you wish, you may touch the Vargon, as well. It won't hurt anyone," the boy assured them.

Jerome placed his hand on the orb. Jessie extended her hand

towards the creature, but she couldn't bring herself to touch it. Daniel looked into her eyes. He put his left arm around her and held her tightly, then, with his right hand, he guided her fingers to the swirling surface of the glistening orb.

"There's nothing to be afraid of here, except contentment and peace," he assured everyone present. After a few minutes, the Vargon began to diminish in size. As quickly as it had appeared and grown, it now vanished from their presence.

"It was so wonderful. Please, can you make it come back?" the Pontiff asked.

"I have no control over it," Daniel admitted. "It has been Kandar's guardian angel for a very long time, but even he doesn't control it."

"Our universe is so full of wonders!" the Pope exclaimed. "The Vargon made me feel so — happy. So peaceful. I can't even begin to describe it."

"It's called the 'choir of souls' for a reason, Your Holiness," the boy assured him.

Jessie pressed her face against Daniel's chest and tears flowed down from her beaming eyes. Even the gruff General's steely eyes glazed over. All of them had experienced the Vargon, but each in his own way.

The Pope reached out to Daniel and Jessie with both of his hands and he placed their hands together.

"Jessie and Daniel, having just witnessed God's greatness here, do you honestly love one another and wish to continue life as one?" he asked them.

"We do," the couple whispered in unison.

"Then your marriage is already blessed," the Pontiff assured them. "You've touched that extraordinary being together and you've chosen to join as man and wife, so, unless you feel the need for a ceremony, there is nothing that I can do to make you any more 'married' than what you already are. May God bless you!"

"Thank you, Your Holiness," Daniel whispered.

*****

"I have seen so much in such a short time," the Pope began with a smile, "and I am so very grateful, but is there any chance that you can let me fly this thing?"

"I'm sorry, Your Holiness, but the *Dorius* only responds to Kandar, Job and myself," the boy replied. "If you tried to fly her, I'd have to wash my hands of the whole business. I just don't think she's ready for a Pontiff pilot."

The Bishop of Rome laughed loudly: "Young Man, you have an irreverent sense of humor, but at least you're well-read!"

"See! This is what I have to put up with!" Jessie deadpanned as she pushed her husband. "Tell him he's a moron, Your Eminence!"

"I think I will stay out of that particular argument!" the Pope answered. "I have seen and heard so much today and there is so much that yet needs to be discussed. My brief contacts with the Vargon and Kandar have served to invigorate my faith. I truly thank all of you for allowing me the benefit of these amazing experiences. I will always treasure this time that I've spent with you."

"Thank you very much for your blessings, Your Holiness," Daniel intoned solemnly.

The General backed slowly down the ramp, hunched over slightly, so that the veil would obscure his face. The Pope walked close behind. Daniel, Jessie and Job followed to bid him farewell.

Then the Pope turned to bless the *Dorius* and his new friends.

*****

Ben was seated in a wheelchair at a window overlooking the Square. He had the cross-hairs fixed firmly on Daniel when he squeezed the trigger. Mr. Jacobs and his team were toward the front of the crowd, ready and waiting to finish the job and board the ship.

The bullet had gotten within twenty meters of its intended target when Job sensed it. Ben was preparing to fire a second round, when his first bullet slammed into his forehead. He was thrown back in his chair, while his rifle slid out through the open window.

"Ben, you missed!" Jacobs muttered into his earpiece. "He's still open. Try it again!"

As soon as the first round had echoed through the Square, Daniel grabbed Jessie and ran her back up the ramp with Job close behind. The dog turned and stood guard at the outer hatch. Jerome threw himself over the Pope and drew his weapon. Jacobs pulled out a pistol and was about to level it at the General when he felt something poke him in the back.

"Drop it!" Banks told him. "The President has other ideas and you 'rogues' aren't part of the plan."

Beckert and several other agents secured the front of the *Dorius*. Jacobs' men attempted to turn casually back towards the crowd and blend in, but the FBI agents outnumbered and outflanked them. Jacobs dropped his pistol and raised his hands slowly.

"Your Holiness, are you alright?" the General asked the Pontiff.

"I'm fine. Was anyone injured?" he inquired.

"I'm not sure, but I need to get you safely into your vehicle!" Jerome whispered.

The old officer helped the Pope to his feet and escorted him

283

towards his waiting car. The crowd made way for them, many of them reacting in horror to the mustachioed, pistol-packing nun in the white habit. As soon as the old cleric was safely inside his bullet-proof limousine, Jerome headed back towards the *Dorius*.

"That's quite some uniform you're wearing, General Bascombe!" Banks yelled.

"Lieutenant Banks, tell your men to 'stand down' or I will shoot my way through them!" the General barked.

"There's absolutely no need for that, Sir," the old FBI agent replied as he slipped his weapon back into its holster and saluted his old boss. "The President is offering all of you amnesty along with his most humble apologies. It seems that there was a lot of confusion and a lack of good judgment in the handling of this matter. He asked me to invite all of you to return home at your earliest convenience."

"Well, isn't that just sweet of him!" Bascombe remarked. "Does he know that his own Vice-President is in cahoots with these creeps?"

"No, Sir, I'm not aware that he is — but he will be shortly!" Banks responded.

The General walked up to his old friend and shook his hand.

"If you'll excuse me, I'd like to change into something a little more comfortable!" the old man told him. "And, whatever you do: don't try to board this ship and do not, I repeat: *do not* 'tick off' our dog! Bad things happen to people who upset that dog."

"Here are your orders, Sir," Banks pulled an envelope from his pocket.

"My orders?" the old officer asked incredulously.

"Yes, Sir. If you're not dead and you haven't resigned or retired, then you're still a commissioned officer," the agent advised him.

"You wouldn't happen to be AWOL, now, would you, Sir?"

The General smiled. "Actually I was scheduled for leave when this particular circus started."

"Very good, Sir!" Banks snapped to attention. "I hope you're enjoying Rome."

The old man ascended the ramp and Job followed him into the cargo bay. The outer hatch closed and all of the noise, confusion and madness of the outside world was abruptly replaced with the peace and quiet of the *Dorius*.

"I'm *really* getting too old for this!" General Bascombe muttered as he plopped onto the couch.

"I hope you realize that if those agents had seriously threatened you, Job would have teleported you onto the ship?" Daniel asked.

"Well, Young Lady, you'd better be very glad that he didn't!" he advised Jessie. "Because if you had seen me naked, you would have been scarred for life!"

"Hey, now that isn't fair! So everyone gets to see me naked, but I never get to see anybody else?" Jessie complained with a giggle.

"Unless you're into scars and faded tattoos, you're not missing a thing!" the General assured her.

"Actually, it's pretty hard for me to imagine you looking any more ridiculous than you do right now!" she laughed.

"Don't pay any attention to her, Jerry. I think you wear it rather well!" Daniel joked.

*****

A week passed before Daniel and his companions felt confident that they could return to America without adverse consequences. There were many discussions among the occupants of the *Dorius* and nearly as many with Banks and the local American Ambassador. A long phone conversation with the genuinely-apologetic President finally persuaded them that they all would be both welcome to return home and secure from prosecution for any alleged crimes.

In fact, the American media was now extolling the crew of the *Dorius* for saving the earth from the alien invasion. The government had attempted to deceive the public with so many disparate lies that the truth eventually had to be told and resignations from several high-ranking officials needed to be tendered. All of the witnesses to the war with the Bardokians were being freed from "protective custody."

The Pope and the Monsignor had enjoyed several visits to the ship, and they too had offered Daniel sanctuary within the boundaries of Vatican City, but he didn't think it was fair to Jessie, the General or their respective families to keep them there. On the day of their scheduled departure, the crowd around the ship numbered in the hundreds of thousands.

Having said their "goodbyes" to the throngs of well-wishers and all of their new friends, Daniel secured Jessie and Jerome in their seats for the return trip. The boy and his dog rose the steps to the cockpit and took their positions. Daniel pulled down his "shades" and closed his eyes for a moment before he gripped the controls of the ship.

"Ready, Job?" he asked his friend. "Let's do this!"

The *Dorius* began to hum and the multicolored lights flashed around the thruster rings as the ship slowly lifted from the Square before the massive old cathedral. The Swiss Guardsmen held the crowds back with their halberds until the saucer disappeared into the clouds. Many of the visitors to the spectacle were signing themselves with the Cross and kissing the ground where the *Dorius* had rested. For some people, there was peace to be found in the knowledge that there were greater life-forms than themselves and that not all of those creatures were a threat to life as they knew it.

*****

Within seconds, the *Dorius* was positioned once again behind Daniel's old shack. The boy and his dog descended the steps to the cargo bay and entered the crew's quarters. Daniel helped Jessie and Jerome to release their seat-belts. They both seemed stunned that the flight had ended so quickly.

"We're home," the boy whispered.

"Hey, Uncle Danny, my step-Mom here was telling me about those little books that you wrote," the General began. "Do I get to read them, too?"

At the sound of the words "step-Mom," Jessie stuck her fingers in her ears and attempted to drown him out with her humming.

"I suppose if you really wanted to, you could read those and all of the rest of them, too," Daniel replied while smiling at his wife.

"No, no, *no!* I am *not* a step-Mom to a geriatric General!" Jessie insisted.

"Don't say that! You're going to hurt our little Jerry's feelings!" the boy laughed. He got up and walked towards the door to the cargo bay, while Jerome snickered.

"Whoa, whoa! Wait a minute! What was that about 'all the rest of them'?" Jessie asked, totally shocked by this new development. "You mean there's more?"

"What? So, you thought that those four little books encompassed everything that I had to say for nearly two centuries?" Daniel asked with mock offense.

"No, but—?" Jessie began to protest.

Daniel opened a cabinet and removed a large box. He set it on the floor in front of his two companions and opened the flaps. The box was nearly filled with thin leather-bound volumes. "You're both welcome to read all of these," he told them as they looked on in amazement.

"Those are all of your adventures?" Jessie gasped.

"Yeah, me and Job. Of course, the Vargon helped a lot, too," the boy admitted. "Some of the stories involve Kandar and Shahlaya and their adventures on Ionus, as well, but those are just what I could transcribe from his memories."

"Wow! This is incredible!" Jerome interjected as he peered into the box. He pulled a volume out and read the title aloud: "*The Life of Daniel.*"

"Let me see that!" Jessie grabbed it out of the old man's hand. She riffled through the pages quickly and exclaimed. "Hey! This is a cheat! All of these pages are blank!"

"No, not quite," Daniel assured her. "Read the dedication."

Jessie set the book on her knees and found the first yellowed page. She read the dedication quietly: "To my dearest Jessie: the woman of my dreams, my wife and my one true love. However and whenever you come into my life, I'm certain that I will know you when I see you."

"That's so beautiful. When did you write this?" she asked the boy.

"It's written at the bottom of the page in tiny print."

"It just says: 'Spring, 1855.'"

"That sounds right," the boy assured her. "That's just about when the dreams started."

"The dreams?" she asked.

"I think that the Vargon set that particular 'carrot' in front of my eyes, just to keep me going," Daniel responded. "The Vargon defies time and space. It let me dream about you, not that I would remember a lot of specific things, but just enough so I would know that there was love in my future and that my life was worth living."

"But why are all of the other pages blank?" Jessie wondered aloud.

Daniel knelt down in front of her and kissed her lightly on the lips.

"Because my life didn't really begin until I met you!" he whispered.

Editor's Notes on
Pop Culture References:

On page 1, the song "Had to Cry Today" is cited. It is a great song by a legendary band, Blind Faith, from their eponymous album. It is sung by Steve Winwood who also composed it. [It would have been nice to quote the actual lyrics, but it seemed too daunting a task to acquire the necessary permission.]

On page 41, Daniel signs in as "Wilbur Post and Ed." This is a direct reference to the TV show Mister Ed (1961-1965) on which the lead character Wilbur Post owned a talking horse named Mr. Ed. [Note: Job is *indeed* a *very* BIG dog!]

On page 99, Jessie reads the lyrics to "She" - *not* actually written by Daniel Johnstone, but by the author William A. Rich, who reserves all rights. He (Mr. Rich, *not* Mr. Johnstone) will (hopefully) release a recording of it sometime in the near future.

On page 104, Daniel mentions the movie "Alien." This was the 1979 sci-fi horror film by director Ridley Scott and followed by at least two sequels: "Aliens" and "Alien 3."

On page 272, Jessie mistakes "wimple" for Whipple — *Mr.* Whipple, that is — the immortal spokesman (1964-1985) for Charmin, a major toilet paper company, as seen in their many TV and print ads. [Note: In referencing toilet paper, this editor does not suggest or condone any such use for this book.]

About the Author

William A. Rich grew up in a near-west suburb of Chicago. As a child, he excelled at school and demonstrated great potential as an artist. Unfortunately, at the age of 12, he came down with "rock'n'roll," an insidious disease that eventually took over his life. In the summer between 6th and 8th grades, he started taking drum lessons and began his schizophrenic life as a "rock & roll" drummer and scholar.

When he graduated from high school, he received the Principal's Math Award, which was the primary reason for his majoring in math at college. He earned a Bachelor of Science, Honors degree (magna cum laude) and the Fr. Gerst Memorial Mathematics Award from Loyola University. He also earned a full fellowship to the Graduate School of Northwestern University to pursue a doctorate in mathematics. During his first year there, he once again fell victim to that debilitating disease and resigned the fellowship to pursue a career as a songwriter.

Mr. Rich was a high school math teacher, which at the time offered no benefits and little more in pay, before taking a temporary job with the U.S. Postal Service. He has written nearly 400 songs and in 1996 released "EcLECTrIC SONGSMITH" his first CD as a singer, songwriter and multi-instrumentalist. When some critics considered that first album to be little more than a joke, he reinvented himself as a humorist. Unfortunately, it was only then that they took him seriously.

Daniel and Job is his first effort as a novelist.